DEAD SIZE

DEAD SIZE

A NOVEL

SAWNEY HATTON

DEAD SIZE Copyright © 2012 by Sawney Hatton

Published by:
Dark Park Publishing

Cover design by:
J Caleb Clark

1st Ebook Edition: January 2013
1st Print Edition: July 2013

This Print Edition ISBN: 978-0-9886444-3-4

To Erin

I was extremely tired, and with that, and the heat of the weather, and about half a pint of brandy—that's what your father drinks—*that I drank as I left the ship, I found myself much inclined to sleep. I lay down on the grass, which was very short and soft, where I slept sounder than ever I remembered to have done in my life, and, as I reckoned, about nine hours, for when I awakened, it was just daylight. I attempted to rise, but was not able to stir. For, as I happened to lie on my back, I found my arms and legs were strongly fastened on each side to the ground, and my hair, which was long and thick, tied down in the same manner. I likewise felt several slender ligatures across my body, from my armpits to my thighs. I could only look upwards. The sun began to grow hot, and the light offended my eyes. I heard a confused noise about me, but in the posture I lay*—much like you boys are lying now—*I could see nothing except the sky. In a little time I felt something alive moving on my left leg, which advancing gently forward over my breast, came almost up to my chin, when, bending my eyes downwards as much as I could, I perceived it to be a human creature not six inches high, with a bow and arrow in his hands, and a quiver at his back...*

Excerpt from the novel *Gulliver's Travels* by Jonathan Swift, as read aloud, for the last time, by Harold Huggens to his sons Dale and Gulliver before their bedtimes on June 6th, 1985.

PART 1

THE LITTLE THINGS

1

Gulliver Huggens awoke once again tied down, face up, on his back lawn. It was the third time in as many weeks, though with the arrival of June at least the weather was mild now. He was loosely bound with cooking twine threaded around numerous golf tees staked into the ground. Gulliver did not play golf, nor did he ever cook anything more complicated than scrambled eggs or grilled cheese, neither of which required trussing. Where they'd found the items to bind him was a mystery.

In contrast to the budding boughs of the cottonwood tree looming above, the parched lawn beneath him was brown and crunchy, more straw-like than grassy, yet it had somehow dampened his roller-skating elephant pajamas. Or that may have been from his own sweat. Gulliver sweated a lot.

Rankled, he sat up without much struggle, yanking the tees from the earth. He unraveled the string and wadded it up into a ball.

Gulliver wondered what time it was. He didn't want to be late again. As long as he performed quality work and met job deadlines, his boss was generally laid-back about his occasional tardiness (and lapses in hygiene), but he preferred not to test the limits of his employer's lenient nature.

"Mornin', Gulliver."

Gulliver turned his head. Mr. Jensen was watering his newly planted flowerbed beyond the short chain-link fence separating their yards. He was a stocky old man with floppy, doorknocker jowls and wisps of silver hair combed over his balding pate. Fond of wearing plaid shirts under bib-and-brace overalls, it gave him an authentic enough bucolic look without having to cultivate anything more ambitious than marigolds and chrysanthemums.

"Good morning, Mr. Jensen."

Normally, Gulliver would have been embarrassed to be seen in his roller-skating elephant pajamas, or the parachuting monkey or toy-making elf ones, but by now Mr. Jensen had beheld his entire bedtime wardrobe under basically identical circumstances. His neighbor was polite enough to never poke fun at him either.

"Little people lash you down again, eh?" Mr. Jensen asked, less out of a genuine interest than as a conversation starter.

Gulliver nodded. After the sixth or seventh time Mr. Jensen had witnessed this sort of occurrence, Gulliver had felt obliged to explain, if only because that seemed the neighborly thing to do. And Mr. Jensen had been very understanding, nary batting an incredulous eye.

"Ever wonder why you don't wake up?"

"I'm a heavy sleeper."

This was true. Gulliver once slept through an F3 tornado that near about destroyed Mrs. Vogler's house down the street. Some people had likened it to a scared-shitless herd of cattle stampeding through their yards, quaking their houses, but Gulliver might as well have been drowsing on some tranquil beach thousands of miles away. He didn't even realize that Fanny Kessler's uprooted laundry rack had impaled the wall due north of his slumbering head until he had risen the following morning and banged his brow against it.

"Not so heavy a troop of tiny folk can't carry you, eh?" Mr. Jensen quipped, har-harring at himself.

Gulliver forced a smile, not wanting his neighbor to think he was nettled by him. He rose to his feet and brushed himself off.

"Gonna be one fine summer," commented Mr. Jensen, assessing the clear cerulean sky while spraying his crocuses. "I can tell."

Gulliver nodded amiably, wished his neighbor a good day, then headed into his house, blades of dry grass tickling the soles of his bare feet.

The inside of Gulliver's house looked much the same as it had when he was growing up there. It retained most of the same furniture, the same fixtures, and virtually the same décor from as far back as he could remember. Even Gulliver's bedroom still bore remnants of his preadolescence: a Robby the Robot talking alarm clock on his nightstand, pictures of magnificent machines both real and imagined adorning the walls, and a ceiling replicating the Milky Way galaxy painstakingly painted by his father.

The only differences throughout the house were the burgundy curtains that had replaced the torn bishop's sleeve drapes in the living room, some added frilly pillows on the sofa (crocheted by his Aunt Augusta as Christmas gifts to him over the years), a refurbished 27" Zenith television his boss gave him his first month on the job, and the twin-sized racecar bed Gulliver had hauled out of their room—now, just *his* room— and into the crawlspace. It wasn't a large residence by any means, just a simple cottage house with two bedrooms and one bathroom, but it suited Gulliver fine living there on his own.

After coming in from the yard, he locked the rear door leading into his kitchen, more out of nightmare-fostered habit than necessity. Ever since he had come back home, Gulliver had recurring waking dreams about a skeletal Grim Reaper, reeking of decayed flesh (or pickled cabbage), weighed down by a baggy monk's robe and floor-thudding hobnail boots. The Angel of Death always visited him in the wee hours of the night to remind him it still coveted his immortal soul, having failed to nab it the first chance it had all those years ago.

Gulliver admired its tenacity, though in his opinion, its rude manners were quite uncalled for.

Skipping his shower and shave once again, Gulliver had just enough time to throw together breakfast before catching the bus. He poured himself a glass of SunnyD and a bowl of Honey Nut Cheerios. He also put in the toaster two slices of rye, which he managed to burn to near cinders. Plumes of smoke billowed across the ceiling. He unplugged the toaster and speared the charred pieces with a fork, lifting them from the slots and dousing them under the sink faucet. He coughed, cracked the window open. The smoke coated his nostrils and throat, smelling to him, as all smoke did, like scorched vinyl…

His father drove the four of them to a movie. It was Gulliver's ninth birthday, and he wished to see The Goonies *on opening day, playing at the Prestwick in Sulfur Springs. The night was dark and drizzly, the roads slick. Their car, taking a curve too fast, skidded off the macadam, smashed head-on into a white-barked tree. Gulliver had been thrown from their Ford Fairmont moments before it burst into flames.*

His mother and father, he later learned, died on impact. His aunt had told him his brother did too, but Gulliver knew better. He remembered all too vividly, as he lay battered and dazed on the muddy shoulder of Highway 40, seeing his older sibling trapped inside the wreckage, engulfed in flesh-searing flames. Dale was screaming at him. For him. Then Gulliver passed out, his eyes welling with the blood trickling from the nasty gash on his forehead.

The pale, L-shaped scar above his left eye, bisecting his eyebrow, remained as a grisly souvenir. Not that he needed one to be reminded of that horrible night. He could never forget, the memory imprinted in his brain. As for the Grim Reaper— who still came clomping up to the bed while Gulliver trembled under his covers—that bastard would never let him go either.

Gulliver spent the latter period of his juvenescence being raised by his Aunt Augusta, nicknamed the Pillow Lady, both for her exquisite craftsmanship making them and for her prodigious, pendulous breasts. She lived on a Nubio-Bavarian goat ranch with her quadriplegic husband, thirteen dogs, and eight cats in a rural community so far up the Northern Peninsula it might as well have been another country.

For Gulliver, life at Aunt Augusta's was not unpleasant, though its rules were stringent. He rose at five each morning before sunup to feed and water the animals. At eight sharp, he began his lessons in reading, writing, and arithmetic, followed by Bible study, all with his aunt, who had been similarly home-schooled to her self-extolled benefit. At half past four, he set the table for supper. Bedtime for the whole household was at nine, even when he was well into his teens. Gulliver's other daily chores included shearing, shoveling, washing, dusting, and folding whatever needed to be sheared, shoveled, washed, dusted, or folded. And while Gulliver was hardly a feckless boy, he did have his bouts of stubborn indolence, for which he was punished with a strapping from his uncle's rawhide belt, administered to his naked thighs. Aunt Augusta meted out the physical sentence, as her husband was paralyzed from the neck down and could neither dress nor feed himself. Gulliver did not resent those acts of corporal discipline. They were always warranted—earned—like Auntie's fig pudding.

Gulliver had long believed he would always live with Aunt Augusta and Uncle Larry. He knew what they expected of him, and he had expected nothing more. Everything was defined and underlined for him; he didn't have to think for himself, only learn what was taught him. Foremost, he'd felt safe there, with no harbingers of death or familiar screams of agony haunting him.

He hadn't realized such bliss carried an age limit.

Gulliver was twenty-five when, at the behest of his aunt ("You're a man now, and a man must forge his own path, following in the Lord's footsteps"), he had returned to his inherited childhood home at 16 Klunghoffer Street in Laymon Township.

The Little People were already there, dwelling behind the walls, beneath the floors, and above the ceilings, behaving like they owned the place.

Initially, Gulliver thought the house infested with mice. He would often hear the muffled patter from armies of tiny paws, as if hundreds of Tic Tacs were spilling down the inner drywall. Sometimes he would discover the groceries in his cupboards raided, the linens in his closet pillaged.

Gulliver surmised the missing pillowcases and hand towels were being claimed for nesting material, his filched cookies and beans likely cached in some dark, dank recess long unseen by human eyes. Dumb as these lower-lifes may be, they still had encroached upon his domain, helping themselves to his creature comforts. Such impertinence he could not abide.

Gulliver bought a bushel of rodent traps from Hap's Hardware and set them along the baseboards behind the furniture and in nooks and crannies throughout the house. For bait, he first used cheese—a Double Gloucester—then bread, peanut butter, chocolate, even dog kibble. To Gulliver's astonishment, over the course of a week none of the beady-eyed buggers had tripped the deadly spring-loaded hammers, never so much as nibbled at any of the appetizing morsels. He figured they were either very clever or very finicky. Either way, he would not underestimate them again.

Gulliver collected the traps and painted them charcoal black. He then cooked up some beef brisket, seasoned with Mrs. Pinch, and diced it into mouse-bite sized pieces. He baited the camouflaged traps and reset them in the deepest niches he could reach.

This round yielded a near miss.

Gulliver heard the whip crack of the trap shortly after midnight, just as he was dozing off. It took him almost half an hour to pinpoint which one had been sprung. To his chagrin, no mouse had met its neck-broken, spine-snapped demise.

What he did find, however, was puzzling. Disturbingly so.

Caught under the hammer was a shirt, a tiny white shirt, not much bigger than his thumbprint.

Gulliver wrenched it from the trap and examined it. The miniature garment appeared to have been stitched together from two cutout swatches of cloth, most likely from one of his pilfered pillowcases. The fabric was speckled with red, pin-head sized splotches. Blood.

After downing a couple of juice glasses of what was left of his father's best brandy, Gulliver drifted off to sleep on the beige Ultrasuede sofa, the pullover fit for a finger puppet clamped in his palm. He dreamt of a moribund Mouse King beneath his floor, sprawled on its hacky sack deathbed, its ribs shattered, its guts ruptured. Its whiskers twitched terribly as it delivered a final edict to its gathered subjects: they would rain merciless vengeance upon the one who had engineered their revered emperor's assassination.

Gulliver also dreamt about boobs.

He didn't stir until early afternoon when the sunlight lanced through the bay windows and slapped him across the face. Listlessly he rose from the sofa and shuffled toward the dining table, frowning at the empty brandy bottle on it. He fetched an unopened bottle of fourteen-year-old scotch—which by now had to be almost triple that age—from the cherrywood-veneered liquor cabinet.

Gulliver unscrewed the cap and poured a shot into his unrinsed juice glass from the night before. Knocking it back in one foul-tasting swig, only then did he notice the bloodied doll's shirt was no longer cupped in his hand.

He scanned the path he had taken from the sofa to the dining table. Gulliver recognized, jutting from beneath the faux-Tiffany mission floor lamp, the patch of white. He stepped forward and bent to pick it up. Dust bunnies (or were they fur balls?) clung to it. He shook them off.

That was when Gulliver spotted the Scrabble game set up on the glass-top coffee table. It was the Deluxe Edition, with the rotating board and raised surface grid. A few letter tiles had already been laid out on it, not placed there arbitrarily, but not part of an ongoing game either.

It was a message.

By the time Gulliver turned six, Scrabble had become a Sunday evening tradition in the Huggens household.

His father believed it imperative that one communicate articulately and persuasively to survive and thrive in this regressively illiterate world. Words were no less than weapons. Scrabble, in building your vocabulary, built your arsenal. *"More than ever, the pen is mightier than the sword,"* Father would quote to them, after which Dale would whisper into his brother's ear that he'd choose a sword over some stupid pen any day if he were facing off with a Cyclops or Jack the Ripper. Gulliver had to concur.

Eccentricity came standard in the Huggens gene package. Grandpa Hobart had been a travel writer who only reviewed locales that had been decimated by a historic natural disaster: San Francisco (earthquake), Pompeii (volcano), London (plague), and so forth. Cousin Roscoe, a rodeo announcer, feared running water and storm drains and gypsies. And Gulliver's own father never spoke without first being spoken to, postulating it gave him the advantage in any conversation that might—and commonly did—segue into some ornery squabble.

No wonder then Father had chosen employment with the U.S. Forest Service as a horticulturalist. Metaphytes never bickered with anybody.

Altogether, Harold Huggens's quirks tallied with his profound, if excessive, respect for the power of language. Scrabble served as a primarily educational, secondarily fun tool for their family, though Father often monitored the game with such fascistic rigor he usually spoiled the fun part. Points were never as important as precision. Deliberately made-up words would not be tolerated. If a word were put down that did not exist, Father would penalize the offender by denying him TV. Only after learning by rote a full page of spellings and definitions from *Webster's Dictionary*, including etymological origins, would his viewing privileges be reinstated.

Their mother, in her discreet way, had been far more reasonable than their father. Or perhaps, being sixteen years his junior, she was just more empathetic toward the boys. When her husband was away at work, she would allow her sons to watch television, even if it was at the time verboten, as long as they pitched in with the household chores. She was also apparently exempt from the "no made-up words" rule. On one occasion, she had concocted the word "boogain," which she asserted meant "a bargain so good it's scary." Both boys challenged her, but Father let it slide then, saying it was a colloquialism. He thenceforth proclaimed colloquialisms banned in Scrabble, as he later did with street slang, brand names, and select onomatopoeias.

The message on the Scrabble board read:

NO KILL US

Gulliver deduced these were not your average unwelcome vermin he was dealing with, but rather a far more sentient creature.

He searched his home, peering over, around, and under his furniture, rummaging through every cabinet, closet, and cubbyhole, even sifting through boxes of cereal and detergent. He spied nothing out of the ordinary. Yet somebody had brought out the Scrabble box from the hall closet and arranged the game on the coffee table.

And that somebody, whoever they were, wanted to let him know they didn't appreciate his recent efforts to exterminate them.

He again heard the rat-a-tat-tat of tiny scuttling feet near where he stood. Again, he could see nothing amiss. Growing riled and a mite alarmed, he decided to take a more direct—and vocal—approach.

"Who are you?" he inquired apprehensively. Then, more peremptorily, "Who are you, I said! Answer me!"

There was no answer. Gulliver felt a bit foolish anticipating one.

Then came a faint, high-pitched squeak, much like a fingertip rubbing a balloon. Coming from somewhere within the house, Gulliver was certain.

He darted from room to room, flashlight in hand, methodically inspecting every possible hiding spot, no matter how small or inaccessible. More than an hour later, he had uncovered nothing but a red checker piece, some coins, and a copper button he had lost from a jacket he no longer owned. Frustrated, he returned to the living room where he had first heard the peculiar, untraceable noise.

The Scrabble board imparted a new message:

WE NO WANT HURT YOU

Gulliver's anger escalated, bristling the vellus hairs on the scruff of his neck. How dare someone invade his home and threaten him! If there were any hurting to be done, he would damn well be the one doling it out.

"Show yourselves!" he roared. "Or so help me I will smoke you out. Or choke you out. Whatever I have to do to take you out!"

Moments later, they came out.

2

They crept out from behind the Queen Anne hutch, popped up through the knothole in the pinewood floor, and clambered down the chandelier light, perching on its brass saucer-shaped bobeches.

Gulliver figured they numbered about a hundred. Actual little people, none taller than his pinky, looking much like he had imagined the Lilliputians did. Father had often read Dale and him passages from *Gulliver's Travels* as bedtime stories. So enamored was Father with these fantastical tales of giants, floating cities, and the abominable Yahoos that he named his youngest son after its titular character. (The elder son had been named after a cartoon chipmunk, his mother's preference.)

Gulliver took a few tentative steps toward them. The Little People held their positions, on their collective guard.

Upon closer scrutiny, he noted their faces and hands, on males and females both, were much hairier than the typical humanoid. They resembled itty-bitty werewolves, lacking the menacing fangs but compensating with the biggest, brownest eyes. They had only four raccoon-like fingers on each hand.

Their simple garments, as he suspected, were assembled from articles appropriated from his closets and cupboards— pants and shirts sewn from assorted linens, shoes formed from hollowed-out coffee beans. Some even sported toothpaste cap helmets. One cradled its bandaged arm in a twist tie sling, likely the casualty of Gulliver's mousetrap.

They all stared at Gulliver curiously, timorously, his dumbstruck reflection captured in each of their huge, burnt umber pupils.

"H-hello," Gulliver stammered.

They cheeped an indecipherable greeting in response.

And that was the beginning of their remarkable alliance.

Over the ensuing five years, Gulliver learned much, though probably a fraction of everything there was to be learned, about his primitive housemates. They had lived there through eleven winters, after migrating from somewhere they called the "nether hills." (The city of Laymon was nestled—some would describe it as sunken—in a wide valley surrounded on three sides by lush evergreen mountains, the most famous being the twin Devil's Horns.) They had resettled in Gulliver's then-unoccupied house because it offered them a safer haven, one not vulnerable to freezing, flooding, or predators.

They had taught themselves to write rudimentary English by decoding and studying the bounty of books, most of them worn mass-market editions of classic literature, on Gulliver's living room shelves. Gulliver, however, could never interpret the Little People's spoken language, whether they were attempting the English tongue or not. To him their vocalizations fell somewhere between a whistling teakettle and a wheezing asthmatic. At best, he could tell when they were laughing and when they wanted his attention. If more explicit communications were required, they used the Scrabble board.

Once they grew acquainted with each other, Gulliver gave the Little People his blessing to run freely about his home, though at that point he questioned whether he really had any say in the matter. He also agreed to share his foodstuffs, particularly his Decadent Darla's snack cakes and jelly packets hoarded from Roberta's Hot Pot Café, as well as pass on any discardable fabrics or other salvageable materials. He even maintained the household thermostat at a temperature most comfortable for them, which frankly was a few degrees cooler than what suited Gulliver. Still, it was a minor compromise, with Gulliver only having to don a sweater more often in the nippier months.

For recreation, the Little People enjoyed watching most anything on television, except the news and talk shows, and having Gulliver read to them. They seemed most enthralled by Dickens and Shakespeare, but even Drs. Spock and Seuss riveted them. He also amused the toddlers with hand-shadow shows, simulating menageries of romping goats and geese and rabbits and rhinos (though shadow snakes frightened them). There were dozens of thimble-sized children among their clan, to whom Gulliver had only been introduced after their chiefs—those with the sparkly aluminum foil coronets—had assured themselves he posed no hostility.

For Gulliver, the most galling idiosyncrasy of the Little People—and there were scores to choose from—was their delight in playing pranks on him. Their favorite was carrying his deep-dozing body outside to his yard and then fastening him to the lawn, the cottonwood tree, or the house's rainspout. Or, while he showered, they'd strategically set on the bathroom floor an uncapped tube of toothpaste, which he would mash when stepping out of the tub, squirting cinnamint dentifrice across the white tiles. Or, in the middle of the night, they'd reset every clock in the house two hours forward so Gulliver would rouse earlier than he had to, in more than one instance groggily arriving at his place of work while the rest of the townsfolk were still burrowed in their beds.

The unbridled glee the Little People derived from these fatuous antics generally irritated, and sometimes infuriated Gulliver, but they always made amends by tidying his home, cooking his meals, or polishing his shoes. He found he couldn't stay sore at them. They were only having fun, he reasoned, and no real harm was done aside from the loss of a couple hours' sleep now and then.

All in all, it was a mutually beneficial, mostly gratifying arrangement. More than that, the Little People became the first true friends Gulliver had ever had.

No, that wasn't right.

His first true friend had been Dale.

They had shared everything there was to share—toys and treats, jests and jibes, backyard and beyond adventures, even parental punishments (for it was always better to be grounded together, both accepting responsibility for the same infraction, whether committed jointly or not). They contracted the same illnesses at the same time. They were fans of the same science fiction TV programs, read the same science fact magazines. They wished for the same things for Christmas.

In the summer of '84, the Huggens brothers snuck off together. Their father had once again refused them consent to go to the annual Captain Calico's Carnival, ranting about it being operated by con men, ex-cons, and other miscreants. Not even Mother could convince him to change his mind, due in no small part to the carnally inclined carnies having years before flipped flirty remarks toward Mrs. Huggens, husband present be damned. "Well, damn them all!" Father seethed. His decision was absolute, set in proverbial stone.

But, driven by their insatiable appetite for fun, Gulliver and Dale defied the patriarchal dictum. Both feigning after-dinner tummy aches, they tucked themselves into their beds early in the evening. Right after the solstitial daylight finally waned, they slipped out their window and sprinted all the way to Shiloh's Field, dazzlingly lit up like a Fourth of July fireworks show.

The traveling carnival featured a variety of flashing, clanking mechanical rides: the Disk'O, Gravitron, Zipper,

Hurricane, Orbiter, and Tilt-A-Whirl, plus a kiddie choo-choo, Ferris wheel, tea cups, Frankenstein's Funhouse, and, of course, Captain Calico's Pirate Ship. Tinny Dixieland music blared from pole-mounted speakers. The screams and laughter of thrilled patrons pierced the air just a decibel or two below the amplified barking of the barkers, enticing their marks with deceptively simple games of chance and all those Taiwanese-made toy prizes to be won. Every few feet there were mouth-watering refreshments to be bought—spun cotton candy, dipped caramel apples, and kettle-cooked popcorn sold from rolling carts, and hamburgers and wieners grilled at the rickety concession trailer. The gross effect was an assault on the senses, and Dale and Gulliver reveled in being beaten to a mirthful pulp.

The boys had been enjoying themselves for less than an hour when they glimpsed their mother and father weaving through the crowd, seeking them out with a bloodhound's doggedness. Anxiously aware they were in more trouble than they had ever gotten themselves into before, they were not keen on incurring their parents' wrath.

So they fled.

Hunkered in a thicket of huckleberry bushes by the Porta-Potties, they waited for their parents to pass. They watched them split up by the swing carousel, both heading away from the boys' hiding spot.

"C'mon," Dale murmured to his little brother, leading him into the woods bordering the field.

For the remainder of that night and well into the after-noon of the following day, Dale and Gulliver survived by their Budgie Scout training and boyhood gumption. They camped on the glacially shorn top of a boulder, taking turns sleeping and keeping vigil beneath the rustling canopy of trees, which let through just enough moonlight to see by. Come dawn, they constructed a blind from plucked flora and woven twigs, hunting squirrel and quail with spears stone-whittled from tree branches. While they waited for quarry, they subsisted on wild raspberries, a hunk of smoked sausage Dale had in his jeans pocket, and fresh water from the creek. No varmints ever ventured into their sights, but they had a grand time anyway. They felt like frontiersmen of yore, borne out of a James Fenimore Cooper novel.

The search party found the Huggens brothers shortly before dusk. Thirty-three townspeople had been combing the territory since morning. When Caleb Schuster, the town pharmacist, veered away from the group to relieve himself, he came within earshot of the children's animated voices. Dale and Gulliver, debating whether Godzilla could trounce King Kong in a pentathlon, were too busy to notice their "rescuers" until they had been cornered.

Deputy Boone, smelling of maple syrup and Old Spice, drove them home in his squad car. He lectured them about how worried their mom and dad were, how dangerous it was to wander off into the woods prowling with bears and mountain lions, and how much bother they had caused everybody in general.

Their parents met them at the front door. Mother, her eyes red and swollen from crying, hugged both boys and ushered them inside. Father, scowling, halted Dale at the threshold, clasping a firm hand upon his son's shoulder.

He then slapped him hard across the face.

Gulliver heard it echo throughout the house and turned around. Dale stood there stunned a moment before his tears began to flow in rills. Their father did nothing to console him. As the elder of the siblings, he expected Dale to be more responsible. He expected him to be obedient. He expected him to present a meritorious example for his younger brother.

It was the only time he ever hit either of them.

They were both grounded for the month and had to bear the entirety of their summer recess without TV or dessert. They were, however, permitted to read books, provided they lacked illustrations, and, as a veritable institution in the Huggens household, they could play Scrabble. Dale and Gulliver had played the game often during their incarceration. They bonded through words, the words begetting jokes, the jokes begetting stories, and the stories begetting secrets shared only between them.

Later that same month they made their verbal pact to never desert one another, or else may the deserter suffer the unspoken—or rather, as yet undetermined—Huggens family curse. They sealed the agreement with a gloppy handshake, mingling their spit.

Gulliver now wondered if Dale, upon his death, had been cursed, in some way, for eternity.

Or by cheating a fate designed for them all, was it Gulliver who now lived the cursed existence? Yes, he should have died. Yet he didn't. And so this cursed life of his lingered on.

As it was, when Gulliver lost his brother, he eschewed any need for companionship, for closeness. While he got along affably enough at the most superficial of levels with the folks he encountered throughout his day, nobody could get past the barrier he had erected within himself. He guessed most thought him stodgy, introverted, or just plain weird. So be it. He became a loner by choice, for his own emotional and mental well-being, espousing the belief that if you didn't get too close to someone, you wouldn't miss them when they were gone.

This heavily fortified wall shielded him from pain… from *more* pain. Not even the Little People could scale its nebulous heights, though they seemed content enough with Gulliver cast in the symbiotic role of benign landlord.

But then he met Kat, and for the first time in many years he longed for somebody to break through the ramparts that sequestered him inside himself.

It was a crisp, light jacket autumn morning when she introduced him to the Caramallow Cocoaccino, and, by extension, to herself.

Gulliver had left for work at his usual time without encountering any of the Little People's impish hijinks. He locked his front door, unlocked it, then locked it once more, feeling that modicum of satisfaction he always did at how smoothly all the internal components—cylinder, cam, spring, tang—functioned together.

Glenn, his mail carrier, greeted him on his walkway.

"Hiya, Gully. Off to work?"

"Yeah." Gulliver paused, reluctantly, in a semblance of courtesy.

"How's business?" Glenn asked, flashing that used car salesman smile of his.

"Same, I guess."

Glenn was rail thin and almost comically short, his hefty mailbag making him look like he'd mugged Santa Claus on Christmas Eve. He was about Gulliver's age, though much worse for wear. The postman wore the stock gray-blue uniform of his profession—though it surely would have better fit somebody with regular measurements—and eye-magnifying Coke bottle glasses, its wire rims kinked from being sat on more than once. His joints made wet snapping noises when he walked. Throughout his life, doctors had variously diagnosed him with rheumatoid arthritis, ulcers, eczema, hypertension, hemorrhoids, chronic halitosis, athlete's foot, and premature hair loss. Despite his excess of afflictions, Glenn vaingloriously embraced his unrivalled status as the most renowned ladies' man in Laymon. His ingratiating, and wholly manufactured, charm went a long way.

According to him it did, anyway.

"I got a hummer from Greta Heffenstauffer last night."

"That's nice." Gulliver teetered on his feet impatiently. Glenn, for some reason, perceived him as a kindred playboy.

Gulliver proffered many a subtle hint to the contrary, but subtlety was as foreign to Glenn as a clean bill of health.

"She'll be a pro when the braces come off."

"I don't want to miss the bus. See you later, okay?" Gulliver was already inching away from him.

"You bet. We should go out for a beer sometime. Scope out the minxes."

"Sure," Gulliver shouted over his shoulder as he scooted up the sidewalk toward Fairview Avenue. "If I can."

"Let me know!" Glenn hollered back while stuffing that week's flyers into Gulliver's chuckwagon-shaped mailbox.

The public bus route stretched twenty-nine miles, from Laymon in the north to Sulfur Springs in the south.

The S.S., that is, Sulfur Springs, was a trendy spa resort town named after its famed fart-scented curative water aquifer, the kind of getaway to which well-to-do middle-aged urbanites flocked to recapture youth sapped from them by too much sun tanning, alcohol benders, and prescription drug popping. It was three times as densely populated as Laymon, with fifteen times as many antique boutiques, gift shoppes, and cafés. It also boasted Aberdeen County's only first-run movie theater, the five-screen Art Deco Prestwick.

The avocado-green, rust-pocked, exhaust-spewing transit bus Gulliver rode had been running daily between the two cities going on three decades, the latter two-thirds driven by the indefatigably gregarious Mr. Russ. The burly, hazelnut-skinned former doo-wopper had thick cornrowed hair and freckles not much darker than his complexion. He could have been in his forties, fifties, or sixties, but as he always told folks, with his sly grin and Barry White voice, he was "forever twenty-one, baby, and built to boogie." Mr. Russ himself had ornamented the bus's interior with Astroturf, gold and silver garland, smiley faces, and collectible 45rpm records. While driving, he often played old school hip-hop and R&B cassettes on a scuffed-up portable radio, its bass cranked up to the max, earning the vehicle's appellation as the Boom Boom Bus. The locals never groused about the volume, and out-of-towners seldom did either. It just seemed fitting.

At a quarter to ten, the bus lurched to the curb at Fairview and Elkwood, its last posted stop in Laymon before it circled around and headed back to Sulfur Springs. The doors jerked open. Gulliver, the sole passenger, stepped off. The bus always picked him up in the mornings and dropped him off in the evenings on the corner of Fairview and Collifax near his home. Not an official stop, but Mr. Russ made an exception for Gulliver. He liked the boy.

"You have a good day, Gulliver," Mr. Russ crooned.

"I'll try. But I'm sure it'll be the same one I always have."

"Maybe today will be different."

"How?"

"Well, you can do something different."

"Like what?"

Russ swished the question around in his pumpkinish noggin. "You dig scuba divin'?"

Gulliver scrunched his face. "Not particularly."

Mr. Russ pondered a moment more, then shrugged. "I got nothin' else."

Gulliver chuckled.

The driver waved and swung the doors shut.

Gulliver trotted up Fairview Avenue, downtown Laymon's main street, lined with a smattering of quaint small shops and mom-and-pop restaurants, a fair share of dollar-draft taverns, and a surfeit of properties for rent that had been moldering on the depressed market for months or more.

The city's prosperity had taken a steep downturn in '94 when its lumber industry abruptly shut down. That was the year the region had been declared a federal wildlife refuge, owing mostly to its endangered eagle population, thus protecting what remained of their eroded habitat from further deforestation. As a consequence, over two hundred lumber-jacks and mill laborers found themselves without jobs and unable to support their families. Many relocated to Sulfur Springs, securing employment in its thriving hospitality and service sectors. Others landed logging work further north and to the west. A handful, those nearing retirement, stayed in Laymon, where they planned to die with all the dignity they could afford on their modest savings and severance packages. The eagles had since multiplied threefold, while Laymon's human population dipped below two thousand, a third of what it had been in better times.

Still, the city endured. Two Laymon attractions helped keep their current economy partially buoyant, each drawing dozens of tourists monthly: the eagle-watching guided hiking tours ($30 per person, $15 for children fourteen and under), and the Martin Van Buren Meteorite, the only known space rock resembling a U.S. president. Unearthed by prospectors on the East Devil's Horn in the early 1900s, it weighed eight hundred pounds and since '57 had been on exhibit in the Laymon Town Hall lobby beneath a shatterproof Plexiglas cube. While not as celebrated as the Lunar Liberace in Vegas, Laymon's did offer the advantage of free admission. (The penny smasher machine cost a dollar per penny pressed.)

As part of his workday routine, Gulliver always stopped at the Beanie Roast, its savory and soothing aromas reminding him of the home-cooked breakfasts his mother once made. The coffee shop's décor had been inspired by an English teahouse, with its rose-patterned wallpaper, chestnut stained woods, and accents of lace doilies under china vases and Brown Betty teapots. The only feature antithetical to this theme was the art on its walls, a series of patently American cowboy-life lithographs.

It was here Gulliver first laid eyes on her, bustling behind the counter in a periwinkle bib apron, whipping up froth for a latte as if it were a magic trick. He figured she must have been new in town, for he never could have overlooked somebody like her, the most beautiful, most exotic specimen of femininity Gulliver had ever come across.

She was a full head taller, a good twenty-five pounds slimmer, and maybe a few years younger than he was. Her porcelain skin glowed ethereally, her arms adorned with tattoos of hellish flames, screaming skulls, and bug-eyed monsters. On the dimple of her left cheek was a dime-sized crimson heart. Satiny raven hair cascaded down to her shoulders like a German helmet. Her succulent lips were painted so sultry a red they could coax even the most devout of celibates into spending a night inside her silky, snug den. Her eyes were a hypnotic iridescent green with flecks of brilliant blue that twinkled in the light—two prized marbles you'd never trade for anything. She wore a tiger-print top with provocatively placed slits over very gropable breasts, a short white skirt that showed off her sleek, toned legs, and suede ankle boots with burnished silver buckles.

Gulliver's eyes latched onto her with invisible grappling hooks. He watched her, unblinking, as she served three other customers before directing her attention to him.

"May I help you?" Her smile was as alluring as a box of crystal diodes, her voice that of an angel's with a few bits of empyrean gravel caught in its throat.

"I think so... I hope so."

"Whatcha in the mood for?"

"I'm not sure." Gulliver mulled it over, glancing cursorily at the menu board above him, but his brain was too muzzy to decide what beverage most appealed to him at that moment. He gave up. "Surprise me?"

"Okay." She stepped closer to him. He smelt maraschino cherries and wild roses on her. "You want something to pick you up, something to chill you out, or something to sweeten your day?"

"Sweet," he blurted. "Please."

"Small, medium, or large?"

"Large. You only live once, right?" Gulliver grinned goofily.

"You got it."

Gulliver studied how she moved, mesmerized. So elegant was she preparing the espresso, steaming the milk in a stainless steel carafe, adding it to the cup with the coffee, drizzling chocolate and caramel syrups into it, spooning creamy foam onto the top, and sprinkling it with mini marshmallows.

"I call this a Caramallow Cocoaccino."

She handed her creation to Gulliver.

He sipped it. It was delicious.

"Sweet enough for you?"

"Yes. Thank you."

"That'll be $4.25."

Gulliver dug into his pocket and fished out a five-dollar bill. Their fingers touched tantalizingly for an instant as he handed it to her.

She rang him up at the single cash register, snapping up coins from the till.

"Oh. Keep the change."

"Much obliged, good sir." There was that smile again. So maddeningly sexy.

She dropped the seventy-five cents into a mason jar with the label "IF WE'RE TOPS, PLEASE TIP."

"You share tips?" Gulliver asked.

"Yeah. We divvy it up between whoever's working the same shift."

"Is somebody working with you now?"

"Becky is. She's still on her break, so I'm flying solo here."

"It's just that I want you to have my whole tip… because I meant it for you."

She snickered and licked her upper lip. "That's mighty generous of you, Daddy Warbucks. But I don't mind splitting it. Really."

"Okay. Just so long as you know it was all for you."

She put on her best Southern drawl. "You're makin' me blush, mister."

"Gulliver. I'm Gulliver."

"Kat." She bobbed her chin toward her plastic name badge. It had devil horns glued to the top, vampiress fangs on the bottom.

"Is that short for Katherine?"

"Katrina. But never call me that. It's a princess's name. And I'm no princess."

"I haven't seen you before."

"Only been here two weeks."

A couple of customers entered the shop then, a pair of bushy mustachioed men in head-to-toe L.L. Bean outfits, clearly tourists, chatting livelily about near-death experiences they'd had. They both ordered medium decaf coffees and inquired about the pastries in the display case.

Becky, a chubby, pimply twenty-something shoehorned into a polka dot gingham dress advertising her canyonesque cleavage, came back from her break. One of her eyes was bloodshot, and she babbled on about this trippy *Twilight Zone* episode she had watched the night before.

That was from *The Outer Limits*, one of the mustached customers corrected her.

Whatever, Becky answered, tying on her apron. Aliens creeped her out.

Gulliver waited for Kat to resume their conversation, until he began feeling awkward just standing there.

"I'll see you around, Kat," he finally called out as he eased toward the door.

She glanced his way. "Nice meeting you, Gulliver." Then, back to one of the mustached customers, "No, sir, those are raisins."

Gulliver beamed. She had remembered his name.

That had been over six months ago. Since then, Gulliver frequented the café at least once a day, sometimes making sublime small talk with Kat while ordering drinks for himself or his boss. Most times, though, she was too preoccupied with other customers for anything beyond a cordial greeting and the obligatory, usually rhetorical "How are you?"

Other times, Gulliver would gaze at her from outside the shop window, much as a cat would when tempted by the fan-finned showpiece in an aquarium. If she noticed him, he would quickly avert his eyes and scurry off, ripples of shame trailing him like sticky webs.

"You're late, Huggens," Gulliver's boss rasped without looking up.

Gulliver slipped behind the counter, turning sideways to scooch between it and a chest freezer with a faulty compressor. He checked his wristwatch. "I'm ten minutes early."

The older man glanced at his own watch while he joggled a pair of needlenose pliers. "So you are. Fix the clock on the wall, would ya?"

Gulliver's employer for the past five years was Reggie Knox, owner of Knox Electronix, located downtown at the intersection of Fairview and Stagg. The shop had been there going on a quarter of a century. Not much about it had changed since Mr. Knox opened it, financed with a nest egg he'd saved up during his carefree days of dope dealing and motorcycle customizing. Knox's was *the* repair service in all of Aberdeen County for any electronic gadget in existence. (His motto, available on complimentary pencils and refrigerator magnets: "If Knox Electronix can't fix it, it ain't worth fixin'!") Televisions, radios, cameras, clocks, calculators, computers, and kitchen appliances cluttered the narrow rows of gunmetal gray shelving, some items stacked four or five high. Business wasn't booming, but enough money flowed in to support Mr. Knox's unfussy lifestyle, as well as covering Gulliver's wages.

Knox was seated on a bar stool at the worktable, operating on the entrails of a TV with his scarred and callused hands. Knox was an outlaw biker without a gang, the majority of his rebel brethren in the Razer Eaterz Motorcycle Club having some time ago swapped out their Midwest real estate in favor of more consistent temperate climes in the South. His wavy mane of more-salt-than-pepper hair was tied back in a ponytail with a rubber band, so taut it smoothed the many ruts of wrinkles on his forehead. The rest of his face imitated the rough texture and tawny hue of broken-in buckskin from decades of hard riding and harder partying. He wore a hell-travelled pair of Harley-Davidson zip boots, and faded and frayed denim ensembles that wouldn't make the grade for a homeless donation bin. He was a dinosaur and damn proud of it.

Gulliver sorted through the pending invoices on the countertop.

Mr. Knox rose from the stool, scratching his stubbly chin with ragged fingernails yellowed from nicotine.

"I need you to finish hooking up the tube on the RCA here. Make sure you test out all the dials." He wagged a crooked finger at an antiquated stereo console on a shelf, one with a still operational turntable. "And take a gander at that hi-fi. Think the speakers are blown. And call Mr. Giles, tell him his goddamned toaster is ready. You know he called twice yesterday? Sonuvabitch must love his toast."

Knox threw on his weather-flogged denim vest with the "Razer Eaterz MC" patch emblazoned on the back. The patch depicted a tusked wild boar, either snarling or smiling, festooned with coils of barbed wire. "I'm taking the rest of the day off. Getting the finishing touches done on my tat."

Mr. Knox hitched up the sleeve of his white T-shirt, revealing a gaudy tattoo of a busty nude woman with outrageously long, luxurious hair and octopus tentacles for legs, neither of which had yet been colored in. Her bosom and tentacles undulated when he flexed his granitic bicep.

"How's it look?"

Gulliver appraised it. "Kind of freaky."

"Good. Chicks dig freaky."

Gulliver grinned at him.

"Still amazed an old coot like me would want to get inked?"

"I didn't say anything."

"You listen to me, son," said Mr. Knox soberly. "Three best ways to keep yourself young are sex, speed, and tats."

"I hate needles. And I don't have a car."

"Then you better hurry up and find some velvet highway to pave before you run out of gas."

Gulliver reddened. "Jeez, Mr. Knox, I'm not *that* old."

"What is it they say? After age eighteen, your body's on the slow road to a cold grave." Knox chortled through his ocher-stained teeth. "Don't forget to lock the place up. You can close a few minutes early if it's dead."

"'Kay," Gulliver nodded as he walked over to the gutted television on the worktable.

"See ya tomorrow, Gulv."

Mr. Knox moseyed out the entrance door, dinging the small brass bell above it. After lighting one of his unfiltered, bonus tar, cancer-be-damned cigarettes, he mounted his '65 Harley-Davidson Panhead out front, modified with chrome pipes, ape hanger handlebars, and a gator hide saddle seat.

Kick-starting and revving its powerful 1200cc engine, he launched up the street with a window-rattling roar.

Somewhere nearby, a dog barked to salute his passing.

Gulliver tweaked the settings on the reassembled RCA television, rotating each of the knobs beneath the screen to correct the spectral double-image of Angela Lansbury in a *Murder, She Wrote* rerun.

The bell over the door jingled. A customer, he presumed, without yet looking up.

"Hi, handsome," said a familiar voice, one saucy and seductive.

This wasn't a customer. It was Kat, in a scandalously indecent Catholic schoolgirl's uniform—unbuttoned-to-her-navel white blouse, pleated tartan miniskirt, black high heels, and incongruous, but not at all unappealing, fishnet stockings.

"H-h-hello." Gulliver's voice scrambled for footing. His eyes bulged so far they could have ventured off on their own. He gulped. "M-may I help you?"

"I've got a broken blinker." Kat's pink-ribboned pigtails swayed each time she coyly cocked her head. "Can you take a peek at it?"

Gulliver didn't drive, much less repair automobiles, though Mr. Knox had given him a few ill-advised motorcycle-riding lessons many months ago.

"I don't really do cars."

"But can you do me?" Kat mewed through pouty lips.

She parted her blouse, baring her breasts to him. They were as round and firm as a pair of honeydews, almost befitting a Frank Frazetta barbarian queen.

Almost, except for her nipples. Each had a teardrop-shaped Christmas light screwed into them.

The left one shined a bright red. The right was unlit.

"I don't know what's wrong," Kat frowned. "It just went out." She gazed into Gulliver's eyes. "Think you can fix it?"

Gulliver gulped again. "Ummm... I can try." He raised his hand, letting it hover centimeters away from her defective teat-light. "May I?"

"Go ahead," she answered enticingly.

His hand glided to the bad bulb. He unscrewed it, slowly, from its pink puckered areola.

Kat squirmed, shutting her eyes and biting her bottom lip. She moaned.

"Am I hurting you?"

She shook her head. Her fingers twiddled the mother-of-pearl buttons of her blouse.

He disconnected the bulb and examined it between his fingertips. A blue-green crust caked its electrical contact.

"You have a little corrosion here... See?" Rolling it in his palm, he let her inspect it for herself. She hmm'd.

"I should be able to clean it off."

Gulliver picked up a sheet of sandpaper from the work-table. He buffed the threads. Fine powder like polluted snow dusted the countertop.

"There," Gulliver said, blowing off the contact. "That should do it."

He twisted the bulb back into Kat's boob-socket. It flared a vibrant ruby red, matching its mate.

Kat smiled. "You're a genius."

He shrugged his shoulders. "It was nothing."

"How can I repay you?"

"Don't worry about it." He faltered for words a moment. "It was my pleas—"

Kat seized Gulliver by his collar, pulling him to her warm, tender lips. She kissed him hard and deep, their tongues tangoing in one another's mouths until his was stewing in her molten hot saliva.

Sparks flew out of Gulliver's ears. His hair smoldered. His face boiled and bubbled, the flesh melting away from his skull. Kat licked it, slurped him up.

He moaned.

Gulliver awoke with a gasp, unpeeling his cheek from the table as he jolted upright on the stool. He gawked at his own ghostly reflection in the glossy black screen of the TV in front of him, drawing his fingertips across his sodden scalp. The indistinct outline of his sweaty head evaporated from the lacquered tabletop, as if it were residue of his dream.

His incredible dream.

His groin throbbed.

He peered out the store window, across the street. At the Beanie Roast.

He was in a desperate mood for coffee.

3

Gulliver started marching across the street with the conviction of Don Juan. (Or was he more Don Quixote?)

He rehearsed aloud some potential icebreakers:

"Hey, your hair looks great."

"Hey, awesome outfit."

"Hey, you smell pretty."

"Hey, I'm such a dork."

Gulliver sighed. With each step, his stomach roiled more and more fiercely as a storm of anxiety surged through him.

Today, he vowed to himself, would be the day he asked Kat out. Today would be the day she said yes. Today would be the day they would always remember as the day the seed of their ever blooming love found purchase and germinated.

Yes, today *would* be that day.

Yet if today were anything like yesterday, or the litany of days before that, Gulliver's romantic ambitions would be thwarted by his own nagging self-doubts and physical aversions to rejection, humiliation, and garlic, all of which could make him break out in unsightly rashes. It was these persistent and perhaps prescient misgivings that likely made his skin itch as it did now, why he was scratching his arms and neck raw.

Though maybe, he hypothesized, if he scratched deep enough, a better, braver Gulliver Huggens would emerge.

When Gulliver entered the Beanie Roast, his heart froze.

Kat's arms were wrapped around another man.

He had one of those grotesquely disproportionate bodies, a preternaturally paunchy middle ballooning from much slenderer arms and legs that resembled the air valves on tires. He was ginger-haired and bulbous-nosed, ugly as a Yahoo from the land of the Houyhnhnms, wearing an atrocious triple plus-sized Hawaiian shirt (with coconut palms, woody wagons, and hula girls) that hung down to the cuffs of his cargo shorts. Worst of all, he sported Birkenstock sandals over white athletic socks.

At that moment, he was choking on a biscotti.

He stood bow-legged by one of the round mosaic-topped café tables, gagging and jiggling. Kat wrestled to bring her hands around the man's rotund waist from behind, but was about a foot shy of being able to interlock her fingers. Valiantly she pressed at his abdomen using sharp spastic squeezes, which only made him jiggle more and did nothing for his gagging. She released him and, trying another technique, slammed her fist between his shoulder blades. This sounded like she was pummeling a cold slab of beef and proved just as ineffectual.

Gulliver watched dumbstruck, the scene conjuring up a mental image of some alien mating ritual between two biologically incompatible species.

Kat looked toward Gulliver in a panic.

"Help me!" she pleaded. "I think he's dying!"

Gulliver vacillated, glancing around him. He was the only other person there. He considered seeking out more qualified assistance—anybody really—but quickly concluded time might be of the essence, since the fat guy was indeed turning an alarming shade of violet. He dashed toward them.

"Excuse me," he said to Kat, rather meekly.

She stepped away. Planting his feet on the floor behind him, Gulliver girdled his arms around the man's midsection, forming a fist with one hand and clutching it with the other.

He thrust upward once, twice, then a third time, until the soggy brick dislodged from the man's throat and splatted on the tabletop.

"Thanks," the big man mumbled, transferring the buttery slobber oozing down his chin onto his wrist. He flumped down into his chair and resumed devouring the remaining portion of his biscotti, now taking an extra couple of precautionary sips of coffee before swallowing each bite.

"Are you okay, sir?" Kat asked, appearing far more shaken than he did.

"Yeah, I'm fine." He held up his cup. "Can I get a refill?"

She took the cup, circled around the counter, and poured him more black coffee from a silver pump pot thermos.

Kat turned to Gulliver, still standing in the same spot.

"Can you give this to him?"

She passed the cup to Gulliver. He set it down on the table before the man chewing his biscotti like it was cud.

Kat breathed a sigh of relief, though for a while thereafter she kept her eyes trained on the customer, half expecting him to have a cardiac arrest, cerebral aneurysm, or herniated disc next.

"That was pretty amazing." She smiled at Gulliver, who had sidled up to the counter to be nearer to her.

"I just did what I had to." For some reason, he became neurotic his nose hairs weren't trimmed, so he kept his face bashfully downward.

"Well, you deserve a free drink, at least. What are ya having today?"

"Oh... how about your special?"

"You got it. One Tall, Dark and Hot. Extra sweet?"

"Please."

She winked at him and went to prepare the extreme java cocktail. The "Tall, Dark and Hot" was a large dark roast coffee with a triple shot of espresso and hot fudge. It was Kat's original recipe, aimed at those jonesing for the beverage equivalent of a caffeine-and-sugar injection directly into their veins.

"Room for cream?"

Gulliver shook his head. He never diluted Kat's creations.

She handed him the steaming cup.

"Thanks." He sniffed it. "Smells like a chocolate factory."

"Yeah, chocolate on steroids."

Gulliver chuckled.

"That was intense, wasn't it?"

He nodded while sipping her concoction. It was so hot it scalded the roof of his mouth, so sweet it made his teeth ache. It was perfect.

Kat raised an eyebrow at him. "So, you save people often?"

"No, I don't," Gulliver answered, more earnestly than her question called for.

Kat peered over at the morbidly obese customer again. He had finished off the biscotti unscathed and now sat nursing his coffee while poring over a comic book titled *Fire Foxes*. There were many b&w panels of hard-bodied, hardly clothed ladies shooting big guns in it.

"Guess he gets to live another day to chow down another cookie."

"Every day counts," Gulliver replied. He wasn't entirely sure what he meant by it, but it sounded positive and profound to him. Maybe it did to Kat too.

Gulliver cleared his throat, rallying the kind of courage one derives from knowing he's just impressed a girl. "Hey, uh, I know this might be coming out of nowhere…"

Right then, two groups of customers filed into the shop. First came four teenagers, a set of identical twin cheerleaders with identical twin laughs, hanging onto the brawny arms of two swaggering, spiked hair jocks in college football jerseys. Then came an older couple in matching checkered coats in the midst of an argument concerning his bleeding rectum; she insisted he should consult a doctor, while he blamed it on her too spicy cooking. Both groups approached the counter, switching conversations to what drinks would slake their thirsts and, as applicable, wouldn't irritate a certain some-body's bowels.

Kat pursed her lips, trying to mask her annoyance. She hated when they flocked in at once. "Can I help anybody?"

None of them were ready to be helped yet.

Before his nerves fizzled on him, Gulliver prattled off what he wanted to say, a condensed version of it at any rate, in a machine gun staccato. "I was just wondering if maybe we could go out sometime. For a cup of coffee. But not here. And it doesn't have to be coffee."

Staring down at a tea-stained wooden stirrer on the countertop, Gulliver realized he hadn't looked at Kat once while proposing his starry-eyed intentions.

He lifted his eyes in line with hers.

Kat was gawping at him as if he'd exposed a part of himself she had no desire to see. Which, in a way, he had. Gulliver now wished he could lasso his ineloquent, inane wooings—"oral excreta" Father would've called them—and reel them all the way back into his brain, grind them up into mulch, and shovel the stinking pile into some fathomless abyss, never to be found.

But, of course, it was much too late for that.

"Are you asking me out on a date?" Kat asked in the prickliest of tones.

"Uh... yeah."

"Oh." She froze, like a spent mechanized toy needing to be wound up.

"Excuse me, miss," a customer interjected. It was the wife of the man who shat blood. "We're ready to order."

Kat shifted her focus to the couple. "Just a sec."

She then turned back to Gulliver. "Let me think about it, okay?"

"Alright." Gulliver figured she was snubbing him, but at least he could appear nonchalant about it. *Play Johnny B. Cool*, as Mr. Russ would say. "I work across the street, at the repair shop—"

"I know," she said, this time unmistakably dismissive. "I'll talk to you later."

With that, Kat whirled away from him, giving her undivided attention to the customers hankering for their lattes and frappes.

Gulliver frowned. Gripping his "Tall, Dark and Hot," he shambled out of the Beanie Roast, his heart retreating into the farthest, loneliest refuge within him, a destination he often visited when he felt he belonged nowhere else.

When Gulliver had returned to Knox's, he busied himself with wiping and wiring, soldering and screwing, degaussing and gluing. Anything to keep his mind off Kat. Anything to keep his mind off himself.

He supposed he should have been proud just for being able to muster up the courage to ask her out. But the failure on her part to acknowledge this singular achievement dissolved whatever newfound feelings of confidence he might have garnered from it. It was like gambling everything you had in your wallet and not only winning zilch, but also losing the wallet through a rip in your pocket.

All he could do now was move on. Forget.

Perhaps later—much later—he would fantasize an alternate outcome, one where he and Kat were kneeling side by side milking a nanny goat, squirting each other from its engorged teats, whooping and laughing, before rolling around together, fondling one another, making love on the hay-strewn floorboards...

Of course, he would only be deluding himself. Fantasies were just that. A frisky goat-milking rendezvous was not in their future.

Growing up in veritable isolation on his aunt and uncle's ranch in the boondocks, Gulliver had very few opportunities to interact with persons of the opposite sex. Once, Aunt Augusta invited her church chum Joyce over for toast and tea. Joyce was a dotty old biddy with impossibly long and bony fingers, much like a chimpanzee's. She liked to point at things with them. She had brought her tomboyish daughter along with her. "Dear Ethel," as Joyce always called her, had a bowl haircut and buckteeth, and was developmentally retarded. Though her body exhibited all the voluptuous curves of womanhood, she had the cognitive faculties of a seven-year-old—albeit a horny seven-year-old. Gulliver, who was ten at the time, had to guard his crotch from her relentlessly roving hands while they'd played *Chutes and Ladders* in his room. When she got around to unveiling her own jungle-thatched chute to him, he bolted from the room and tattled on her. It was the last time Dear Ethel ever paid them a visit.

And then there was Sara.

Gulliver's aunt drove his uncle into town one January morning for his weekly electrotherapy sessions, which had improved the wiggling of his toes. Gulliver stayed home to care for the animals. He was filling the goats' trough with wilted veggies and grains when he spotted her trudging out of the woods, bundled up in enough coats to make her look inflated.

She had stumbled upon their ranch after trekking miles across the foot-deep crust of freshly fallen snow, avoiding the plowed roadways and, specifically, her stepfather. Gulliver ran up to her. She about collapsed at his feet.

He hoisted her onto his back, her arms draped limply over his shoulders, and carried her into the house, setting her down in front of the kerosene heater. He helped her off with her coats, gloves, and boots. The harsh winter chill had bled through all those puffy layers, her skin deathly cold to the touch.

Her name was Sara, she'd told him through chattering teeth and chapped lips. She was fifteen and, though three years older than Gulliver, was half his size. She was also perhaps the loveliest creature he had ever seen, with cherubic cheeks and an otariid nose. Her eyes were a faceted emerald green, her hair a ringleted brown reminiscent of ripples of wind-swept, sun-baked sand. Beneath her heavy outer gear, she wore summery khakis and a baby blue camisole with white chenille trim. Under her yellow slicker boots a single pair of men's woolen socks covered her frostbitten feet.

He fed her his aunt's home-baked oatmeal raisin cookies and some sourdough bread, served with mulberry marmalade and a glass of stove-warmed goat's milk. He could tell, as famished as she was, that she could have scarfed down everything at once. Whatever dining etiquette had been ingrained into her had won out, as each dainty bite was chewed thoroughly, then washed down with a moderate sip of milk.

After her hunger had been sated and she was sitting cozily on the settee, Gulliver asked her why she had been walking all by herself through the dark, freezing woods. She was running away, Sara replied. Why? Sara's countenance turned somber. Because her stepdad Jesse was mean as a cougar, meaner still if he were drunk and lonely. She wouldn't elaborate any further than that, and Gulliver didn't press her. He saw the overlapping purple welts, like Rorschach tests, blotting her arms.

What about her mom? She never noticed anything. Or she didn't want to, 'cause Jesse took care of them.

Tears welled in Sara's eyes.

"Where are you going?" Gulliver then asked.

Sara shrugged, squeegeeing her tear-streaked cheeks with her knuckles. "Just away." As far as she could go. Where Jesse couldn't find her.

"But where will you live?"

"Anywhere," she answered. It didn't matter.

Gulliver could tell Sara was scared about not having planned things out, but she was much more scared of her stepfather. He was a bad man who did bad stuff to her.

Gulliver could have hidden her in the musty hayloft of the barn or cleared a livable secret space for her in their cluttered attic. Or he could have loaded her up with enough sandwiches, snacks, and sodas to sustain her on her journey to someplace, anyplace, better. He could have even run off with her, to keep her company, to keep her safe.

He could have done any of these things, but he didn't.

Instead, he told his aunt about Sara when she got home with his uncle. He told her that Sara was in trouble, that she needed help.

Aunt Augusta spoke to Sara privately on the veranda for nearly fifteen minutes. Then she drove the poor, resigned girl back home. Back to Jesse.

"They'll work things out," Aunt Augusta, an armchair psychologist, reassured Gulliver. It was normal for a child to resent her mother's new husband, seeing him as a competitor for her affections. It was normal for Sara to fabricate stories of emotional and physical abuse to sully him, to drive a wedge between her mother and stepfather. It was even normal for her to hurt herself, her bruises lending credence to her fibs.

Not three months later, after the spring thaw, hikers spotted in a gulch Sara's body, or rather her gnarled, desiccated hand, protruding from an eroded mound of soil and forest detritus. She had been slowly strangled and hastily buried.

Someone had tried to hide her after all. Someone other than Gulliver.

Jesse and Sara had both disappeared the month before, abandoning Sara's mother without warning or explanation. She'd reckoned Jesse might have kidnapped her "little flower-bud" and had reported this presumption to the authorities. She had wept uncontrollably, like any good mother would, willing to concede maybe Jesse actually was the bad man Sara had claimed him to be.

Now she knew for sure.

They never caught Jesse.

And Gulliver never forgot how he had failed to save Sara... how he had failed to save his brother Dale... how, when he was sixteen, he had even failed to save his three-legged cocker spaniel Rondo from darting into the path of a snow-plow...

Gulliver shook off these memories and, with the ageless guilt still clawing at his viscera, resumed tinkering with the chaotic innards of the hi-fi stereo system, losing himself in its multi-colored network of wires and tubes.

The tiny bell above the door jingled. Soft footsteps approached. Gulliver didn't look up from the worktable until he caught the familiar fragrance of exotic roses and cherry resin. Eau de Kat.

She sashayed toward him, her vampish eyes locking with his spellbound stare. She stepped up to the counter, leaning so far forward her breasts all but flopped out from her low-cut green-sequined V-neck.

"So. I thought about it," she said. "And I'm free tonight."

Gulliver paused as his lust-addled mind processed her words.

"Oh. Great. That's great. So am I. You wanna go out?"

There was a playful gleam in Kat's eyes. "I think I already said yes to that."

"Oh, yeah," Gulliver replied with a titter. "Guess you did."

Recognizing his awkwardness, as cute as it was, Kat mercifully turned her head away from him, scanning the shelves of disabled electronic equipment.

52

"You fix stuff here, huh?"

"Yes," he said, rising from his stool. "TVs, microwaves, radios, anything electronic. And I can even build new stuff from old parts."

Both Gulliver and his brother had, from early on in their lives, demonstrated an innate aptitude for gadgetry. Gulliver wasn't so much intrigued by what a device did, but rather how it did it—how a bulb or bell connected to a socket connected to a wire connected to a battery connected to a switch that, when thrown, would generate light or sound. Each element was a factor in a challenging equation for which he sought a solution. Once he figured out the logic of the design, its function was merely a practical footnote. Dale on the other hand had had more creative inclinations. By age ten, he'd constructed a huge outdoor pulley-operated sun scrim to keep the Huggens' home cool in the swelter of summer, and a model train-based delivery system that not only transported a three-course meal via tracks to any room in the house, but also kept hot food hot and cold drinks cold by its temperature-regulated platters. He could be, as Father would say, bogglingly inventive.

"You're quite the handyman. I like that." Kat grinned. "Bet it comes in handy."

Gulliver, flushed, floundered for a response.

"You make really good coffee."

Kat snickered. Balancing on her toes, she leaned even farther over the countertop, closer to Gulliver, squeezing her boobs together between her upper arms for augmented cleavage. It compromised his ability to engage in conversation, and she knew it. She knew how to work a man, what buttons to push on him. Kat was a woman who embraced her libidinous impulses, her wanton urges.

She hadn't met a man yet who didn't appreciate that about her.

"Wanna know my secret?" she said invitingly.

Gulliver nodded.

"I pour four scoops into the machine, flick it on, and it does the rest by itself. Pretty hard to screw up."

"Well, I've had some nasty-tasting coffee before. You must be doing something right, whether you know it or not."

Kat smiled again. The fluorescents above reflected in the irises of her eyes and washed out her alabaster skin even more, giving her a bewitching android appearance.

"Got a pen?" she asked.

Gulliver picked out a blue Bic, missing its plastic cap, from the Harley-Davidson coffee mug beside him. He passed it to her.

She grabbed his wrist. Along his forearm she jotted something with the pen.

"Here's my address. Pick me up at eight."

Gulliver looked at his arm. Gasped.

"I don't have a car. At the moment. I m-m-mean... I'm between cars."

"Then I'll pick you up. Got a home, I hope?"

"Uh, yeah. Sure I do." Gulliver reached for one of his personalized Knox Electronix business cards off the stack on the counter. He wrote down his address on the back and gave it to her.

"I live on Klunghoffer Street, by Collifax Road."

Kat studied the card a moment. "Gulliver Huggens? Killer name." She said it like she sincerely meant it, her official stamp of approval.

"See you tonight, Gulliver Huggens." She then did a lazy pirouette away from him and strolled out of the shop, her flawless oval buttocks swaying with each step, keeping tempo with her own sensual beat.

Gulliver was smitten.

Her scent hung over him like a euphoric haze. He could still feel the tingly tickle of her touch on his wrist, could still see the glimmer of her eyes in front of him, the lusciousness of her lips, the ripeness of her breasts. It took several seconds for these phantom sensations to recede and his mind to register that she was indeed gone.

It took a few more moments for him to comprehend she had been seducing him.

At least, he thought she'd been.

He had had a couple of girls brazenly hit on him since returning to Laymon. There was the plump-limbed cashier at the Eagle Market who bagged his groceries and always offered him her tutti-frutti gum, straight from her mouth. He declined every time. And the fifty-something platinum blonde divorcee at Po' Pappy's Bar & Grill who dressed like she was still seventeen, flaunting her expired goods. She'd bought him an overture of a cocktail called Sex on the Beach. He had thanked her and hurriedly left, acting as if he'd suddenly remembered a life-or-death matter he'd neglected to tend to.

But Kat was doing much more than such elementary coquetries. Indubitably, she had earned her MFA—Master of Flirtatious Arts—with advanced certifications in cosmetic appeal and, Gulliver suspected, holistic lovemaking.

Oh yes, he was certain of it. She'd definitely been seducing him.

He wondered if he would ever get to see her naked.

4

Gulliver closed up Knox's. With eight o'clock only three hours away, his belly once again began to pitch and roll, as if he were standing on a ship's deck while crossing a turbulent sea. But instead of a sea, he was crossing Fairview Avenue, toward his haircutter. His nerves were wreaking havoc on him as well, sending tidal shockwaves throughout his body, making him foggy-brained and jittery.

A car braked with a screech in front of him, honking angrily. Gulliver scarcely noticed.

He had to get ready.

Of course, he was excited too. How many other times in his life had he the enviable opportunity to date such a remarkably beautiful woman… or any woman? None. Ever. And he wasn't going to squander this chance, nerves be damned.

Seven Seas Styles was one of two haircutting places in Laymon. Unlike the no-frills, women-catered Darling Do's, Seven Seas had a kitschy atmosphere Gulliver found fun and endearing. The entire shop, inside and out, was decorated with tropical and nautical motifs—dried palm fronds stapled over the ceiling, marbled aquamarine tiles on the floors, and out front an Easter Island moai statue chiseled from a cigar store wooden Indian by Seven Seas Styles' longtime proprietor, the pathologically ebullient Vic. On the wall was an authentic hardwood captain's wheel which, when spun by a "wee lad" or "wee lass," could win the child a piece of saltwater taffy, a rubber fish, or a plastic flower lei, depending on which ship-shaped label the arrowed handgrip peg landed on.

Vic, sporting his signature Vandyke beard and admiral's cap with golden anchor insignia, draped a maroon cape over Gulliver. The spry sexagenarian had never seen an actual ocean in person, much less sailed on one. But someday, he boasted, after he retired, he planned to buy the biggest boat he could afford and voyage around the equator, docking at every white sandy beach and blue water cove he came upon. And though consensus was that Vic never *really* intended to retire, everybody wanted to believe in his seafaring pipedream anyway. He was just that kind of good ol' joe you rooted for.

"I need to look stellar, Captain Vic," Gulliver said as he settled into the vinyl-upholstered hydraulic chair. A block and tackle dangled from the headrest. "I have a date tonight."

The barber clucked his tongue, then nodded assuredly. "In that case, I'll give you my special 'Handsome Devil' cut. I'll just leave the horns off."

Vic spritzed Gulliver's hair with a spray bottle and slicked it back with a comb.

Regarding himself in the wall mirror, Gulliver thought he resembled a young Marlon Brando, minus the leather jacket and machismo.

"Who's the lucky gal?"

Gulliver smiled. "She's a dream. I can't stop thinking about her."

"Those are the best ones," Vic hailed, making the first snip with his scissors.

Gulliver, clean-cut as a congressman, exited Seven Seas Styles right as the Town Hall tower clock tolled six (which, being five minutes fast, indicated it was 5:55). This allowed him just enough time to catch the Boom Boom Bus, which arrived every hour on the hour, though inclement weather and Russ's compulsive indulgence for convenience store hot dogs and Coca-Cola slushies could affect the schedule. As it was, Gulliver only had to wait six minutes at the stop before Russ clunked up to the curb and creaked the doors open.

The bus was near empty except for one hand-holding elderly couple in hooded windbreaker jackets sitting on the rearmost bench and, of course, the inimitable Mr. Russ at the wheel. He was grooving to Parliament's funk track "Glory-hallastoopid" on his Reagan-era jambox.

"Afternoon, Gulliver. How was your day?"

"Great," Gulliver answered jauntily, taking the seat behind Russ. "I have a date tonight."

"Congrats, Casanova." He shot his palm up. Gulliver high-fived him.

"Remember to bring protection," the driver counseled him, pulling the lever to shut the doors. "I recommend a crucifix."

Gulliver chuckled. "I don't think she sucks blood."

He spied Russ cocking an eyebrow at him in the rearview mirror. "She's a woman, ain't she?"

The instant he got home, Gulliver commenced his fastidious, if largely improvised, primp-and-preen ritual. For it was not a ritual as such, this being the premiere circumstance to merit upgrading his appearance beyond what organically resulted from his erratic sleeping habits, his every-other-day shower and biweekly shave, and his pedestrian fashion sense. Considering all this, he was surprised he could have attracted Kat at all.

With his "Handsome Devil" haircut shielded underneath a plastic baggy skullcap, Gulliver showered for a solid hour, soaping and scrubbing every cleft and cavity of his body. By the time he stepped out of the bath, his skin was as raw and red as the meat in a butcher's case, which he presumed meant he was optimally exfoliated. He moisturized himself with an aloe-oatmeal lotion that stung his more sensitive well-loofahed areas. (The lotion and loofah had been giveaways years before at the grand opening of Blair's Beauty Barracks downtown.) Gulliver plucked his nose hairs, swabbed his ears, smeared maximum-strength antiperspirant under his arms, and rinsed his mouth with spearmint-flavored Listerine.

Deciding what to wear proved the most daunting of all his self-ministrations. Gulliver knew he wasn't the handsomest of men, but he was quite sure he wasn't the homeliest either. Realistically, he judged himself to be aggressively average in all aspects—average height, average weight, average build, average hair, average everything, from his almond brown eyes to his size 10 shoes.

Only his scarred brow perhaps set him apart.

Like Frankenstein's Monster.

Thus, his outfit had to make him look debonair. Distinguished. It should say something about him, something *above* average. But what?

He had a knack for electronics. He enjoyed reading, watching TV, and grilled cheese sandwiches with Dijon mustard—only Dijon mustard, never the yellow kind.

None of this sounded all that fascinating to him, and probably even less so to Kat.

He began to worry again, or rather, worry even more. What would they talk about? What did they have in common? What would they *do*? He had no time to plan anything. Then again, he also had scant time to think about what could go wrong. And with only forty-five minutes left before her arrival, he resolved not to start brooding over that now. There was still so much to be done!

Gulliver, displeased with his own meager and mundane wardrobe, resorted to rifling through his father's closet.

His parents' bedroom remained immaculately preserved, kept precisely as it had been before they had died. Gulliver had never moved or removed anything, not the furnishings nor the pictures nor their clothes. Nothing. He did clean the room once a week, dusting off the Franciscan cedar bureau/bedside table set and the Moroccan ceiling fan, vacuuming the afghan bedspread and Berber carpet, and wiping down the windows and doorknobs.

If he hadn't known better, it would've appeared as if his parents still occupied the space, the room waiting for their inevitable return. Sometimes Gulliver swore he caught a whiff of his mother's lavender perfume or his father's Clubman talc wafting on a fleeting draft, as though one of them had brushed past him.

But Gulliver did know better. They were never coming back, at least not in any corporeal form. He would have to be satisfied with their ghosts, be they real or mere fragments of his distant but never dormant memories.

He put on a vintage '70s paisley polyester shirt, buttoning it up to the collar, paired with starchy pinstriped turquoise slacks. A wave of melancholic nostalgia swept over him when he appraised himself in the full-length mirror. Dear God, he *was* the spitting image of his father as a young man. And, like him, Gulliver looked goshdarned good all gussied up. Somebody might even find him irresistible.

Oh, how he hoped so.

It was already 7:55.

Gulliver paced his living room, plagued by clammy palms and twinges of nausea. The house felt suffocatingly languorous to him, and he fretted over dust motes clinging to his polished skin. He chose to wait outside.

After slipping on his father's slightly saggy tweed blazer, which he'd found still wrapped in its dry cleaner's paper sheath, Gulliver checked himself over one final time in the gild-frame mirror in the living room. Resisting the urge to run his fingers through his impeccable hair, he instead whisked invisible crumbs from his jacket. Adjusted the mudflap-wide lapels. Tugged at the cuffs. A deep, quivery breath later, he headed for the front door.

An asynchronous chorus of high-pitched peeps caught Gulliver's attention. He halted and turned around. On the coffee table, placed alongside the Scrabble board, was one of its wood racks neatly set with seven lettered tiles: a *Z*, a *Q*, a *C*, an *L*, an *F*, and two *I*s. Not the best selection to build words from, especially if you led off the game. The Little People, however, relished going first, even if they had slim pickings as they did now. They deemed it some great honor, so Gulliver always accommodated them. He usually won anyway.

"Can't play tonight," Gulliver said to them, less apologetic than brusque. He again made his move for the door.

The Little People's collective groan of disappointment shrilled in response.

"No. I got a date."

The cloth drawstring pouch full of Scrabble tiles spilled out from the tabletop onto the hardwood floor, scattering like casually cast runes.

"Stop it!" Gulliver snapped, as if he were scolding a disobedient dog. "Don't be petulant, or I won't ever play with you again."

Silence answered him.

Gulliver sighed compunctiously, shifted his tone to one more paternal. "And stay out of trouble, please. I might be home late." He reached for the doorknob, pausing. "I'll read you another chapter of *The Count of Monte Cristo* when I get back," he said, then let himself out.

As Gulliver waited restlessly on the stoop, a brisk evening breeze brought the aromas of pine and frying bacon. It calmed him somewhat, though it also reminded him he hadn't eaten anything since breakfast and was now starving. But all the butterflies swarming in his gut would likely make him barf up whatever he might snack on before Kat came. He sat down on the single step, trying to concentrate on the creaking wood of the porch posts and not on the gurgling in his stomach.

Minutes ticked by. He noted the white paint peeling from the posts and the sides of his house, leaving curlicue chips strewn about the perimeter. He listened to the soughing wind vibrate the glass panes on the rustic lanterns beside the front door, causing the orange bulbs within to flicker. He glimpsed something, perhaps a bat, flit from the trees toward the slice of moon above.

Although it was not even summer yet, Gulliver thought it almost autumnal out here. Like a Halloween night. Which was rather appropriate, since he really didn't feel much like himself right then—more like somebody pretending to be this different, dapper version of him.

After he glanced at his watch for the tenth or eleventh time—it was now 8:08—Kat cruised up in a firetruck-red Mustang convertible, canvas top down, muffler belching, wheel wells spattered with mud. The stereo blasted raunchy rock 'n' roll that might have been George Thorogood, but Gulliver didn't recognize the song.

He rose to his feet, needlessly swatting debris from his pants as he walked toward her. Putting on his rendition of a suave smile, Gulliver's tensed facial muscles seemed almost frozen. He worried he looked like a demonic dummy.

"Hi," Gulliver said, loud enough to be heard over the radio.

Kat lowered the volume a notch. She wore a candy-striped, form-fitting halter top that revealed more bare breast than Gulliver had ever seen on a clothed woman, along with a tight black miniskirt and burlesque stiletto heels. Her nails were painted magenta to match her glittered lips. Mascara-spackled lashes stood out against her powdery skin, her hair adorned with a ruby-studded barrette resembling a piece of a broken tiara.

Gulliver swore she was the sexiest woman he had ever laid eyes on.

"Hey, stranger," she purred. "Want a ride?"

Gulliver, beaming like a kid on Christmas morning, opened the passenger door and hopped into the cheetah-print seat. Kat smirked at him as he buckled his seatbelt. She then thrust the car into gear and stomped on the gas pedal.

Although they doubled the speed limit on his street in less than six seconds, making the probability for a collision nail-bitingly high, Gulliver's eyes were glued on the flexed calf belonging to the very foot in control of their imprudent acceleration. He didn't even care that the wind was wildly mussing his hair. The world zoomed by at a breakneck blur, but Gulliver was in no rush to tear himself away from that stunning leg of hers.

Until she noticed him ogling it.

"See something you like?"

He looked up at her, sheepish.

"No... I-I mean, yeah. I think so."

Kat laughed, not at all scornful. "You let me know. Maybe I'll let you take a test drive later."

Gulliver didn't know how to respond to that, so he just smiled at her again, sank back in his seat, and enjoyed the dizzying ride.

"You've lived here all your life?" Kat asked before downing the last of her wine.

"Mostly," Gulliver answered. "I lived with my aunt and uncle for a while up in Sawquelle."

Kat's blank expression suggested she had no idea where that was.

"It's about four and a half hours north of here."

Kat refilled her glass, her third, draining the bottle of Chianti even before their entrées arrived. "I think we're gonna need a bigger bottle." She giggled.

Gulliver still nursed his first glass, too absorbed in everything she was saying to savor it, too focused on trying to say something witty or profound or interesting. Anything that would keep her interested in him, and yet he was terrified he might say the wrong thing.

"I've lived all over," Kat drawled, her eyelids fluttering. "New York City, Los Angeles, Austin, Vegas, Phoenix." She was charmingly tipsy, on the verge of boisterously blitzed, her ruddy cheeks mimicking a Kewpie doll's.

"You plan on being buried here, Gulliver Huggens?"

"Not alive, preferably."

Kat laughed. Gulliver felt proud of himself.

Jörgen's Jolly Meatball, providing the finest in Swedish/Italian fusion cuisine since 1976, was the fanciest eatery in town. Snow white tablecloths, leather-bound menus, sprigs of assorted herbs in crystal vases. Couples having their first, and sometimes last, dates there was a Laymon tradition. It was also *the* hot spot for wedding anniversaries, family reunions, and the increasingly infrequent business luncheon. As it was a busy Friday night and they didn't have a reservation, Gulliver and Kat had been fortunate to nab a small table under the *ABBA in the Giardino di Boboli* mural by the restrooms.

Their meals came on warm bone china plates, brought out by an effete, tuxedoed server. Gulliver had ordered the Swedish meatballs and linguine, sans garlic, Kat the osso buco with a lingonberry reduction.

"I was born here, grew up here," said Gulliver, wiping his chin with his napkin after taking an explosive bite of a bleu cheese-infused meatball. "My house is here. It's comfortable."

Kat studied him. "Don't you have an adventure streak in you? Don't you ever want to experience new things and new places and new people?"

"That's what television is for."

Kat chuckled halfheartedly, as if she couldn't decide if he were kidding or not. "No offense, but that seems really boring."

Dammit, Gulliver thought, I'm losing her.

"If I'm so boring," he mooted, "then why did you agree to go out with me?" Gulliver grinned, in case he came across more defensive than he'd intended.

"Something tells me there's more to you than watching and mending TVs." Kat deliberated on this further. "You're not a serial killer, are you?"

"N-n-no," Gulliver stammered. "I'm not."

"Relax. I know you're not, doofus."

Gulliver caught the mischievous gleam in her eyes.

"Sorry… But I am a cereal *eater*," he quipped. "Finished off a bowl of Cheerios this morning."

Kat rolled her eyes and tittered.

A lull passed between them as they ate their meals. Gulliver genteelly spun his pasta around his fork, making a conscientious effort not to overstuff his mouth. Meanwhile, Kat mutilated her veal, slurping up the morsels from a spoon without a pretension of dining etiquette, even using her fingers to rescue any greasy shreds that dropped onto the tablecloth.

Gulliver found her enchanting.

"What about you?" he asked. "What brought you to Laymon?"

"A ramp off the highway." Kat sucked sauce from her fingertips.

Gulliver sensed she might be parrying his question, not just joshing him. Still, he thought it a topic worth another coin in the slot.

"Small town like this doesn't seem exciting enough for a big city girl like you."

"It's not. But it's as good a place to lay low as any."

Gulliver furrowed his forehead. "Lay low?"

"I was in this bad relationship back in Seattle."

Her eyes strayed from Gulliver's, roaming the dining room in quest of some visual oasis. They fixed on the glowing EXIT sign above a potted ficus plant. "Really bad."

"I didn't mean to pry."

"No, it's okay."

Under the table, Kat briefly stroked his leg with her foot. Gulliver wondered if this were unintentional, or encouraging.

"I was doing double duty as my ex's trophy bimbo and punching bag," she continued. "I finally got fed up, packed all my shit in my car, and kept driving until I felt like stopping."

"But why here?"

Kat shrugged her shoulders, absently raking her fork across her plate, making swirls in the purple sauce. "This seemed like the kind of place where nothing bad happens." She managed a rueful smile. "I needed that."

Gulliver nodded in understanding and wished that it were true.

Gulliver and Kat strolled a quarter of a mile to the raw timber footbridge spanning Silias Creek, named after Horace Silias, a memorial to the man who *almost* claimed the land that became Laymon Township.

The legend goes, so narrated Gulliver, Jebediah Laymon, a Virginia plantation owner, had laid claim to the valley that would bear his name mere hours before Silias, a Boston shipping merchant, attempted to do the same. Their arrival times that day in 1878 were substantiated by the footprints each novice explorer had left in the snow; having reached the area first, Laymon's tracks had accumulated more newly fallen powder than Silias's. Sympathetic toward the justifiably sullen Silias, Jeb proposed christening the not-yet-named Devil's Horns Mountains after his contemporary. But Silias, much too querulous to accept the magnanimous offer, instead challenged Laymon to a duel with pistols, the victor winning exclusive rights to the territory. After Jeb shot Horace dead in a fair contest—thanks primarily to Silias's weapon jamming—Laymon, ever the Southern gentleman, baptized the narrow meandering creek that flowed through the valley after the late, late Silias.

"Could've also called it Crap Luck Creek," commented Kat.

They leaned against the log railing of the bridge, gazing down at the dark mirror of water reflecting the starry skyscape above, the crescent moon illusorily anchored just beneath its surface. They listened to the purling of the water along the reedy banks, heard the occasional splash of a leaping fish. A fine mist created gauzy halos around the sodium-vapor lamplights suspended from arcing steel posts. It was a postcard perfect scene, except for the crumpled Beanie Roast cup caught in a small whirlpool inside the cluster of mossy rocks below.

"You live by yourself?" Kat inquired.

"Yeah," Gulliver answered. A gentle gust of wind glanced off the creek, twirling the mist around them like nimble wraiths, ruffling Kat's hair.

"Have any brothers and sisters?"

"I had... a brother." Gulliver dithered over elaborating, not wanting to spoil the serenity of the moment, then felt ashamed for it. "He was killed in a car crash."

Kat let out a faint, heart-wrenched "Oh." Then, louder, "That's awful." While Kat's commiserative eyes were able to shine through the gloom in his soul, they could not repel those inextinguishable flames of the past.

"Dale was eleven. I was nine... He was only a few feet away, right there in front of me. In the fire." Gulliver's hands furled into useless fists. "But I couldn't save him."

"You were a kid. You're not Superman, all invincible and fireproof."

"Superman wasn't invincible. Kryptonite hurt him."

"Well, there ya go. Point is, it wasn't your fault, Gulliver." Kat's warm hand clasped his forearm, yet he shivered at her touch, his mind juggling between rekindled pains and foreseen pleasures. It made him woozy.

He changed the subject. "You play Scrabble?"

"That word game?" Kat shook her head. "No."

"I used to play with my brother. Beat him a few times, too. Or maybe he let me win. Whatever, it was fun... I miss that."

Kat stared back down at the creek, removing her hand from his arm. Their connection broken, Gulliver lambasted himself for being so daft to waste such an intimate moment talking about, of all things, Scrabble.

He contemplated how to salvage it...

Gulliver remembered sitting side by side with his brother on that same bridge, their bare feet dabbling in the brook. It was their last summer together. Mother was visiting the church nearby, and she let them take the pebble-paved path to the creek to play. Night had fallen, the light of the full moon streaming down on them.

Dale picked up an empty beer bottle, discarded by partying teens or cuddling lovers. "Know how to catch the moon in a bottle?" he asked his little brother. Gulliver shook his head, naturally curious. Dale held up the clear glass bottle in front of Gulliver's eyes so the younger boy could view the luminous satellite through it. "See? I caught the moon in this bottle."

Gulliver scoffed, "The moon ain't actually in the bottle."

Dale shrugged. "Depends on how you look at it. Look at something the right way, and it can be anything you want it to be."

Gulliver scoped around the bridge's truss. There were no bottles to catch anything with.

"How deep do you think this river is?" Kat asked.

"About three or four feet. But it's deeper closer to the lake."

"Wanna go skinny dipping?"

Gulliver turned his head toward her. Kat was watching him eagerly, awaiting his reply. His assent.

Dear God, he was going to see her. All of her. Right there in front of him.

"Okay," Gulliver murmured, poised to disrobe. Right there. With her.

Kat looked away from him. "You wish you were that lucky."

She donned an adorably wicked smile.

It was a joke, of course. Yet Gulliver couldn't help feeling duped. For a moment, she let him believe he would see her naked, maybe even let him touch her nakedness. Maybe she would touch his. But it was only a tease, a lark. And it wasn't funny. It was damn cruel.

He wanted her so bad.

Kat then guided her face toward his and kissed him with a burgeoning desire that fed off his own. Her tongue flicked at his lips, demanding entrance. He shut his eyes and opened his mouth. Their tongues met and danced clumsily, amorously. She tasted of wine and berries. The steamy exhalations from her nostrils could have singed his cheek. She laid her palm on his chest, kneading it, reminding him to breathe. And when he did, he breathed her all in, filling himself, his lungs, his heart, his blood, with Kat. And when their lips finally disengaged, Gulliver was rendered speechless.

Kat had gotten his tongue.

5

They didn't speak the entire trip back to Gulliver's house.

Kat lead-footed the gas with no respite, taking circuitous right and left turns to dodge any red lights and stop signs, careening down Laymon's straightaways like she was aiming to rewind time. To erase their date from her mental archives. Gulliver predicted an imminent future where he would be dumped off and forgotten, Kat leaving him and 16 Klunghoffer Street far behind, as fast as her drag radials could take her.

After their kiss ended—a kiss so electrifying it might've been visible from space—Kat abruptly, icily, declared she was taking him home. No explanation, no apology.

Gulliver hadn't a clue what had soured her mood. Was he too stilted, too vapid, just too plain *ordinary* for her? Had he inadvertently done something to upset her? Did he, despite all his preparatory labors, still smell odious to her, of some sub-epidermal stink he could never wash off no matter how hard he tried?

Whatever it had been, she wouldn't say, no matter how much Gulliver tried to wheedle it out of her. Thus Gulliver acquiesced, or rather surrendered, to the now inexorable termination of their first and, odds were, final date.

Kat pulled the Mustang alongside the curb in front of Gulliver's house, braking with a jerk that bounced Gulliver from his seat. She killed the engine and swiveled her body toward him. Her eyes were dark orbs with twin sickle-shaped glints in their centers.

Still she said nothing, only stared at him with those unreadable eyes.

"So," Gulliver broke the inscrutable silence. "I had a great time."

"So," Kat parroted him. "You gonna invite me in?"

Gulliver's pulse quickened. "Ummm... sure. Yeah... Why not?"

"Such enthusiasm," she razzed.

Gulliver, not picking up on her frivolity, worried again he had offended her.

Yet he was even more trepidatious about the Little People scaring her off.

He'd never had a guest over, never let anybody inside his house ever. It was too risky. Having tacitly and unequivocally assumed custodianship of the Little People, Gulliver found himself very protective of them. That and their frustrating capriciousness lent to him adopting supremely cautionary measures, segregating their world within his abode from the one outside it.

He could hope the Little People would respect his privacy and tend to their own non-Gulliverian affairs while Kat was there. But he likewise dreaded they'd initiate some random ruckus. Since Gulliver never before had reason to address such a situation as this, he'd never had the opportunity to test them. They might behave themselves. Or they might not.

Gulliver decided it—she—was worth the risk.

"It's n-not you," he spluttered. "It's a bit m-messy inside."

"A messy bachelor pad? How bizarre!" Kat playfully slapped his arm. "Don't be embarrassed, Mr. Fix-It. If I'm grossed out, we'll just turn the lights off."

Gulliver thought he saw fiery tendrils flail in her eyes, inflamed by the prospect of sinfully lubricious activities to come. He nodded and nearly tumbled getting out of her car. His muscles in a twitter, he escorted Kat to his door and, after fumbling for his keys, led her into his sanctum.

The Little People, blessedly, were nowhere in sight.

Kat excused herself to grace his bathroom. Gulliver, in the meantime, fetched them drinks. He didn't have any beer—he detested hops, which to him had the mildewy bouquet of goat feed—and he didn't think serving hard liquor would send the appropriate message, even if he wasn't certain what that message might be. Fortunately, in his fridge he still had a four-pack of unobjectionable wine coolers Mr. Knox had pawned off on him the previous summer, leftovers from a Laymon Chamber of Commerce party. (His boss had been one of only six attendees there, counting the rent-a-clown.)

Gulliver brought the Day-Glo orange beverages into the living room. Kat was there now, browsing the Huggens family memorabilia exhibited on the walls and shelves. He handed one of the uncapped bottles to her.

"Thank you." She read the label. "Ooo," she cooed. "Fizzy Navel."

Taking a sip, Kat gestured to a walnut-framed photograph set on the uppermost shelf of the hutch. In it, a much younger Gulliver posed with his brother and parents, all in their Sunday finery, beside a scraggly fir tree bedecked with plastic popcorn garland and glass ornaments that had flaked metallic paint like festive dandruff. It was their last Christmas together. Gulliver had gotten the Laser-Action Mars Command building blocks, and Dale was given Professor Poof's Kosmos of Kemistry (its educational value trumping the egregious misspelling). While their mother cooked the turkey with all the trimmings, Father joined his boys outside to build a robot snowman. After inserting a Fisher-Price walkie-talkie in its tinfoil-antennaed head, the threesome went back inside the house, huddling by the front bay window with the other two-way radio. From there, they wished "Merry Christmas" and sang off-key carols to many baffled passersby. Once, Dale roared ferociously, frightening off a stray mutt that dared pee on their SnoBot. They'd all laughed a lot. Just a day later, the sun had razed their creation, reducing it to a pile of quasi-robot parts. Gulliver still lamented nobody had the foresight to take a picture of it beforehand.

"That your family?"

"Yeah. At Christmas." *Obviously.* Gulliver grinned like an imbecile.

Kat scrutinized the photograph, comparing its background to that of the house she stood in now. Nothing had changed, as far as she could tell. It was the same wood paneling, the same brass chandelier, the same colonial hutch.

"So this is the house you grew up in."

Gulliver nodded.

She sniffed the air. "It smells like you."

Or was that the telltale wet canine stench of the Little People? Where were they?

Kat sashayed across the room, setting her wine cooler down on the coffee table next to the Scrabble board. She eased down onto the sofa, crossed her slinky legs, and patted the cushion beside her, ensnaring Gulliver with a beguiling come-hither gaze.

"Come. Sit."

Gulliver did a sort of wormy two-step toward the sofa and sat down beside her, allowing for a few inches of decorous personal space between them. He thumb-stroked the sweating bottle in his hand, humming a microtonal scale of his own anxious invention, before placing his drink down next to hers. He then settled back, his spine rigid, his palms cupping his knees to still his fidgeting legs.

Kat leaned her face toward his, studying him. "You have such nice skin." She caressed the contours of his jaw with the tip of her index finger. "Like a baby's."

She inched nearer, her lips agonizingly close to his cheek. He once again felt her breath, hot and humid and citrusy. Goosebumps surfed up his arms. Then she pressed those pillowed lips, gently, against his flesh. He inhaled sharply.

She pinched his chin and spun his face toward hers. Then she kissed him, tender at first, as if testing her footing, before snaking her tongue into his welcoming mouth. She wove her fingers through his hair while he navigated his hand to her waist—

The television flashed on, pounding out the theme to *Hawaii Five-0*.

They stopped kissing and regarded the TV like it were some crass, drunken party crasher. Gulliver shot up from the sofa, vaulted across the room, and smacked the off button. The image of the majestically coiffed Jack Lord shrunk to a glowing pinpoint before fading to black.

Gulliver returned to his place on the loveseat beside Kat and without missing a beat resumed their frenzied petting. Soon their hands were exploring more sensitive, more intimate areas of each other's bodies—rubbing the small of an arched back, groping the inside of a supple thigh, grazing the nub of a hardened nipple. His heart pumped at full throttle, hurtling toward a finish line he had, up until this glorious moment, only dreamt of. Their temperatures rose in unison, and Gulliver began to perspire. Sweat dripped from the tip of his nose onto her bare shoulder, which only seemed to fan Kat's libido more, his musk saturating her pores.

The TV disrupted their lust-making yet again, louder this time, blaring a commercial for Sergeant Sparkles Floor Polish. Sgt. Sparkles, in his crisp olive green uniform with white-mop epaulettes, postured imperiously over a shiny kitchen floor, barking, "It ain't clean till I darn well say it's clean!"

Gulliver growled.

"Dammit." Pulling away from him, Kat checked under her butt. "Is one of us sitting on the remote?"

"I don't think so." The Zenith's remote controller had been lost long ago, probably annexed by the Little People for some indeterminable use in their lair, though they'd denied any knowledge of its whereabouts.

Gulliver stomped over to the TV, this time yanking the plug from the wall socket.

"Be good," he hissed at the wall, at them.

He then turned to Kat, nodding confidently. "That should do it."

Gulliver sat back down. His brain swooned. His loins blazed. He had never desired anything so much in his life as much as he desired Kat at that very moment. He yearned to lose himself to her, in her.

And he knew by the feral look in her eyes that the yearning was quite mutual. They stared one another down, panting, both transformed into ravenous beasts, uncaged and hungering for each other.

"Where were we?"

Wordlessly she shucked off her halter top, tossing it onto the floor. Her breasts, unburdened by a bra, fell free, a pair of cherry-peaked, grapefruit-sized spheres that seemed to float in their own orbit upon her heavenly body.

Gulliver gawked and gasped.

Kat seized him by the collar of his disco shirt and shoved him down. He caught a titillating glimpse of the sheer pink G-string under her skirt as she swung her leg over his, straddling him. She ripped open his shirt's buttons, popping one across the room where it ricocheted with a hollow ping off the Capodimonte vase. Her fingernails scraped down his naked chest, leaving parallel scarlet trails on his pale skin. His groin thumped insistently against the zipper of his trousers, ready—*no, please, not yet!*—to erupt.

She thrust her mouth once more against his. He breathed into her, splaying his fingers along her ribs as if he were playing some forbidden musical instrument. With her bosom pressed against his own, Gulliver could feel the sync of their racing heartbeats.

Gulliver wondered if she could tell he was a virgin, that she would be his first. As she began to writhe against him with expert marksmanship, his mind emptied of all thoughts but those stoked by the most primal of urges, the most compelling of urgencies.

In their throes of heightening ecstasy, neither noticed the beefeater lamp sliding sideways on the end table beside them, until it plummeted to the floor with a thunderous crash.

Gulliver whirled his head toward the downed yeoman.

"Don't worry about it," Kat bawled, still grinding away on him. She nibbled at his earlobes, sucked on his neck. Undid his belt.

Gulliver ceased worrying.

Until the point of a pencil harpooned his auditory canal.

Gulliver yelped and flung Kat off him, plunking her unceremoniously onto the floor. He sprang from the sofa, plucking the pencil from his ear then probing inside it with his fingertip to assess the damage. He detected no breakage of skin, no squishiness of oozing blood. His forefinger came out virtually as clean as it had gone in.

"What's wrong?" Kat shrieked, cowering against the sofa.

"You could've punctured my ear drum!" Gulliver spat.

"I didn't do anything."

"Not you," he responded to her, mollifying his tone. He swept his arm around the room, gesturing at everything and nothing in particular. "*Them*."

"Them?"

"The Little People!" he blurted.

Kat regarded him with scrunched-together eyebrows.

"They like playing pranks," Gulliver explained with un-containable candor. "And apparently," his voice then rising to an exasperated shout directed at the ceiling, "they're also really friggin' jealous!"

"The little people," repeated Kat.

"Yeah. Tiny. Like three inches tall. They live behind the walls."

"Behind the walls, here?"

He shrugged. "Maybe under the floor. Somewhere." Only then did Gulliver begin to regret divulging what had been his most safeguarded secret. In retrospect, it probably was not a subject wisely broached on a first date.

"Right," Kat sighed, gone frigid. "That's *fucktabulous*."

She snatched her halter top from the floor and rose to her feet, grumbling to herself, "Why do I always hook up with nutcases?"

"I'm not a nutcase," Gulliver answered anemically.

Kat slipped the halter top over her head and shimmied it down her torso. Gulliver could discern the outline of her still erect nipples through the fabric.

"You believe your house is infested with fairies."

"They're n-not f-fairies. They're real."

"Of course they are," Kat replied patronizingly. She scurried across the living room, her heels tramping on the floor. Gathering up her purse from the credenza by the front door, she turned and addressed Gulliver with a tart mixture of sympathy and mockery.

"Sorry, Gulliver, I don't think we're gonna work out."

Gulliver inwardly leafed through his very limited last-ditch options which might rectify the tailspinning situation. In his hastiness, he opted for the worst of them.

"But they'll come around to liking you. I know they will!"

Kat rolled her eyes. "You have issues, Gulliver. And I can't be your girlfriend *and* your shrink." With that, she opened the door and exited his home and his life.

Gulliver's eyes filmed over. He fought off the onslaught of tears and chased after her.

Kat had gotten into her convertible by the time Gulliver caught up with her outside.

"Don't go, Kat. Please."

Keying the ignition, she didn't respond to his plea, acting as if he weren't there. She revved the motor, perhaps to drown him out.

He spoke over it anyway. "Hey, I was kidding. It was a joke. Really."

Gulliver didn't sound convincing, even to himself. He sounded desperate.

"It's alright, Gulliver," she uttered over the galloping engine.

Gulliver's eyes lit up, hopeful. "It is?"

She looked over at him. "I just don't do crazy anymore."

Kat threw the transmission into gear and punched the gas. The rear wheels squealed on the asphalt, kicking up smoke and grit before they found traction. The car barreled up the street and within seconds had vanished around the corner.

Gulliver kept listening for it, until all he could hear was the ping-ponging chirps of crickets. The pungent smell of burnt rubber lingered, stinging his nostrils. The heat of the Mustang's exhaust had dissipated around him, supplanted by the chill of the night air enfolding him in its stiff cloak.

Served him right for being completely honest with Kat, he upbraided himself.

But was it his fault she didn't believe him?

No, it wasn't.

Just as he wasn't to blame for their date having dived headfirst into, as Kat might've put it, Crap Luck Creek.

It was the Little People's fault. They had sabotaged his evening with Kat. No, worse than that. They had detonated an atomic bomb on his love life, embedding more painful, irremovable shrapnel inside him—enough to rebuild those inner bulwarks he had recently let crumble.

He should have never trusted them. He should've been smarter, known better. He should've persuaded Kat to instead take him to her place, or to a motel, or even to Lovers Logs, a field of felled but never harvested red oak trees that young couples had been coupling amongst for years.

He should've. But he hadn't.

And *that* was his fault.

Gulliver did a melodramatic about-face and stormed up the walkway toward his front door. Halfway there, upon spying his snoopy neighbor Mrs. Jensen peeking out her curtains, he modestly buttoned up his shirt and refastened his belt.

Fuming the fumes of a pantheon of angry gods, Gulliver barged into his home and slammed the door behind him.

"You bastards!" he raved, gnashing his teeth. "Couldn't let me be happy for once, could you?"

On that cue, the television switched on again. It was tuned to a syndicated episode of *Fantasy Island*, Gulliver's favorite program. To placate him, no doubt.

Gulliver, too livid to appreciate even the dulcet aphorisms of Mr. Roarke or the doe-eyed venerations of his pint-sized sidekick, rushed the television and spanked the power button. It blinked off.

"Just leave me the hell alone!" he huffed, blue veins throbbing at his temples.

Gulliver flounced to his bedroom, threw himself onto his bed, and sobbed himself to semi-sleep.

That night, as Gulliver laid fitfully in a heap of tousled sheets, clenching his tear-stained pillow, the Grim Reaper, in its grimy monk's robe and grimier boots, dropped by once again to niggle him about mortal matters of his past. But Gulliver was too fraught with his own palpable, inextricable inadequacies to pay it any heed. After a while, his tormentor grew weary of him and, as it galumphed out of his bedroom, Gulliver thought he heard a dispirited sigh whistling through its ossified rictus.

PART 2

THE GIANT PLOT

1

One wouldn't know it by looking at him, but right now the gears in Sheriff Cyrus Roy Boone's brain were ratcheting so fast and furious they could, if its energy were harnessed, power all of downtown Laymon.

This wasn't because he was processing what his deputy was relaying to him about youths blowing up roadkill with M-80s out on Route 29 (a practice the locals called "Bambi Bombing"). Nor was it because he was still reflecting on the tri-county crime briefing he had attended in Millhaven that morning, and not because he was wondering what his wife had packed him for lunch, which he hoped was her chicken salad on rye.

He couldn't recall his deputy's name.

Again.

These lapses in memory began about a year before. They were sporadic and occurred only as it pertained to life's lesser details—people's names, phone numbers, directions to places, the spelling of certain words, and the calculating of mathematical equations. Initially, he had attributed it variously to his overworking, his undersleeping, his diet, changes in the weather, even the miasma of chemical solvents the cleaning lady employed throughout the station. So he'd taken a couple of fishing trips, went to bed earlier, ate only organic foods, dressed appropriately based on the forecast, and dictated only a water and vinegar solution be used to disinfect the surfaces in the headquarters.

None of these measures had helped improve his condition. Rather, it had progressively—if undetectably to others—worsened. Up until now, Boone had been able to deftly smokescreen these absent-minded episodes of his by always looking folks in the eye, nodding tactically, and asking questions or commenting germanely on things that were just said. Nobody suspected he was having problems, not even his wife of thirty years.

Two months prior, he had discreetly made himself an appointment with the doctor, but he'd cancelled at the last minute due to a house fire on Claypoole that had killed Gerald Culpepper, who had been partial to cigars and naps, doing both at the same time one instance too many.

Sheriff Boone never rescheduled with Dr. Habibowitz in Sulfur Springs, because he already knew what the prognosis would be. Like his father before him, Boone knew he was at the onset of irremediable crippling senility, the embryonic stages of Alzheimer's.

He was only fifty-six, damn it.

The sheriff had placed cheat sheets as mnemonic aids around the station. He always kept a roll of his deputies' names on a dry erase board in the main squad room, as well as a paper one in his top desk drawer, which also included all important official and personal contact numbers and mailing addresses. Furthermore, he avoided discussing ongoing investigations unless the case file was set in front of him. And, whenever possible, he had one of his deputies drive him to crime scenes or any other away-from-headquarters police business requiring his presence.

All this to ensure the impression he gave was one of indisputable authority and competency. There could be no glaring cracks in his façade.

A thirty-five year veteran of the force, Sheriff Boone had presided over the Laymon PD for seventeen of those years, always re-elected without opposition. He coordinated a current roster of four deputies based in a building not much larger than the typical public restroom in a county park.

Violent crime in Laymon was rare, ordinarily the result of heavy boozing or flashpoint tempers, or a combination of both, leading to barroom brawls, domestic beatings, and vehicular assaults. There was also the petty thievery here and there, the most notable being a wave of lawn ornament snatchings two winters previous. The items had mysteriously reappeared the following year on the anniversary dates of each theft, though on different properties from where they had originally been taken. Neighbors blamed each other, with some next-door relations becoming downright contentious and, if you asked Sheriff Boone, dang silly about it.

Boone was embarrassed to admit he'd never come close to catching the prankster, dubbed the Pink Flamingo Bandit by *The Regal Eagle*, Laymon's only local newspaper. He was even more red-faced at having been one of the targets, losing his woodland gnome with the corncob pipe. The statuette was eventually returned to him by a neighbor who had discovered the bearded fellow lying under the rear tire of his pickup, the staged victim of an apparent accident.

Which is to say, being the sheriff of Laymon was not particularly demanding these days. But even the cushiest of jobs could be made mighty difficult if one's most valuable asset were on the fritz.

Sheriff Boone strained to remember his deputy's name while the young man sat there before him, reciting what amounted to an oral dissertation on Laymon's rampant juvenile delinquency.

Boone mentally ran through the alphabet until a letter clicked, much as if he were cracking a safe. Was it Cal? No... Carl? Cliff? It was on the tip of Boone's tongue... ah, to hell with it. He nonchalantly slid his desk drawer open, glanced down at his cheat sheet.

Clive. That was it.

Senior Deputy Clive Eriksen was a physically fit, boyishly good-looking paragon of second-in-command proficiency, his conduct well-mannered, his uniform well-laundered, his hair and face well-groomed. There wasn't a thing out of order on him. His buffed-to-perfection gold badge glinted on the breast of his regulation taupe shirt, even in the dark.

Clive took every opportunity to dazzle the sheriff with his self-aggrandized proactivity and thoroughness. Maybe the brown-nosing kid—he was only twenty-six—was gunning for his job. He had the academic chops for it, Boone reckoned, but he was still green under the fingernails. Clive hadn't been digging in the trenches long enough to always know how to smell trouble when he'd unearthed it.

Once, the fool almost let a perp who had robbed a gas station with an antique derringer go scot-free, all because said perp was a redheaded knockout who could play a weak-kneed man such as Clive like a mandolin.

No, Clive wasn't ready to be sheriff. Moreover, Boone wasn't ready to give up the post.

The deputy completed his report. The sheriff dismissed him with a gracious "thank you, Clive." Clive smiled cockily and exited his superior's spartan office. Boone could barely recall more than two words the Boy Wonder had spouted off to him.

The sheriff took a swig from his bottle of sarsaparilla and eyed the triptych of Audubon-illustrated wild birds adorning the wall opposite his desk. Testing himself, he identified each by their popular names: an ivory-billed woodpecker, a great blue heron, and a fork-tailed flycatcher. Hundred percent, Boone congratulated himself. He then leafed through his legal pad, reviewing his notes from that morning's assembly of high-ranking law enforcers. There wasn't much to review.

Clive had been pleased as pie to give him a ride to Millhaven when Boone had asked him to. He told the deputy it would be a good learning experience for him to attend the meeting, not to mention (and he didn't mention it) Boone wouldn't have to fret over directions going there. Clive wasn't at all awkward being the only deputy present. In fact, he looked proud as a groupie getting to hang with the band.

They had sat in the Millhaven station conference room among three dozen other lawmen from small cities and townships within a hundred-mile radius. They'd all traveled there at the special request of the captains of the Millhaven and Gabriel Ridge state police precincts. Millhaven, an evangelical college town, and Gabriel Ridge, a middle-income suburbia, were both in a different county from Laymon, about fifty-five and eighty miles away respectively.

Sheriff Boone, like the majority of the others around him, held no official jurisdiction in either district, but fears were steadily mounting they might soon share a common curse.

That curse was the Potato Sack Rapist, so nicknamed for his modus operandi of overpowering a woman from behind and muffling her head with a burlap bag.

Thus far, the offender had confined his exploits to the two communities, but then he could foreseeably alter his hunting ground to an adjacent area less vigilant, one not yet suspecting such a fiend to prey upon its mothers and daughters.

The visiting officers were quickly brought up to speed on the sketchy facts. The only pattern among the eight female victims was that they all wore skirts at the time of the attacks, ostensibly because it allowed the perp easier access, or possibly it was a fetishistic preference. Other than a predilection toward those under age forty (or looking it), most of the women had dissimilar traits—tall and short, thick and thin, blonde and brunette, demure and dirty. He seemed to favor no specific type. All were fair game.

He struck late at night or, less frequently, right at dawn, when his quarry had been out walking alone in a deserted area, or had parked her car somewhere remote enough that any risk of eyewitnesses was eliminated. He was patient as well as erratic, with some incidents committed weeks apart, others months, over the past year and a half. Whether or not he staked out his victims beforehand was undetermined.

Descriptions of the assailant were, unsurprisingly, lacking. All agreed he was big, over six feet in height and, by some accounts, over eight inches in length. He was strong, using one hand to twist the bag tight around their necks while his other arm pincered their waists as he violated them. He never spoke, never so much as grunted. The bag's burlap reeked of gasoline so harsh it stung the victims' eyes. He always fled the scene with it. He also always left behind his semen, so they had oodles of DNA samples. But without a suspect to trace them to, these were useless at the moment.

And that was all. Sheriff Boone realized, as did everybody else in the room, that it wasn't much to go on. He just hoped he and the citizens of Laymon would never have to contend with the Potato Sack Rapist.

Instead, they would find themselves faced with something even worse.

2

The morning after his calamitous date with Kat, Gulliver sulked around his house, perfunctorily beginning the day as if he were on autopilot. His only incentives for not staying in bed forevermore were 1) he had to go to work, and 2) every room, even those she hadn't been in, exuded Kat's scent. He thought it might've been him, that his hair and skin had sopped up her bodily redolence, but even after showering, bedeviling whiffs of her remained, winged nymphs thrashing him with cat o' nine tails.

The Little People judiciously didn't pester him, not so much as making a peep while he went about his a.m. drill. A part of Gulliver understood how they might have deemed Kat a trespasser, an apparent threat to their peace and security. Another part of him, the dominant part, didn't care a whit about what the furry shrimps might have thought.

They had, to use a popular vulgarism, cockblocked him, and that could not be simply pardoned after some cinnamon-sprinkled oatmeal or bathroom-grout scrubbing or whatever they were conspiring as reconciliation.

There would be repercussions. Punishment. They had to learn who was king of that castle.

No reading to them for a week. No—a month! That was a start.

A disheveled Gulliver made his unmerry way to the bus stop, head bowed, feet shuffling. The sky was, aptly, overcast and dreary, and according to the Top O' The Mountain News 4 weather report, would continue to be so for the duration of the week, with a seventy percent chance of rain on Tuesday.

Gulliver wondered if there would be any sunny days ahead for him ever again.

His mind didn't register the Boom Boom Bus idling in front of him until Russ's buttery baritone voice bellowed a jovial "Good mornin'!" at him.

Gulliver plodded up the bus steps, his sneakers feeling like they'd been encased in concrete. His every movement seemed to require an extra ounce—make that a pound—of effort. He slumped down into the empty handicapped seat and wished he could just shrink away, perhaps transmogrify into some single-celled organism. He was pretty sure amoebas didn't have to deal with these kinds of troubles.

"How'd your date go last night?" Russ asked him.

Gulliver sighed. "I think I scared her off."

"Before or after you did the deed?"

"Sorta during."

"Oh?… Oh." Russ frowned sympathetically, then slapped on an encouraging smile for him. "Well, don't sweat it. There are many more fish in the ocean."

"No." Gulliver shook his head. "Not like this fish. She was different. Beautiful. Awesome gills."

"I hear ya. But if you're freshwater and she's salt, it wasn't meant to be."

Gulliver pondered this while staring at the achromatic world outside the bus window.

"She might be brackish," he finally said, then let his thoughts swim even deeper into the stagnant waters of the lovelorn.

It was either 10:50, 10:59, or 11:07, depending on whether Reggie Knox consulted the microwave's digital reading, his analog wristwatch, or the battery-powered Bakelite wall clock, respectively. Which meant Gulliver either would show up in ten minutes, would arrive any second now, or was seven minutes late for his shift.

He guessed the boy was tardy more often than he harped him about, but that didn't much matter to Knox nowadays. As long as things went down close enough to what he had slated, that was fine with him. His life followed its own clock.

Especially since he'd been put on borrowed time himself.

He had his first inkling something was royally fucked up after he'd hacked up a coal black, spongy lump that had no place being inside of him.

Three separate doctors ran a series of invasive and enervating tests, each one pegging him with the Big C. The advanced malignancy had ravaged his lungs, logically stemming from his inveterate smoking of products the Surgeon General had long warned might cause heart disease, emphysema, or lung cancer (bingo!), and may complicate pregnancy. Now there was a plus—at least he weren't preggo. Still, his outlook was as rotten as a compost pile. Pack your bags in two to three years, they'd told him, you're moving to Dirt Nap Acres!

So he done got himself a terminal illness. Reggie always expected he'd unexpectedly keel over one day, stumbling into his own surprise bon voyage party where he was the only one invited. He had even kind of looked forward to dying peacefully in his sleep, like all those other lucky bastards he read about in the obits.

Instead, for the last two years he had experienced the boundless joys of confronting his own mortality. No hair-robbing radiation therapies, special flavorless diets, or New Age enemas would cure him now. At best, they might buy him six, maybe nine months. Fuck that. Knox wouldn't subject himself to the indignities of losing his Samson Club of America thrice-honored locks, or flushing his ass out with seaweed smoothies, or do anything else that would compromise his accustomed quality of life. If he were going to die, he would do it his way, on his terms. Meaning he wouldn't do a damned thing different, except live harder and fuller, and death could have whatever scraps were left over after he was done with himself.

Gulliver came in, looking like Hell the day after its millennial fire sale.

"What happened to you?"

"Didn't sleep well."

"Somebody use ya as a trampoline all night?"

"I don't want to talk about it." Gulliver's eyes didn't leave the floor. "Sorry."

"That's okay, man. We all got days like that."

Gulliver didn't respond. He took a seat at the worktable and dove into deconstructing a DVD player with a disc stuck in its tray.

Huggens was an oddball to be sure, Knox thought. In that respect, the boy took after his father, who'd stocked up enough ingredients of his own to bake a fruitcake.

Many years ago, Knox would see Papa Huggens strutting about town, always wearing those aviator sunglasses, pastel suits, and, on balmier days, an air-conditioned fez. And the dude hardly talked to anybody. Words, it seemed, came from him at a premium.

Knox had met the man only once, with his munchkin son Gulliver and the older brother in tow. They'd brought in a Sylvania color television with a blown-out picture tube. The tube needed to be replaced, Knox had informed Mr. Huggens. He had a spare on hand. He could have it replaced and ready to pick up the next day. But Mr. Huggens rebuffed Knox's services. His kid could install it himself, he'd said. So he just purchased the part outright and vamoosed. The laconic Harold Huggens uttered, at most, two dozen words throughout the transaction. And none of them included a "hello" or "thanks" either.

To his credit, Gulliver manifested appreciably better social skills than his dad, but he was still no Mr. Personality. Hey, it was a hard cold bitch of a thing getting his whole family wiped out the way they had been. Gulliver turned out damn well adjusted, considering.

Knox liked him from the very inception of their working relationship. When Gulliver moved back to Laymon, he had dropped by the store, wearing a ridiculous seersucker suit, in timid quest of a job. After a nuts-and-bolts interview, Knox hired him on the spot, essentially taking the boy under his wing. Knox had good reason to. For one, having been familiar with Gulliver's history, he felt sorry for him. For another, Knox had been overwhelmed with his project load right then, and here was Gulliver, this self-taught electronic wiz who could repair any gizmo you set down in front of him.

One might say destiny brought them together. If you believe in that shit.

While Knox wasn't much of a mentor, he didn't fancy himself a father figure either.

But he was *something* to Gulliver.

Knox had no surviving family, and he had never nudged himself into starting one of his own. By default, Gulliver became as close to kin as Knox had on this tore-up road that was his waning life. Which was why he had designated the boy his signed and notarized heir, bequeathing him his business, his home, his bike, and all his well-worn worldly possessions. He hadn't told Gulliver about any of this, not even about his cancer, primarily because he didn't want to bum the kid out. Knox supposed he'd have to fess up to him one of these days, but not until he was on the brink of his last breath. He saw no point in stirring up Gulliver's misery prematurely. He'd been through plenty enough already.

"Check this out, Gulliver."

Knox rolled up the sleeve of his "Jesus Looks Holier on a Harley" T-shirt. There on his upper arm was the finished Octa-

Girl tattoo, fully inked, with the new addition of a barnacle-encrusted motorcycle helmet enclosing her head. Just a few strands of her hair, now a fiery scarlet, overflowed from it, faintly obscuring her polypoid nipples.

"You put a helmet on her," Gulliver commented. He wore such a deadpan expression at the sight of the tattoo, his boss thought the boy dosed on heavy lithium.

"She reminded me too much of an ex-girlfriend," Knox explained. "I think it sums me up. Y'know, symbolically."

Gulliver nodded aloofly.

"You going to the coffee shop?"

"I don't know."

"Run over and get me an Americano, would ya?"

Mr. Knox tossed him a crumpled ten-dollar bill he plucked from his jeans pocket.

"And buy yourself something to perk you up. I don't let no zombies work for me. Unless you're a hot zombie chick. Then you can eat me all day long."

Knox chuckled. Gulliver left.

Gulliver's sluggish, hundred-meter walk across Fairview Ave. to the Beanie Roast felt more like a grueling hundred-mile hike over the most rugged of terrain. He seesawed between gut-twisted reluctance and heart-driven intent to see Kat again. Maybe it would be different now. It was a new day, with new possibilities.

Yes, perhaps he could resurrect and rejuvenate his hopes for... for what? He wasn't even sure he should hope for anything anymore. It was too easy to be let down.

Gulliver entered the coffee shop, his mouth gone dry and his knees wobbling. Kat stood behind the counter in her apron tending to the few customers alongside her pudgy co-worker.

It occurred to him that he didn't know what to say to her, or if he should say anything. He could pretend nothing had ever happened, but that seemed disingenuous, almost craven.

He waited in the short line. When his turn came up, Becky took his order for Mr. Knox's Americano and his mochaccino. By the time she served him the drinks, the busy spell had died down.

Gulliver smiled at Kat as he passed her on his way out. She smiled in return like everything was normal. Like nothing had gone off the rails between them.

He stopped and stammered, "L-listen, Kat. About last n-n-night…"

"Let's not talk about it, okay?" Her tone was civil, pacifying.

"I just want to explain."

"Don't bother," she interjected. "Just take your drinks and go. Please."

She stared him down, those once magmatic eyes now gone glacial. She then turned her back to him as she wiped the enameled farmhouse sink behind her with a terrycloth towel.

Gulliver trudged out of the Beanie Roast.

So that was it. They were done. Over. *Fini.* Their date had been like a three-hour movie with the most fantastic buildup to the lousiest ending ever.

The coffees began to burn his palms. He welcomed the diversion of searing pain until his skin grew desensitized to the heat. He wondered if he would ever become inured to all the other pains poking and pinching inside him.

He doubted it.

Gulliver shambled past an empty brownstone storefront, its latticed windows overpapered with sun-bleached Christmas giftwrap. He could still make out a herald angel here, a laurel wreath there, but mostly it looked like a gallery of overexposed film negatives. The store had once been a wedding gown and tuxedo rental shop. Since nobody got married in Laymon anymore, most opting for the glitzy chapels and banquet halls in Sulfur Springs, theirs became just another business that had perished in the city's economic blight. No one even bothered to put up a FOR LEASE sign.

Its entrance door stood wide open.

From the murky interior a godly voice called out to him: "Gulliver Huggens!"

Gulliver halted and looked in the doorway. He couldn't see anybody there.

The voice boomed again: "Please, come in."

Gulliver glanced warily about him. The sidewalks were deserted. An old, green Chevy Impala, driven by an even older, bespectacled geezer slouched over its steering wheel, trundled by him on the street.

"I don't have a great deal of time, Mr. Huggens. If you would indulge me, I shan't monopolize much of yours."

Gulliver once more peered into the storefront's uninviting maw. His enigmatic host remained unseen. The voice, while commanding, was guttural and strangely artificial sounding—like a microphone grafted onto someone's flayed larynx—yet it conveyed neither malice nor menace.

Gulliver's curiosity overrode his caution, and he stepped inside.

After his eyesight adapted to what paltry light seeped in the doorway and through small rips in the holiday window dressing, Gulliver still couldn't see beyond ten or twelve feet into the deep, tenebrous space. There appeared to be no merchandising fixtures left behind, nor any other décor to indicate there had once been a business there. It stank of stale mothballs and herbal cigarettes. A patina of dust coated the floors, with a cavalry's worth of footprints marching through it in all directions. He could make out some of the graffiti scribbled in red and black marker on the walls—"REPENT OR DIE" and "FUCK THIS WALL." The latter tag had an arrow pointing from it to a ragged hole in the plaster.

"Back here," the voice beckoned.

Gulliver moved farther into the darkness, until he could just perceive a shadowy figure standing amongst yet more shadows in the rearmost section of the store. He was tall and broad, wearing a long, grungy trench with bulky gloves, square-toed boots, and a wide-brimmed fedora. His hands were clasped in front of him at the waist. His posture was so rigid he might've had a steel rod running into his crotch to prop him up, like one of those wooden artist's models. His face was an inky void.

"Greetings, Mr. Huggens."

Gulliver stopped. This close, the hoarse, almost inhuman voice caused him to shudder. The figure remained motionless, keeping his distance, which gave Gulliver enough room to flee should he attempt to lunge at him.

"Do I know you?" asked Gulliver.

"Permit me to get right to the matter at hand. I represent some very special individuals who have sent me here to request your assistance."

"My assistance? With what?"

"It has come to our attention that you reside with a community of little people. Is this true?"

Gulliver tensed. Whose attention? And how did they find out? From Kat?

"What is all this about?" he answered, his suspicions fomenting.

"The individuals I speak for belong to a race of Giants, who have been living secretly in the Devil's Horns Mountains for centuries."

Gulliver churned this revelation over in his mind. "No way," he snickered after a moment. This had to be a joke. Kat pranking him, having an altogether different sort of fun with him than the night before.

"They are a peaceful, simple folk," elucidated the faceless stranger, "who prefer their isolation. But circumstances have arisen where we must solicit your help. Your little people, whom we call Micronians, genetically produce a unique virus, harmless to them and your kind. But, unfortunately, quite lethal to Giants."

"You're making this up."

"Hence the Micronians," the stranger continued, unfazed by Gulliver's incredulity, "or rather the virus they carry, pose a significant threat to the survival of our civilization. We wish to suppress that threat."

Okay, I'll play along, Gulliver decided. He wouldn't want Kat to think he was a bad sport on top of being a nutcase. "And how does this concern me?"

"We ask you to exterminate your little people."

Gulliver felt a gulf violently split within himself, one crumbling cliffside still holding onto his cynicism, the other appreciating the gravity of the stranger's entreaty.

"The method we'll leave to your discretion."

"You want me to... to kill them?"

"Yes. Their erasure must be absolute, irrevocable."

This was no joke, Gulliver grasped.

At least, not a funny one.

"I can't do that," he balked.

"But you must," the stranger exhorted. "The Micronians could instigate an epidemic among the Giants, one that would spell their extinction. To put it plainly, it's either them or us."

Gulliver had the unshakeable urge to turn and bolt out of that retail tomb, to ascribe the entire episode to a multisensory hallucination triggered by his emotional distress, or something else just as rational.

Even if the stranger weren't a figment of his imagination, how could he trust this mere shade of a man? The very notion of Giants afraid of tiny tribesmen sounded no less than ludicrous, calling to Gulliver's mind cartoons depicting an elephant terrified of a mouse 1/1,000th of its size. Yet what the stranger so casually proposed was anything but comical.

It was mass murder. Mini genocide. It was reprehensible. Horrendous.

Yes, Gulliver should have turned and bolted. Instead, he stayed and listened, because his instincts further warned him this stranger would neither be disregarded nor refused.

"I understand how disagreeable this must seem to you. Alas, there is no alternative."

"Why d-don't you guys do some research? Find a vaccine to protect yourselves?"

"We do not possess such technological capabilities. Even if we had, there is no time. Our scouts have reported recent sightings of Micronians at the outskirts of the woodlands bordering your village."

Gulliver shook his head. "That can't be. They never leave the house."

"How can you be so certain? Much like your kind, they too might have the impulse to explore, to journey beyond your walls."

"Not that I know of."

But Gulliver knew the Little People—the Micronians—retained an aura of mystery about them, for he could neither see through the walls nor the floorboards. He could not be home all day, nor stay awake all night. He couldn't be privy to their every movement and activity.

The stranger must have known this too.

"Regardless, we cannot afford the risk. The Micronians must be annihilated. And you must be the one to execute it."

"I can't." *He wouldn't.*

"Only you have their trust, Mr. Huggens. Only you are near enough their lair to accomplish the operation without them suspecting anything. That is, not until it's too late."

"This is…" Gulliver scoured his brain for the words that would do *this* justice. "I don't know what this is. But I know I don't like it." He tremulously jutted his chin at the stranger. "Why should I even believe you?"

"Because you have no choice."

"Oh? What if I say no?"

"The terms are straightforward. Either cooperate, or suffer the consequences."

Gulliver swallowed. "What consequences?"

"We needn't address that. Not yet." The stranger's tone remained so blasé they could as well have been discussing upcoming dinner plans. "Suffice to say, you can imagine what unpleasantries a race of Giants can effect."

Gulliver didn't respond, letting the minatory statement sink in. The only thing he could imagine right then was being squashed beneath a size 300 shoe, which he imagined would be quite unpleasant indeed.

"You have until midnight tomorrow to fulfill your part of the agreement."

"But... I-I didn't agree to anything."

"You will, Mr. Huggens. It would be wisest for you to do as we say. We'll be watching."

With that, the stranger swiveled away from him and retreated further into the space, Gulliver losing sight of him in the magnified darkness.

"Wait!" he pleaded.

A door yawned in the rear of the property. Bone gray daylight flooded through it, causing Gulliver to squint. It was open only seconds before the stranger shut it behind him, yet those seconds were enough for Gulliver to glimpse the man's illuminated profile. The skin of his face drooped under his eyes, nose, and jaw, as if it were not attached to anything underneath, like a fluffed-up sheet on a bed. Gulliver figured it must be some ill-fitting rubber Halloween mask, that of an old man, or maybe an alien. It gave him the willies.

After an instant of hesitation—fear—Gulliver raced after him, careful not to spill the coffees still gripped in his hands.

The door exited into a narrow alleyway across from the stuccoed back wall of the Bucks 'n' Butts, Laymon's hunting and smoking paraphernalia shop. There was one cardboard-crammed dumpster and a few dented metal trash cans. Bullet casings of various calibers were scattered on the ground. Chickweeds with white blossoms sprouted from jagged fissures in the concrete. Winged insects flitted about Gulliver, a couple sideswiping his face and buzzing off agitatedly.

The stranger was gone.

Either way he went would take him to Fairview Avenue. Gulliver chose left as the quickest, least bug-ridden route there. After tripping on a crack and sloshing the coffees onto his hands, he reached the sidewalk, peered up and down the street. No sign of the stranger.

Gulliver waxed theoretical about what had happened. He revisited his initial impression, that it was some surreal hoax. However, he now very much doubted Kat had masterminded it. With their date taking place only the night before, she could not have conceived, arranged, and enacted this in half a day. But if she weren't involved, who was behind it? What was the joke's punchline?

Unless it wasn't a joke at all.

Perhaps the stranger was nothing but a madman…

…a madman who knew Gulliver by his full name and all about the Little People!

He purported to represent a race of Giants—real-life Brobdingnagians—living somewhere in the mountains. Yet the stranger couldn't have been taller than six feet himself. Human size. A queer choice for Giants to recruit as an agent. Unless he was a midget Giant. That was possible, Gulliver supposed. And pragmatic, since the Giants wouldn't wish to attract attention to themselves when contacting him.

"Pardon me, son," ribbitted a feeble voice.

Gulliver looked downward to behold a knobby old man—an actual one, not a disguise—the same one he had spotted driving past him in the Impala minutes before. He sported the finest in senior citizen discount day thrift store fashion, his weight supported by a foldaway walker with sliced-open tennis balls clamped onto its front feet.

"Are you lost?" the old man asked.

"No, sir," Gulliver answered.

"Then mind gettin' the hell out of my way?"

"Sorry." Gulliver stepped aside to let him dodder by.

Gulliver dubiously regarded the turtle-faced man before concluding he probably hadn't played a role in any of this. He clicked a mental picture of him anyway, just in case. He then headed back to Knox's, pledging to keep himself on high alert for anything out of the ordinary.

But Gulliver would never see all the eyes watching him, everywhere, waiting for his next move.

3

Huey Humongous (so he had been called after his Goliathan growth spurt as a toddler) didn't know where he was, but he already knew he hated the place.

He squatted on a rocky outcrop on the eastern slope of the mountain overlooking the town. To Huey, it was just another carbuncle on this festering abscess Earth, belching the fetor of putrefaction and pestilence. If the whole execrable sewer, rife with noxious machinery and botched humanity, would implode in on itself tomorrow, that would be hunky-dory with him.

Huey picked at his few remaining teeth with a pine needle, drawing blood from his gums. He then peeled off his shoes to air them out. Judging by how sore his feet and legs were, Huey figured he must've traversed many miles across the wooded highlands. From where, he could not recall. It didn't matter. It was all the same to him.

He loathed it all.

He loathed bright days and cloudy days and rainy days. He loathed the sun and the moon and the stars. He loathed trees and mountains, lakes and rivers, fields and flowers. He loathed all animals, from fish and fowl, to dogs and deer. He loathed every sight and sound that assailed his eyes and ears. He loathed cars and trains and airplanes. He loathed towns and cities and farms. Most of all, he loathed people. All people.

But there was one thing he did love.

Huey Humongous loved sweet things.

Gulliver sat pensively on his sofa in his banjo-twanging frog jammies, staring at a daddy longlegs skittering across the ceiling. He mused about how easy it would be to terminate its life without experiencing a scintilla of remorse. Why was that? Because it was only a spider, which, as far as Gulliver knew, could not intellectualize or emotionalize? What would its death mean to its arachnid brothers and sisters? Would it be mourned, missed? Probably not... but what if he were wrong?

Gulliver wondered if this was how the Giants regarded the Little People, as such lesser, unloved creatures so effortlessly dispatched.

He watched the spider crawl behind the curtain valance.

Gulliver remained perturbed over his encounter with the stranger the day before. He still couldn't reach a verdict on how he should react to it, or if he should even react at all. Eventually he decided to adopt a wait-and-see stance, as there really weren't any other options—ones not utterly repugnant at any rate—for him to consider. Just wait and see what the Giants would do if he didn't do anything.

"*You can imagine what unpleasantries a race of Giants can effect.*"

He'd wait and see.

The Little People's unintelligible castrati voices chirruped up at Gulliver. He looked down at the Scrabble board on the coffee table. A new message was written out in letter tiles:

WHAT WRONG

"Don't worry about it," he replied aloud. "Just got something on my mind."

Moments later, another message appeared:

THE GIRL

"Yeah. That's one thing."

WE SORRY

"I know you are." Gulliver sighed glumly. When he'd gotten home, the Little People had mollified him as best as they were able with a Riverdance-style show on his dining room table. As terrifically choreographed as it was, it didn't resolve his dilemma d'amour.

"I just want her to like me again. Somehow."

FLOWERS

He shook his head. "No. That's too tame for her. If I'm going to win her over, I have to appeal to her wild side." He rose from the sofa and paced the room. "What can I do that screams rock 'n' roll?"

For some constructive accompaniment, the Little People switched on his DaikeSonica AM/FM stereo. The Scorpions' anthemic "Rock You Like A Hurricane" besieged the house.

Gulliver groaned, his fingertips massaging his temples.

"C'mon, guys. Turn that off. It's giving me a headache."

The stereo's radio flipped over to a much less drubbing classical station. Gulliver ruminated a while.

Somewhere between Tchaikovsky's *Capriccio Italien Op45* and Pachelbel's *Canon*, it struck him what he would do to re-ignite Kat's passion for him.

All it would require was shedding a little blood for her.

The following morning, Gulliver bounded out of bed.

Running on no sleep but vivified by a Nebuchadnezzar's worth of adrenaline, he showered and dressed, then called Mr. Knox to tell him why he couldn't be in until the latter half of his shift. His boss approved.

Gulliver left his house and hustled toward Fairview Avenue. He waved hello to Glenn across the street, not pausing to hear the postman crow about his latest sexual conquests. Ten minutes later, he boarded the Boom Boom Bus, informing Mr. Russ that today he was headed into Sulfur Springs. When the driver asked him why, Gulliver beamed with excitement, saying he had something special to do there. He had just enough money saved up to cover the cost, and just enough courage to pull it off.

The procedure took less than three hours to complete. Though not pleasant, it was for the most part painless, and the results, to Gulliver's critique, were masterful.

He got back to Laymon before one o'clock that afternoon. After using Green Valley Fuel's restroom to spruce himself up, he made a beeline into the Beanie Roast. The only other customer there was Olivia Ehrwort, the frumpy file clerk from the Town Hall. She sat at the rearmost table facing the wall, quietly sipping a demitasse of jasmine tea. Prevailing local canards branded her a witch. She did frighten small children without trying. Plus, she cackled.

Gulliver strode up to the counter and rolled up the sleeve of his Tommy Bahama shirt, unveiling his graphic tribute to Kat.

"Hi. Look."

The fresh tattoo on his right deltoid glistened from the antibiotic ointment daubed over it. The skin was still tender, rimmed with a coral red nimbus. The artist instructed him to leave the bandage on at least overnight, but Gulliver couldn't wait that long. He'd removed it in the gas station's bathroom, tucking it in his pants pocket to reapply later.

The three-inch, all black tattoo, selected by Gulliver from the parlor's catalog, depicted a yowling cat's head. It could've well been the mascot for some college sports team.

"What do you think?" Gulliver asked Kat, sounding much like an overzealous grade-schooler vying for a gold star sticker from his teacher. "I got it for you."

Kat rolled her eyes, groaning.

"Jesus fuck," she spat. "Are you gonna stalk me now, too?"

Kat's words, cutting and caustic, sliced through Gulliver's heart. He craved a whiskey to anesthetize it. Or a knife to carve it out permanently.

An emasculated "no" was all he could say in response.

"Good. 'Cause I'm not into you, Gulliver. Never will be."

Gulliver muttered, in the frailest of voices, "Give me a chance, Kat."

"I don't have to give you anything. Besides, that tat's ugly as ass."

Olivia Ehrwort cackled.

Gulliver cupped a hand over the tattoo, his touch stinging it. Wounded, he looked down at some droplets of water on the floor by his feet, realizing a moment later they were his own spilt tears.

"Sorry," he whimpered. Then he withdrew from Kat and out of the shop.

This time, Kat watched him go. Cussing to herself, she stomped out from behind the counter, roughly undoing the knot in her apron strings as she headed for the "Employees Only" door.

"Cover me," Kat snapped at her co-worker Becky, who had just arrived for the second shift. "I'm going out for a smoke."

"But you don't smoke."

"I do today." And she slammed the door shut behind her.

Kat felt shittier than the dog dookie she stepped in exiting the Bean. Sure, Gulliver is a wack job, she thought as she raked the sole of her Creepers across a patch of crabgrass. But he wasn't the first one she'd dated. Nor the worst. Not by a long shot.

Katrina Ronette Klugerschmidt was born and raised in a pretentious Pennsylvanian mining town. Her father worked as a ditch digger, her mother the writer/producer/director of the community theater troupe The Prancing Pigglies. While dad broke gallons of sweat breaking hard earth six days a week, mom received a medley of regional accolades for her original plays promoting old-fashioned values and New Age sexuality. Gail Klugerschmidt, never one to refuse an opportunity to parade about in her off-the-rack designer frocks and costume jewelry ensembles, always got her family the best tables in restaurants and the choicest deals in stores. And her husband Luke absolutely begrudged her for it. The new Cadillac, the Sony Trinitron, his Calvin Klein suits, her Wedgewood dinner-ware—he would've gladly given them all up for a "normal" life. That was, one that didn't feature his celebrity wife being goggled at and gushed upon every day, everywhere they went. He'd dreaded leaving the house with her.

So it was no mystery to Kat why her father had strayed, engaging in a succession of torrid affairs with some of the classiest Botoxed pub trawlers in town. Luke's spitefulness aside, perpetuating the sanctity of marriage was never high on Kat's parents' list of priorities. As her mother didn't seem to care about her husband's infidelities, Kat didn't much either—until she'd turned sixteen and dad began boffing her girlfriends in the backseat of the Caddy. On her seventeenth birthday, Kat bailed on her folks, hopping a Greyhound to New York with only her purse and a knapsack filled with clothes, feminine products, and the three hundred dollars she'd liberated from their bank account. She hadn't spoken to either of them since.

Once in Manhattan, she spent her initial weeks at a flea-bag motel in Alphabet City for $19 a night. She then hooked up with a heroin-addicted, nouveau riche artist in a Greenwich Village piano bar, moving into his obscenely spacious SoHo loft two days later, rent free, on the stipulation she be his muse. This involved suspending her upside down by her ankles, splashing her nude body with different palettes of acrylic paint, then spinning, sliding, and slamming her against an enormous canvas. This arrangement got old fast, so she dropped him for an enterprising law student. He ended up vanishing three months later after launching some capital venture that had competed with a mob-managed money-laundering ring with a more aggressive business plan.

With NYC wearing itself anorexically thin, Kat boarded the Amtrak for Miami. From there, over the next five years, she planted temporary stakes in a dozen cities, shacking up with more than two dozen men of ill repute.

Some lowlights:

There was Pack Rat Pete in Tucson, who had amassed the world's largest collection of secondhand nooses, innocently and incessantly requesting she try each on for size. And the Atlanta minister with a prosthetic left hand with which, at his bidding, she pleasured herself while he leered at her, afterwards beating her with his stump to atone for her sins and his shame. More recently, there was the Japanese-American mayoral candidate in Denver, a fertilizer mogul who, she later found out, had a penchant for soliciting the sleaziest of whores to satisfy his more deviant appetites, those he didn't want to inflict upon the one he loved (and loved to smack around). That was bullshit, of course, so she'd helped herself to his Mustang and eight thousand dollars, saying sayonara in a letter informing Scum-San she had in her possession a memory stick containing pics of him snorting a mound of cocaine shaped like Mt. Fuji. Consider the car and cash farewell tokens of his "love" for her, she wrote. Whatever he'd actually considered it, she knew he wouldn't come after her, not if he cherished a career in public office or anywhere else.

For all the crap she'd been through, all the assholes and dumbshits she'd loaned herself out to, she figured she earned herself a few perks. Money, wheels, clothes, boob job—she was entitled to whatever she could get out of a relationship.

Except maybe love.

Kat was in control of her life, as much as Fate would permit, but Love was not in her stars. That's what a tarot reader had once told her anyway, and she supposed it was true. Most men, from her extensive personal experience, were filthy, idiotic, barbaric creatures. How could anyone fall in love with that?

Kat fired up a joint in the alley, took a deep drag.

Yeah, Gulliver may have been a scoop shy of a sundae, but he was still sweet. Just a goofy, oversexed guy with a naïve, overcompensating crush on her. And while the tattoo may have gone a teensy bit overboard—and it wasn't *that* hideous, really—that didn't mean he deserved to be treated the way she'd treated him. The way she'd hurt him.

Guilt gnawed at Kat, and she didn't know how to handle it at all.

She had thought she couldn't feel much of anything anymore.

As he traipsed out of the Beanie Roast, Gulliver found he felt nothing. And nothing, he discovered, kind of hurt like hell.

He made his way to Knox's, in no mindset to work but with no place else to go.

Mr. Knox was stooping over the workbench, untangling a jumble of wires in an electric mixer.

"What the hell did you get?" he asked when Gulliver entered.

Gulliver looked at him with a puzzled expression.

Knox pointed at the Octa-Girl gracing his own arm, then at the raw artwork on Gulliver's, whose sleeve was still rolled up, the tattoo prominently displayed.

The young man sighed. "It's a cat."

"No kidding?" Mr. Knox answered sarcastically. "Why'd you pick that?"

Gulliver then recounted the early chapters of hope and happiness romancing his barista belle, followed by its trial and tribulation-packed finale. He omitted the Little People's role in the narrative, as his boss remained ignorant of their existence and Gulliver was not yet bold enough to explain to him that particular facet of his life.

"Well, it is pretty ugly," Knox chaffed him.

Gulliver frowned.

Mr. Knox, recognizing he'd plucked a nerve in the boy, backpedalled. "But I've seen uglier."

"Don't think that makes me feel any better."

"Don't take it too personally, kid. If you like it, that's all that matters."

"What mattered was *her* liking it."

Mr. Knox rescrewed the metal coverplate on the mixer. "You wouldn't be the only sap who got inked for a girl who didn't 'preciate it."

Gulliver regarded his tattoo critically, poking at it with his finger. He elected not to put the bandage back on, conjecturing if it became infected the image might flake off.

"Maybe I should start a support group for people with regrettable tattoos."

Mr. Knox chuckled. "That's good, Huggens. Seeing the humor in your heartbreak is the first step to recovery."

"I wasn't trying to be funny."

Mr. Knox, at a loss for further encouraging comments, stood up from the worktable. He tried out the mixer. It gyrated acceptably.

"Man, I'm tuckered," he sighed. "Why don't we close up

shop? I'll buy you a beer, or a soda. Or milk. Whatever you want."

"No, thanks." Gulliver took a seat on the opposite side of the worktable in front of a disassembled flatscreen. "You can go though. I'm going to throw this TV together. I promised Mr. Preston he could pick it up tomorrow."

"Alright." Knox nodded. "See you tomorrow then."

Gulliver, already immersed in his task, didn't reply.

Mr. Knox buttoned up his denim vest and ambled out the door.

Seconds later, Gulliver heard his boss's motorcycle rev powerfully outside, then vroom up the street, a roving gang of leashless terriers yapping behind it.

It took forty-five minutes to re-solder three malfunctioning joints on a circuit board inside the TV. Gulliver plugged its cord into a power strip, inserted the cable line into the set's jack, and turned it on for a test run. Static materialized on the screen. Gulliver surfed through the channels using the controls on the bottom panel. Every station broadcasted the same snowy wall, the same distorted *Om*-like hum.

Maybe their cable was out.

Grabbing one of the many remotes lying around him, Gulliver turned on the 19" office TV propped up on a platform of milk crates across from him. Reception for the Jerry Van Dyke talk show was crystalline. A potbellied woman in a peach bodysuit was confessing to her security guard husband that she'd been cheating on him the past eleven months with his deceased father. Gulliver switched it off before she got into the sordid logistics.

He renewed his attentions to the inoperative flatscreen. Its picture, almost imperceptibly, seemed to have cleared. Gulliver swore he could now discern text beneath the swarms of static. He tweaked the image correction dials, adjusting the contrast, tint, and sharpness, until the words, printed in a sans serif font on a stationary title card, became legible:

By morrow morn all Little blood be shed,
Else 'nother Man Kind ye shall cause dead.

Gulliver reread the demented nursery rhyme three times before it began to flicker, resuming the flurry of winking pixels. He again fiddled with the television's dials until a picture scrolled up and steadied on the screen: Sergeant Sparkles employing a long, sterile corridor in the Pentagon as a Slip 'n Slide, his unsoiled monument-white uniform demonstrating how "darn well clean" his polish left even the most marched upon floors.

Gulliver jabbed the off button.

The store's interior suddenly felt cold to him—meat locker cold—though he was pretty certain this temperature fluctuation was only in his head. What he had seen, however, wasn't a trick of his mind. Or was it?

No, he wasn't crazy. That *was* real.

Pins and needles rappelled down Gulliver's spine while his brain wrestled with the cautionary message, and he very much feared what it might mean to the unsuspecting people of Laymon.

The Giants, it appeared, had declared war.

One hour before Gulliver had received the Giants' ultimatum, Glenn Hammond was driving his postal truck toward Hap's Hardware Road.

All he could think about was one thing: he was fucking impotent.

Glenn realized that was one of those *oxomoronisms*, two words together which contradicted each other, but they sure summed up his sentiments exactly.

The universe had really done a number on him.

It was bad enough he suffered almost every non-fatal medical condition there was. Now for the past month, his vaunted pecker, the joy toy of countless babes, had been out of batteries. He vocally blamed his limp performance on the most recent spate of women he had entertained, criticizing their subpar mouth or ungainly handwork, instructing them to come back when they learned what the hell they were doing.

But he knew they weren't the problem. He couldn't even rise *himself* to the occasion while viewing his favorite gyno porn starring Tatiana Tulips, the Queen of the Speculum. He had scheduled a date with the doctor, hoping she would dole out some of those miracle boner pills he'd seen on those late-night infomercials.

His weekend was shot though. Or rather, he wouldn't be doing any shooting at all. Probably end up getting spacefaced and watching the *Cops* marathon.

Christ on a cracker, was he pissed off.

Hap's Hardware Road was named at the time when residential development in the area, at the foothills of the Devil's Horns Mountains, had been predicted to explode by Y2K. Several local businesses had been approved to sponsor the newly laid streets. Home construction, however, had progressed much slower than anticipated. Only four homes had been completed before the project, known as Blessed Acres, was placed on hiatus due to dwindling public interest. (This after Sulfur Springs put three luxury housing site proposals on the fast track in its own city.) Laymon's lumber mill closing down a year later rang the death knell for Blessed Acres, its last rites written in an official memo that, by that point, nobody even bothered to publish or read.

Hap's Hardware Road was the final stop on Glenn's route. It was also his worst.

The street was almost fifteen miles away from the nearest populated district, making it the most secluded community within Laymon's city limits. Its long neglected pavement was now this crumbling vestige of a trail that jounced Glenn when he drove over it. Every winter and summer, he and the other mail carriers drew stamps from an envelope to choose who would handle delivery to "Hardass Road" the next six months. Glenn had drawn the lowest denomination stamp in January.

He swerved his truck around the blown-up remains of a deer at the desolate junction of Hap's Hardware Road and Bank of Laymon Boulevard. He coasted up to the row of flimsy metal mailboxes, all of them with hammered-out dents from past rounds of mailbox baseball. One of them was just a lidded aluminum waste bin, bolted to a wooden post, with a red number "3" spraypainted on it.

Gotta be some crackpot rubes living way out here, Glenn reckoned. He had never seen any of the houses' residents—three of the four homes were occupied—but he presumed they must all be Unabomber types, stockpiling military surplus and penning their anti-everything manifestos.

He shifted into park, letting the engine idle while he stepped out to deliver the typical quarter-dozen pieces of bulk rate mail, along with a small package from ComputerCo. As he slipped the items into the boxes, he looked up to see half of the Hap's Hardware street sign had been blasted off, so it only said "Hap's Hard".

Lucky Hap, Glenn sneered.

Glenn heard a crunch. Like a heavy foot treading on dead leaves.

What'd that come from?

He froze, waiting, listening.

He didn't hear any more footsteps, or whatever it had been. Maybe he was hearing things. He scanned the copses of deciduous trees around him. All was still.

And this was, now that Glenn was conscious of it, strange. He didn't hear *anything*. No caws of crows, no tweeting of sparrows, no chittering of squirrels. All this woodland and not a peep of wildlife.

It was deathly quiet. Like a cemetery.

He'd never given it much thought before, but come to think of it, Blessed Acres was freaking eerie. It even had a graveyard's name.

Glenn wanted to get the hell out of there.

He deposited the last Narko Drugs circular into the wastebasket mailbox, then hurried back toward his truck.

He halted when he again heard the crunch of trampled detritus. Behind him. And closer this time.

Much closer.

A hulking shadow loomed over him.

Glenn hadn't time enough to turn to find out what it was. Within an instant, his head was enclosed in smothering, pitch blackness.

He scarcely heard the crunch of his eyeglasses, nor his skull, being crushed to splinters.

4

What a perfect day, Sheriff Boone thought.

The sky was a dome of cloudless azure, crisscrossed by a trio of Laymon's federally beloved eagles. The golden sun dipped toward the horizon, balancing on the summit of the West Devil's Horn. A soft breeze blew, whooshing through the trees like a gratified sigh, animating the hand-painted carved animal whirligigs throughout Boone's backyard.

The sheriff, leisurely clad in a camp shirt and chinos, reclined on the white Adirondack chair on his flagstone patio, sipping a glass of lemonade his wife had fixed from scratch that morning. He watched the eagles above perform a ballet of avian somersaults through Bushnell binoculars.

"Do you think eagles are telepathic?" Lorna asked. Sheriff Boone's wife lay on a matching Adirondack chair beside him, peering through an identical pair of binoculars.

"Pardon, hon?"

"They swoop all around together up there, and never once bang into one another. It's amazing. Like they can read each other's birdy minds."

Sheriff Boone smiled. Lorna was wearing her cute safari outfit, minus the Panama hat and snake-proof boots. She had soft eyes and pert lips, her silvery hair cut short like that of her movie idol, Dame Judi Dench. Though only six years Boone's junior, Lorna at age fifty had the sex appeal of a fabulously fit forty-year-old, her natural beauty rivaling even as gorgeous a day like today.

Had they really been together thirty years? Yep. That fact alone should have made Sheriff Boone feel as old as Rip Van

Winkle, but Lorna kept him young at heart. As for the rest of him, while he was now grizzled in places he'd never imagined got grizzled, he wasn't near set to be put out to pasture. Nope. Lorna wouldn't have it. She knew how much the job meant to her husband.

Though not as much as she meant to him.

Lorna Bea Wallace. That was her full maiden name when they'd met, and he swore to himself he'd never forget it.

Yet Boone could only recall snippets of *how* they had met: sledding together, dancing together, a candlelit dinner in front of a tinkling fountain with lion statues. Or were they horses? Where was that, darn it? Colorado, probably. Maybe Utah.

He remembered she had made him laugh. She still did.

"Is that a sapphire-crowned king finch over there?" Lorna asked.

"Where?"

"Top of the big birch."

He raised the binoculars up to his eyes, training them on the wrinkly-barked tree about thirty yards away. A small brown bird roosted on an uppermost branch, preening its feathers.

"Why, yes it is. A female."

"Quite the rare breed, hmm?"

Yes, you are, Boone thought, and he smiled again.

The phone rang within the house.

"I'll get it," Boone said, rising stiffly from his chair.

He opened the sliding screen door and entered their Cape Cod-style home. It was decorated in a harmonious blend of Old West Americana and New Country Minimalism, with, not surprisingly, birds being the predominant motif, followed by antique firearms, ornamental cutlery, and Hummel figurines. Bowls of potpourri sat on every horizontal surface. Everything smelled faintly of cloves.

He answered the rotary phone on the fifth ring.

"Boone abode."

The sheriff listened.

"Who is it?" he asked the caller, his folksy charm gone sober, professional. That of a lawman.

"Lord have mercy." He placed his palm against the wall, drumming his fingers upon it. "Where at?"

Lorna stepped inside, closing the sliding door behind her since her husband had neglected to do so, an oversight she would have chided him for if not for his grim mien.

"I'll come straight by. Make sure no one touches anything before the M.E. gets there, 'kay?" Boone hung up the receiver.

"What's wrong, Cy?"

"I have to go to work."

"But it's your day off. Can't one of the deputies handle it?"

"Not this one," he muttered, heading toward the bedroom to don his uniform, his gut telling him he might not have another day off for quite a while.

There hadn't been a murder in Laymon for over two decades, not since a hysterical wife mowed down her husband with her Buick Skylark after catching him in self-flagrante with a boudoir photograph of her mother. And the last attempted homicide had occurred eight years ago, a bartender viciously beating a customer with a register till in some dispute over a Special Olympics track-and-field betting pool. There had also been a couple of confirmed suicides in the preceding few years, one by bridge bungee hanging, the other by self-immolation during a publicity stunt gone awry at the U CAN BBQ store liquidation event.

But in the city's entire history during which Boone served and protected it, never had there been anything like this.

Sheriff Boone approached the crime scene at the inter-section of Bank of Laymon Boulevard and Hap's Hardware

Road, though neither one had any right to be called a boulevard or a road in this millennium. They could well have been the bridleways to some antediluvian ruin.

Boone found the location without much difficulty, though he had to consult his atlas once or twice. He negotiated his '97 Jeep Wrangler around a deer carcass teeming with bloated flies and mangled almost beyond recognition, as if it had nuzzled a landmine. The sheriff parked outside the area cordoned off with yellow caution tape.

He spotted two of his men, Deputies Clive Eriksen and Toby Darkcloud, a purebred Native American Pokahawnee with plaited hair and, as befitting his birth name, the dourest of dispositions. He regularly prognosticated the impending end of the world by a rain of fire or some such Angry Spirits scenario. The other deputies thought he was a hoot.

Sheriff Boone exited his vehicle and strode up to them. It was still sunny there on the western side of the mountain, but it would remain so for only about an hour more. They'd have to set up a generator and some halogen work lamps soon.

He saw the body lying supine on the dry, bronzy dirt by a row of battered mailboxes, its upper torso beneath a striped Navajo blanket. The exposed bottom half wore recognizable mail carrier trousers.

"It's definitely gotta be Glenn Hammond, Sheriff," Clive confirmed, showing him the postman's driver's license inside a gold pleather wallet.

Darkcloud was assiduously studying the vicinity around the victim, combing for tracks or any other evidence.

"Anything?" the sheriff asked the sienna-skinned man.

Darkcloud shook his head. "One who did this dragged feet along ground while walking. Left no distinct footprints."

"Well, be sure and check out these woods 'round here thoroughly."

The Indian nodded stolidly. You could tell he loved his job.

"Are we sure it's a homicide?"

"See for yourself" was Clive's answer.

The deputy crouched by the covered body. He clutched the hem of the blanket and lifted it high enough so the sheriff, kneeling beside him, could get a good look.

Without steeling himself for the gruesome sight, Boone winced, but recovered his composure quickly. Hammond had been decapitated. No, that wasn't quite accurate—his head had been mashed flat, creating a sludge of bone, brain, and blood.

This was no accident.

Clive briefed Boone. A young couple driving by, seeking a private spot to picnic, found the body. They had made the discovery around 4 p.m., but weren't able to report it until they reached Green Valley Fuel fourteen miles down the road some twenty minutes later. Clive arrived on scene just before five and dutifully set up a perimeter. Darkcloud had taken witness statements from the unnerved teens at the gas station, then joined the other deputy by 5:30, ten minutes before Sheriff Boone got there. No murder weapon had been retrieved yet, though Clive wasn't even sure what kind of weapon they were searching for. Robbery could be ruled out as a motive, as the victim still had with him his wallet (thirty-three dollars and six condoms inside) and a 24-karat gold necklace. The county medical examiner/crime photographer, based out of Sulfur Springs, was on the way.

"Nice work," Boone complimented the deputy.

"Thanks, Sheriff," Clive said, beaming.

Boone could discern the twisted frame of a pair of eyeglasses amongst the gore.

"Looks like someone bashed his head in," the deputy offered, trying to be helpful. "Must've been with something real heavy. Maybe a sledgehammer?"

"I don't think so," Sheriff Boone differed, reexamining the damage. "The head appears to have been squashed by something."

"Like under a tire? Maybe he got run over by a truck." Clive lowered the blanket as the sheriff rose to his feet, brushing off his knee.

"Maybe. Hopefully the M.E. will be able to give us more solid particulars."

The two lawmen stood on tenterhooks over the body as if it were still liable to spring to its feet and saunter off. The sheer amount of blood, though—so much damn blood for such a puny fella—surely confuted that possibility. Death must have been instantaneous, Boone hypothesized. At least he hoped it'd been for the poor guy.

"Who would want to kill Glenn, Sheriff?"

Boone looked around them.

"Don't know, Clive. But we're gonna do our damnedest to find out."

When Gulliver returned home from work that evening, his agitation over the Giants' televised threat was abated somewhat upon being greeted with the epicurean feast prepared by the Little People.

It was a gesture of reconciliation on their part, comprised of a prosciutto, mushroom, and fennel crêpe drizzled with hollandaise sauce, with sides of a small Niçoise salad, grilled asparagus, and saffron rice, and, for dessert, a boysenberry-rhubarb tart. The meal was aesthetically plated on a tangerine Fiestaware dish, set on the dining table along with polished utensils and the Oktoberfest stein from Gulliver's cupboard, filled with quenching grape Kool-Aid. Vermillion gerber daisies, most likely picked from Mr. Jensen's flower garden next door, were arranged in a crackled purple vase as a center-piece. Baroque music featuring flute, violins, and a harpsichord played on the stereo in the living room.

The ambience was pleasant. The food was delicious.

Later, the Little People brewed him a pot of French roast coffee. Gulliver stared catatonically down into the stoneware cup before him on the kitchen dinette. The fluorescent bulb overhead reflected in the black liquid, and Gulliver watched as the luminous circle morphed into Kat's sultry face, eyeing him like... well, a Kat in heat.

"Sooooo hot," she moaned, steam venting from her lips, kissing his.

Gulliver didn't need to be tormented any more than he already was. He added milk to his cup, stirring it with a spoon. Kat's face dispersed within the swirling whorls of white, cooling both her and the coffee off.

He rose from his chair and made for the liquor cabinet, producing a new bottle of Jack Daniel's from it. Returning to the kitchen, he sat back down and unscrewed the bottle's black cap, poured a shot's worth into his coffee. Gulliver chugged the cup, then refilled it with just the whiskey, guzzling that down too, letting the eighty proof elixir warm his body and numb his brain. He slumped in his chair, lulled by the soporific tick-tock of the rooster clock on the eave over the sink.

When he reopened his eyes, Gulliver found himself on the kitchen floor. He had also somehow become, judging from his extreme perspective—which could be described as an ant's eye view—appreciably tinier. Not quite ant tiny. Little People tiny.

Petrified wads of ages-ago chewed bubblegum hung from the underside of the chair above him like carious megateeth. The Maytag refrigerator looked like a towering white monolith advertising a selection of Disney magnets on it. A gigantic blue jay (or rather, a normal-sized one, if Gulliver had still been normal-sized) pecked hungrily at the kitchen windowpane from outside, its gunslinger's stare fixed on him.

Gulliver felt a newfound degree of vulnerability. Rats, snakes, even leaky hot water pipes now posed mortal hazards to him. Actions as basic as climbing stairs and flipping wall switches presented vexing challenges for the severely height disadvantaged. Changing a light bulb seemed nothing less than impossible, like extracting a sword from a stone. And what about food? It wasn't as if he could simply open his refrigerator or cupboards anymore, nor even grab an apple or granola bar off the countertop like he used to without having to embark on an onerous ascent. His life had suddenly become altogether altered and foreign to him. It was overwhelming. And scary as hell.

"Lord Gulliver," a brogued voice called out to him.

Gulliver spun around, reflexively assuming a defensive posture.

Peeking out from a floor-level cabinet was one of the Little People. A chieftain as evinced by his crinkly silver crown and mauve toga, fashioned from one of Father's "U.S.F.S." monogrammed silk kerchiefs. The elder also wore charcoal-ash lipstick and eye shadow reminiscent of Coptic glyph figures, and a beehive wig that appeared to have been woven from Gulliver's own hairs.

"Come," the chieftain said in perfectly comprehensible English, beckoning Gulliver with his four-fingered hand. "You'll be safe with me."

Gulliver loped toward the cabinet and climbed inside the chemical-reeking space beneath the sink, the jay cawing disapprovingly at his departure. He followed his guide behind the drain cleaners and dishwashing detergents, then through a ragged mousehole in the wall.

They wended their way through a murky warren of wood and wire passages. These soon became illuminated by strands of red, green, and white Christmas lights strung up along the sides, giving the corridors a *Star Trek*-ish vibe. There were also more Little People, all extending Gulliver a reverential bow of the head as he passed them.

"I am Ambassador Kyak of the Micronians," the chieftain introduced himself without breaking his stride.

"How is it I can understand you?" Gulliver asked.

"You are one of us now, my Lord."

"Why do you call me 'Lord'?"

"Because that is your title among us, as ordained by our High Council, as foretold by the Prophecy of King Jamus Bibble."

"Oh. Did this prophecy say anything about me once being bigger?"

"Aye. And that you possess the fifth digit of the Sacred Ones." Apparently, having five fingers merited automatic nobility in the Micronian hierarchy.

"Do you know how I became..." Gulliver, unacquainted as he was with the protocols governing Micronian political correctness, tried to be tactful, "...your size?"

Ambassador Kyak effusively explained how Gulliver's "blessed transmutation" precipitated from the extraordinary synthesis of an interdimensional umbilicus, a psychogenic energy nexus, and the artificial sweeteners in Gulliver's kitchen drawer. It was all impressively scientific and, according to Kyak, also divinely mandated. It was also enough to make Gulliver—Lord Gulliver—swell with irrepressible hubris. He wondered if his exalted new position came with its own cool scepter.

The ambassador led him into a grand hall, which Gulliver could tell, by the ceiling of parallel wood slats, was located beneath his front porch. Here throngs of Micronians, mostly commoners judging from their bumpkinish attire, bustled to and fro, going about whatever business Micronians did. The few who espied Gulliver promptly genuflected to him. He had to smile.

In the center of the space he saw two sizzling meaty globes suspended on toothpick spits, rotating over a tinfoil brazier. They were each about four feet in diameter (or, if measured in normal human size proportions, approximately two inches). Whatever they were, they smelled scrumptious.

"Hark, fellow Micronians!" Kyak heralded to the crowd upon entering the chamber. "I humbly present our appointed heir to the royal throne, Lord Gulliver!"

Those that weren't yet kneeling did so, their faces cast downward.

Some seconds later, Kyak, who was slightly shorter than Gulliver, craned his neck to whisper into his ear. "You may instruct them to rise, my Lord. If you wish."

Gulliver nodded, embracing the spirit of the ceremony. "Rise!"

His subjects rose in unison, all wearing expressions of elation and awe.

Ambassador Kyak clapped his hands together. "Everyone, finish preparations for the feast!"

The crowd recommenced their activities with renewed vigor and purpose. Matchbox tables were set, thimble seats were placed, and a throne molded from candlewax awaited their new king beneath a larkspur petal canopy. Micronian chefs sedulously basted and seasoned the browning spheres, which Gulliver ascertained were to be the banquet's main course.

"We've anticipated this day for so long, my Lord. We only hope you are pleased with our celebrations in your honor."

Gulliver smiled again. "So far, so good."

Ambassador Kyak beamed, giddy with delight.

"Tell me, what are those round things?" Gulliver asked. "Some kind of meat?"

"Aye. They be the fruit bearing your seed."

"Pardon?"

"Your Pearly Nuggets, my Lord."

What was this? Some sort of riddle?

Gulliver frowned, clueless.

Kyak now regarded him as if he were a moron as well as their monarch.

"Your Cream Jewels?"

Realization hit Gulliver like a cannonball to his gut. His eyes widened. His jaw dropped. He stretched the elastic waistband of his pogoing snake pajama pants and received horrifying visual confirmation.

"You cooked my balls?!"

"Aye, my Lord. Do you not approve?"

"Of course I don't! Are you people insane?"

Panic caused the ambassador's eyes to bulge cartoonishly. "But you had not been using them, my Lord. And they *are* a delicacy."

"I don't care! STOP COOKING THEM!"

"Aye, my Lord!" Kyak scampered toward the barbecue pit, waving his arms frantically, screaming for the chefs to cease fire.

But the damage was done, and Gulliver fainted as the team of hirsute Bobby Flays began carving slices from his broiled testicles.

Gulliver awoke bleary-eyed and naked in his tub, slathered in Mrs. Butterbean Maple Syrup.

A neoteric Little People gag.

Ordinarily, this would have irked him greatly, but upon finding his Pearly Nuggets right where they should be, and him back to his accustomed five foot eight inch self, he felt as content as a bear lolling in a king-sized ceramic honeypot.

Despite showering most of the treacly goo from his body, when Gulliver left for work that morning his armpits and inner thighs remained sticky, with amber gobs still clotted in his hair. He made his way to the bus stop. Bleak pewter clouds dominated the sky, with even more ominous ones drifting toward Laymon from beyond the Devil's Horns Mountains. The air was oppressive, promising a rainstorm.

He should go back for an umbrella, Gulliver thought as a postal truck puttered by him. He raised his arm to wave at Glenn before seeing the driver was not Glenn after all, but rather some husky woman wearing a Mark Knopfler headband. She waved back at Gulliver with a mittened hand.

Glenn must have taken the day off, Gulliver presumed, even though the mail carrier never took any sick days—he would not give his mutinous body the satisfaction—and he vacationed only in the month of August to attend the annual Erotica Expo in New Zealand.

Gulliver encountered another unprecedented irregularity upon getting on the Boom Boom Bus. Every one of the half-dozen passengers on board was engrossed in Tuesday's edition of *The Regal Eagle*. The biweekly newspaper was more of a community happenings pamphlet, with a predominance of ads, ninety percent of them for businesses in Sulfur Springs. Today was different though. *The Regal Eagle* had published legitimate front-page news, not the typical mundanities about the long-delayed Laymon Town Hall repainting project or the Sacred Valley Church's monthly raffle and cookoff.

"Crazy shit, huh?" was how Mr. Russ cheerlessly greeted Gulliver.

"What is?"

"You didn't hear?"

"Hear what?"

"Somebody in Laymon got murdered yesterday."

Russ handed him a copy of *The Regal Eagle*, splashed with the sensational headline "MURDER ON THE MAIL ROUTE!"

Gulliver read the accompanying article, then reread it. It covered all the Journalism 101 bases, spiced up with the newspaper's standard tabloidesque flourishes. (Who? Glenn Hooper Hammond. What? A murder most heinous! When? At the cusp of dusk. Where? In the creeping shadow of the Devil's Horns. How? A savage blow to the cranium. Why? A mystery most baffling!) The account culminated in a pithy obituary enumerating each of Hammond's professional and personal accomplishments, including his third runner-up award at the State Mah-Jongg Championships in '92.

Glenn continued to be the main topic of conversation at Knox's.

"He was your mail guy, eh?" Mr. Knox asked while trying to unclog a vacuum cleaner with a wire brush.

"Yeah," Gulliver replied. "And we had gone to the same elementary school. On Old Mill."

"Friend of yours?"

"Not really. He played with the girls mostly."

Gulliver supposed it would have been proper for him to experience some measure of shock or grief over Glenn's death. Instead, he concluded the only thing he'd miss about the guy was the mail, and that issue had already been sorted out.

Mr. Knox plugged in the vacuum and switched it on. Its motor revved like it was simultaneously grinding quartz, baby chickens, and a constipated Richard Simmons. He shut it off and threw up his hands.

"Piece o' crap."

"Want me to take a stab at it?"

"No. This one's my cross to bear. But mark my words, this Electrolux's gonna be gagging on my high-pile by the end of today."

Knox rambled on some more about making the "damned dirt-sucker" his "bitch." He then asked Gulliver if he would go fetch them coffee.

Gulliver nodded unenthusiastically. His boss gave him a ten-dollar bill and told him to get him his usual. And one of those blondies with the cranberries in them, if they had any.

Once outside, Gulliver dawdled on the sidewalk across the street from the Beanie Roast. He stared down at the toes of his right sneakered foot, the ball of which he grated against the concrete, back and forth, back and forth. He wouldn't go in, he eventually decided. It was a matter of principle. Of pride.

And of cowardice. Admittedly, there was that.

Was he overreacting? What was the worst that could happen? Most likely Kat would just take his order. Or ignore him altogether. Or berate him like a child who'd peed himself in public.

Mock him.

Slap him.

Humiliate him.

Castrate him.

The stuff traumas were made of.

Gulliver didn't chance it. Trauma collecting was a hobby he wished to forgo.

He returned to Knox's carrying a cardboard takeout tray cradling two cups of coffee.

"About time," Knox grumped. "I was ready to send out a search party."

Gulliver set the tray down on the worktable. "They're both the same, so, whichever you want."

Mr. Knox lifted one of the Styrofoam cups. On its side was the Dudley's Donuts logo—a Rastafarian Sasquatch with a beatific, Boston crème-lathered grin.

"You went to Dudley's?"

"They make good coffee there. It's a gourmet blend." Gulliver spoke with all the authority of a java connoisseur; in truth, he had simply memorized the description off the bakery's placard. "It has robust flavor, with a roasted chest-nutty aftertaste."

"Okay. But Dudley's is over a mile down the road."

Gulliver shrugged. "I was in the mood for a walk."

Knox shot him a skeptical eye, notes of wry amusement playing on his lips. "It's that gal over there, ain't it? You're avoiding her."

"I j-just didn't want to m-make her uncomfortable. She's, y'know… working." Gulliver tried to sound insouciant about it, but came off to Knox as the third-rate bullshitter he was.

"Man, she really did a number on you, boy." His boss shook his head, chuckling as he took a sip of his coffee.

"Not bad," Knox said before glaring over at his chastened employee. "Though ya could've brought back some crullers."

Vic calculated he was now less than one year away from buying himself the forty-three foot Sea Wasp motor yacht he had been eyeing for the past decade. While he'd only seen photos of it in magazines, he'd known in his gut from the get-go this was the vessel he would one day be captaining, with its roomy interior, ample sleeping accommodations, breathtaking cockpit view, and powerful twin 8.1 S gas inboards. Aye, she was a beaut, and soon she would be his.

Vic, at the helm of Seven Seas Styles barbershop for some forty-odd years, understood most folks in Laymon nowadays regarded him as just this sweet, silly codger clinging onto his youthful dreams of sailing the seas of Sinbad. But they didn't know him well.

Not well at all.

It was ten minutes before three o'clock. Vic hadn't had a customer for over an hour and a half. Might as well close up shop for the day, he decided. He bolted the entrance door, flipped the painted plank hanging by a chain in the window from "Ahoy, Mateys!" to "Gone Sailin'," and retired to his back office. He shut the louvered wood door behind him, latching it.

Vic reached up and took down the Queen Conch shell mounted on a nail high on the wall, right above the brass porthole clock. He extracted from its orifice a rolled-up plastic bag. It was filled with five grams of premium grade Bolivian marching powder. His personal stash.

Sitting at his desk, he poured a generous portion onto a large hand mirror, cutting the mound into three thin lines with a straight razor. He then sucked up every last flake into his left nostril through a dried horsetail reed he'd clipped from the riverbank.

His commercial stash he kept elsewhere, inside a hollow rock with a false bottom that sat inconspicuously in his yard amongst a stack of other stones marking the gravesite for Skipper, Vic's late "Beloved First Mate Kitty" that, incidentally, never existed. Vic figured nobody would desecrate a pet's final resting place, and in the twenty-or-so years he'd been stowing his coke cache there, nobody ever had.

For those very same twenty-or-so years, Vic's dedicated supplier had been Jokkum, a small-time drug mule as well as Sulfur Springs's most popular Zsa Zsa Gabor impersonator, performing on alternating weekends at the Galleria. Since he was a teenager, Vic had spent the majority of his free time in the S.S., mostly picking up the upper-class ladies who visited its pristine and malodorous health spas, offering his once virile coital expertise to all those lonely lasses and discontented wives. Vic had also befriended and partied with a host of wealthy and, in some circles, unsavory characters who conducted regular business in the town. He was introduced to Jokkum at an after-hours club and eventually they struck a deal for Vic to be Laymon's exclusive peddler in blow. It was darn good money, especially when the mill was still operating—lumbermen had accounted for eighty-five percent of his clientele. After it had shuttered, business slowed to an IV's trickle, but by that time Vic had accrued over $400,000 in the bank. Now, just twelve thousand more and he could finally develop his sea legs in earnest.

He supposed he would miss this place though. Yes, the barbershop had been an ingenious front, but he genuinely enjoyed shooting the breeze with Laymon's steak-and-potatoes citizenry. Especially when he was hopped up to the gills.

If they only knew! Some of them would probably capsize themselves.

Vic tossed his head back, sniffing spasmodically. His heart thumped in his chest like God's gavel, his blood pumping through him at a Nascar pace. Within minutes, the euphoric effects kicked in. He felt incredibly alert and superhumanly alive. He was positive he could run fast enough to defy gravity, sprinting up the wall, across the ceiling, and down again, emulating Fred Astaire. With jet boots.

He wouldn't attempt it though. Not again. One broken ankle in his life met his quota. Instead he sat back in his rattan chair and let the sounds and smells of the world around him ricochet throughout his hypersensitized brain.

Something heavy as a bowling ball banged against the wall right behind him. It knocked his glass-encased British Colonial maritime map onto the floor and jolted him out of his opiate-induced bliss. Vic whirled his head around, frowning at the shards of shattered glass now strewn all over his Persian rug.

Whatever it had been, it must've hit the wall from outside. More annoyed than alarmed, Vic stood up, left his office, and headed to the shop's rear exit.

He threw open the door and peered out into the alley.

There, only a few feet away from him, was a huge, hairy beast. It was twirling a metal trash can around—most likely what had impacted with the wall—in some delirious primal dance, grunting rabidly.

Bigfoot, Vic whispered to himself.

But he hadn't whispered it inaudibly enough. The thing heard him and stopped its manic mambo.

The two locked stares, frozen.

Then the creature roared and, flinging the trash can aside, charged at him.

Vic screamed. He retreated inside his shop. He hurtled to the front door, unbolted it, and fled out into the street, wind-milling his arms like an epileptic Muppet. He raced across the road toward Hap's Hardware.

Hap was sorting his latest shipment of key blanks onto the hooked display board when Vic barged into his store. The barber dashed up to the counter, panting and puffing, eyes wide with fright.

"What's the matter, Vic?" Hap asked. "You seen a ghost?"

"I seen Bigfoot, Hap! Out behind my shop!"

"What are you yappin' about?"

"Must've been nine feet tall," Vic jabbered on. "Hairy as a bear!"

"You sure it weren't a bear then?"

Vic shook his head emphatically. "It was wearing a sweatsuit."

"Bigfoot was wearing a sweatsuit?"

Vic nodded, also emphatically.

Hap studied him, then had to ask, "Are you high on somethin'?"

The men had known one another since grammar school and had shared some memorable, if regrettable, wild times. Hap was one of the few folks who had knowledge of Vic's sideline. On occasion, he was even a customer of his, but never made a habit of it. Not like Vic did. But that was Vic's business, Vic's life.

Now though, Hap thought his buddy looked downright unhinged. Having some kind of mental breakdown, had to be. Maybe his newest stuff had been laced with something, or tainted with a bad bacterium. Didn't some molds make you trip out? Did cocaine get moldy? Whatever it was, it sure as hell was messing with Vic's mind.

"I'm not hallucinatin', Hap!"

Hap computed how best to calm a person freaking out on drugs. "Why don't you have a seat, Vic?"

"Have a seat? With that monster rampagin' out there?"

Hap considered hog-tying Vic with the phone cord next to him, in case he might go and hurt himself, or even Hap. Might have to call for an ambulance too. Who knew what poisons were fouling up Vic's system.

"Are you listening to me, Hap?"

"I hear ya, Vic. But—"

"But what?"

"Holy damnation," Hap muttered as he gaped over Vic's shoulder.

Bigfoot was coming in.

5

Sheriff Boone finished the last bite of his ham and Swiss on pumpernickel sandwich his wife had prepared for him that morning, washing it down with a bottle of apple juice. It was one of his favorite lunches, though he hadn't savored this one much. But it kept him nourished, his mind firing and focused.

Namely, on investigating a murder.

A murder with no leads thus far. At first, Boone had expected it would be relatively easy to ferret out the culprit, considering the victim's reputation as the town Lothario. Most likely a jealous husband or a spurned lover. But none of the women questioned who were known to have fraternized with the victim, nor any of the men who may have taken exception to their fraternizing, panned out as viable suspects. They all had either rock solid alibis or, like Pastor LaFey, characters beyond reproach. A few of them were physically incapable of committing the crime. One, a hostess at Po' Pappy's Bar & Grill, carried the victim's baby, though she hadn't yet shared this news with him. Never would now.

The sheriff sat at his desk, scrutinizing each of the crime scene photos the M.E. had taken, looking for something he might have missed on site. But there was nothing. No tire tracks, no footprints, no cigarette butts, no candy wrappers, nor anything else of prospective evidentiary value.

Which left Boone with diddlysquat.

He supposed it might have been a random act of brutality, perpetrated by a random individual. Something committed extemporaneously, out of rage or for kicks. The wrong-place-at-the-wrong-time scenario. This was a theory that screamed

Unsolved Case, and Boone didn't want to go there. Not yet. To do that would be acknowledging the chance of failure.

No, there *had* to be a motive for someone to want to kill the postman, and Boone hoped such optimistic thinking would generate positive results, sooner or later.

His senior deputy... Clive... rapped on the doorframe, a manila file folder clasped in his hand.

"Got the coroner's report, Sheriff."

"That *was* fast." The M.E. had promised he could give the examination his highest priority, his second highest at that moment being a half-consumed burrito.

Sheriff Boone took the folder from the deputy and opened it on his desk. He skimmed over the preliminary physical descriptive details and zeroed in on the more salient empirical assessments and speculative conclusions of the report: "Cause of death: acute head trauma." (Who would've thought?) "The victim's head was compressed on both sinistral and dextral sides with a force of no less than 30,000 psi, possibly indicating a mechanized or hydraulic jaw device was employed, though no trace residuum of lubricants or metallic particles were detected." Boone flipped to the next page. "Perpetrator had been significantly greater in height than victim, as victim was standing when attacked, based on blood spatter analysis of victim's clothing."

The sheriff mulled all this over. The report didn't add much to what he had already surmised. It did conjecture some kind of vise may have been used as the murder weapon, but without any tangible evidence this was hardly irrefutable.

What else could he distill from the forensic analysis? The victim displayed no defensive wounds, meaning he must have been taken by surprise by or he knew his attacker, and the perpetrator had been taller than the victim, which was really no surprise since Glenn Hammond had been only 5' 3".

Which still left Sheriff Boone with diddlysquat.

"Maybe he's a bodybuilder," Clive said.

"Huh?" Boone's mind had wandered a spell, fantasizing about Lorna's homemade peanut brittle.

"The perp. I figure he must've been exceptionally strong to be toting around a Jaws of Death or whatever he used to off Hammond."

"Could be."

"Maybe I should re-question everybody. Ask if they'd ever seen Glenn associating with a muscular person or persons."

Boone didn't believe this line of inquiry would amount to much, but without any other leads to act on, it couldn't hurt.

"Fine idea, Clive. Let me know if you come up with anything."

"Yes, Sheriff." The deputy, thinking he had impressed the boss with his deductive talents, grinned like a Cheshire cat who caught the Cheshire mouse.

Clive turned to exit Boone's office. His way was blocked by Kris Greeley, appearing in the doorway and nearly colliding with him.

"Afternoon, Sheriff Boone!" he caroled.

Greeley represented the androgynous reporting half of *The Regal Eagle*, while the butchier Anthony—Kris's partner in business as well as, according to never repudiated rumors, in the bedroom—managed the publishing and advertising chores. The periodical reigned notorious for its commonplace cringe-worthy inaccuracies, such as the "Eagle Hunting Season Open" article—they'd meant "Hiking"—and the flagrantly erroneous story about the town council voting to outlaw live Christmas trees in the plaza (allegedly to eliminate the cost of cutting one down each year). The mulish duo never printed corrections or retractions for any of their errors, probably out of reluctance to admit journalistic fallibility. They had a very lofty opinion of their profession and of themselves.

"How many times have I told you not to barge into my office?" Boone snapped.

Kris stepped into the office anyway, albeit deferentially.

The feathery-haired newshound dressed in vernal preppy garb: a fuchsia polo shirt, white capri pants, and penny loafers without socks. Today he also sported a sateen ascot, as he did on those occasions when he claimed to be having a flare-up of his so-called "cervical rashes," which most everybody was certain were, in actuality, man-hickies.

"Sorry to interrupt, Sheriff."

"Don't be sorry. You know you talk to Deputy Quinn for any official statements."

"He was the one who allowed me to see you."

"He said he had acquired information he could only tell you, Sheriff," Deputy McQuinn called out from the squad room. Quinn—Boone often dropped the "Mc" prefix—was the greenest officer in the department, but as the only one with a college degree (in liberal arts) and the voice (and hair) of a young Ted Koppel, it made him the most qualified point person for any public relations tasks. A responsibility he apparently shirked this time.

"I think he misunderstood me," Kris clarified. "I'd said I *required* some information only *you* could tell me." This was malarkey, of course. Greeley was as tenacious as a starving wolf outside a padlocked henhouse.

"I'll only take a smidgen of your time."

"You've already taken it."

"Just a smidgen more then. After all, the public has a right to know of anything that might present a danger to them. Such as a killer on the loose."

Boone gritted his teeth and shot Kris Greeley his most withering stare. "Don't even think about starting a panic in my town. If you stir up so much as the tiniest tizzy that hinders my investigation, I'll have you in cuffs, y'hear."

Greeley didn't wither, didn't so much as rustle an eyelash. "I do have a constitutional right to report the facts."

"Facts are fine. Fear-mongering ain't. If you keep shakin' that torch, my men might just have to devote a portion of their time making sure you're obeying every letter of the law. I don't care if it's some obsolete ordinance that's been on the books since the first Thanksgiving. If you break it, you're gonna pay for it. Do you understand me?"

Kris squinched his lips. "Clearly, Sheriff."

"Good."

"So *are* there any new facts in the Hammond case?"

"No. And we'll let you know when we get any."

"Yes, I'm sure you will. But I'll be checking in, with your Deputy *Mc*Quinn, just the same."

"You do that. Now if you'll excuse us, we have a—"

"Sheriff!" Deputy McQuinn interjected, craning his neck over the shoulders of Clive and Kris. "There's an assault in progress at Hap's."

Boone tensed and wondered, what the hell was happening in this town?

Sheriff Boone reached Hap's Hardware, followed by Clive in his squad car, as the Town Hall clock tolled four.

Deputy Cavett, a born-yet-again (his sixth rebirth to date) Christian, had roped off and blessed a perimeter around the immediate area, where a bevy of bystanders stood bystanding. Though they had left the station at the same time, somehow Kris Greeley had arrived at the scene in his cobalt blue Miata before the sheriff. Deputy Darkcloud was keeping the reporter at bay behind the yellow tape with a CB antenna he declared accursed by some vengeful ancestral spirit.

Boone parked his Jeep at the curb outside Narko Drugs and made his way past the barricade toward Cavett's vehicle. His path was cut off by Hap "I Got Hardware On The Head" Harrison, yammering at him with frantic eyes and a frothing mouth.

"Sheriff! You gotta do something!"

"I mean to, Hap," Boone replied sternly. "As soon as you gimme the gist of what's going on here."

"He's crazy!" Boone thought Hap himself was doing a fair impersonation of somebody certifiable. "Bustin' up my store worse than an angry bull."

"Who is?"

"This giant, stinky feller."

"Ever seen him before?"

"Never. And you couldn't miss this guy. Think it must be one of them hoboes passing through. Lots of 'em have mental problems."

"Any reason you know of why he might want to vandalize your store?"

"No, sir. He just charged in and started wreckin' the place, throwing shit around, like he's possessed or something such." Boone reckoned that might explain why Hap's coveralls were splattered with caulk and reeked of turpentine.

"Did he have any weapons?"

"None that he'd brought in with him. But now he's got his choice of the largest selection of top brand-name tools in the county!" Hap's voice had segued into sounding like he was doing one of his local cable commercials. Force of habit, Boone guessed. "Got Craftsman, DeWalt, Black & Deck—"

They heard the cymbally crash of metal clashing metal inside the store, punctuated by a primeval howl of rage, or of exultation. Hap flinched.

"You gotta stop him, Sheriff! He's gotta be costin' me a fortune in damages."

"Leave it to us, Hap. In the meanwhile, you just wait across the street there."

Hap clammed up and nodded, resigned to having to endure a torturous combination of helplessness and working-hour sobriety. He stepped away as directed, regarding his store as if it may be the last time he would ever see it.

Sheriff Boone joined Cavett by his patrol car. The pear-shaped deputy was crouched behind its trunk, pistol drawn, hawk-eyeing the store like he anticipated the Virgin Mary to materialize in its window. Or maybe the Devil, which would better justify the gun.

The sedate storefront belied whatever mayhem was happening beyond it. The window reflected a kaleidoscope of vague, shimmery shapes around a flashing red neon hammer striking a blue neon nail, these giving the shop a touch of adult boutique tawdriness. The "HAP'S HARDWARE" stencil above the window had turned translucent from multiple seasons of sun and snow so one could now make out the brickwork beneath.

Boone knelt down beside Cavett. "What've we got?"

"We have one large—very large—deranged white male inside, pretty much smashing up the place willy-nilly."

"Have you tried communicating with him?"

The deputy nodded. "When I poked my head in there, he threw a plunger at me. So I went and asked him if he thought the Lord would approve of his behavior. And he threw a bunch more plungers at me."

"Then what?"

"I fell back here." Cavett shrank a bit under the sheriff's deprecatory gaze. "I didn't want to get hit. The rubber on those things is hard."

Deputy Eriksen crab-walked up beside them, clutching his Remington twelve-gauge rifle.

"A shotgun, Clive?" Sheriff Boone questioned.

"A big gun can scare the biggest of men."

Couldn't argue with him there.

"Are we going in, Sheriff?"

"That's a sensible plan, seeing as he likely ain't comin' out to greet us."

Sheriff Boone, his Smith & Wesson .38 primed, and Deputy Eriksen, his rifle pressed against his chest, slipped into the store through the entrance, though they needn't have bothered being so stealthy since the electronic chimer trilled the General Lee's theme-horn when they opened the door. Fortunately, the subject was out of sight, and hopefully out of earshot.

And what a sight he had left in his wake—a one-man war waged against the largest selection of top name-brand tools in the county. The floors were littered with Hap's sundry goods, most of them bent or broken or spilled, toppled from the over-turned shelves. A wall of product once arranged on pegs had, judging from the crater in the particleboard, been taken out by a catapulted Gasco generator.

Emanating from somewhere farther within the store was a series of thunks, like bullets hitting dry earth, but without any gun report. Each thunk was instead accompanied by an almost baby-like shriek, from what'd have to be one *very* big baby.

Boone, with Clive on his heels, moved cautiously toward the sounds. They passed by three aisles—Plumbing, Electric, and Garden, all equally devastated.

The fourth aisle revealed their subject.

He was at the other end, his immense, unkempt body literally filling the passageway. He could've been mistaken for a wooly mammoth that had roamed out of *The Lost World* and decided it might as well do some shopping. Boone thought he looked a bit like that wrestler... who was that? Andy the Giant? The subject looked like a castaway'd Andy the Giant, in a soiled red tracksuit and disintegrating moccasins, after years without seeing soap, scissors, or razors. Boone could smell him from where he was, twenty feet away. Campfire smoke and stale urine, with a base note of patchouli.

Peeking around the corner of the aisle, Boone and Clive observed the subject for several moments. He was meticulously picking through drawers of miscellaneous nuts and bolts and screws, hurling the ones that met his criteria (or perhaps the

144

rejects that didn't) down at the floor. Most bounced off the tiles, fracturing them. A few embedded themselves into the linoleum, each of these eliciting a whoop of triumph from the subject, scoring points in a solitary game of Madman's Darts.

"What should we do?" Clive whispered to the sheriff.

"We arrest him."

"Don't you think he'll resist?"

"Won't know 'til we try."

Boone stepped partially into the aisle, just enough so the subject could see him and the upraised gun.

"Hey there!"

Andy the Giant froze like a dreadlocked deer caught in a high beam.

"You stop these shenanigans right now and put your hands up!"

The kook appeared to mull over the sheriff's command, canting his head like a bemused dog, before scooping up a handful of hex bolts and pitching them at Boone. The sheriff ducked behind the shelves out of harm's way. The projectiles punctured a couple of spray paint cans merchandised in a steel mesh cage along the wall. Bursting mists of "graphite" and "terracotta" coated Boone and Clive's slacks. The enormous man chortled at them—a laugh more akin to a foghorn than something from human vocal cords—then returned to sorting his gamepieces.

"Suppose we'll have to take him more directly."

Clive's jaw twitched. "You mean, shoot him?"

Boone gave the deputy a sideways glance. Clive had never ever shot anybody—probably didn't have the cojones for it— but the sheriff didn't hold that against him. Squeezing off a trigger at someone was a measure of last resort, and Laymon, thank God, had never been a last resort town.

"I was thinking something a li'l less deadly."

"He's gotta be near four hundred pounds. And strong as a gorilla, I bet. We can't tackle him down by ourselves."

"I aim not to even get within arm's length of him."

Boone holstered his pistol and lifted a galvanized metal lid off one of the aluminum waste bins displayed on an endcap.

"Let me borrow your club."

The deputy slid from his belt his baton, always polished to an obsidian-black sheen, and passed it to the sheriff, who never carried one of his own because it often made it a pain to sit down anywhere.

Gripping the lid by the handle like a gladiator, Boone stepped out once again into the aisle. Wielding Clive's sturdy stick at shoulder height, he whistled at the subject.

This time Andy the Giant did not hesitate to launch a bombardment of zinc-plated nuts at him. Boone cowered, protecting his head and trunk with the lid. The nuts deflected noisily off it, which greatly amused the subject, inducing a convulsion of baboonish laughter from him.

Boone took advantage of the cease-volley by slinging the baton. It spiraled through the air, clonking the subject squarely in the forehead. Andy's body cramped up, his lips mouthing something incoherent. He teetered and tottered on his anvil-sized feet for a few seconds before the pupils of his eyes floated upward into his brainpan and he slowly tipped over like a chopped down sequoia.

Sheriff Boone lowered his shield. He and Clive regarded the inert giant on the floor, now resembling a heap of matted animal pelts swaddled in a red tarp.

"Better cuff him, Clive. Before he comes to."

Clive gulped and nodded, advancing warily toward the subject.

That would earn the deputy his merit badge for the day, thought Boone. And they didn't have to shoot nobody neither.

And if they were really lucky, this bundle of fat and fur would be their break in the Glenn Hammond homicide.

A slavering Mr. Russ slathered his hot dog with artery-clogging chili and liquid cheese, topping it off with dollops of sweet pickle relish.

The Sha Nom Nom Mart had the best franks—sausages, really—in the county, hands down. If he were on death row, they would be his last meal, along with a saucy rack of ribs and an Oreo milkshake.

He refilled his jumbo-sized cup with Very Berry Extreme from the slushy machine (the Coca-Cola flavor dispenser was, sadly, out of order), grabbed a two-pack of Chocodoodles, then paid Stax, the pompadoured clerk at the cash register.

"See ya, Stax."

"Later, Pipes."

Pipes. That's what folks used to call Russ. Nowadays only a Motown aficionado like Stax still did. The guy had just been expressing his admiration for him, Russ knew. That's why he had never redressed him.

But Russ preferred "Russ." Because "Pipes" might as well be dead.

By the time he exited the convenience store, the sky had become dark as soot, pelting Russ with a hard rain. With his face down and his shoulders hunched to shelter his dinner, he speed-waddled through the minimart's lot and across the road to the Boom Boom Bus, parked in a gravelly turnout under a streetlamp that blinked on and off intermittently.

Russ climbed aboard, closing the pneumatic accordion door behind him. After toweling off the water caught in the gutters of his cornrows, he set his food and drink down on the dashboard and plopped down in the purple velvet upholstered driver's chair. Normally he would have flipped on his radio's cassette player and grooved to some tracks while he ate, but during a storm like this he dug listening to the rhythm of the raindrops drumming the skin of the bus's hull.

For nineteen years, Russ had worked the Sulfur Springs/Laymon route. And all these years had been a gas, mostly, even if every once in a while he could still feel them boogie bugs strumming his strings.

He knew *those* days were long behind him. The memories, though, weren't.

'Cause some memories, like scars, are forever.

Back in the mid-'70s—a buried-and-paved-over epoch ago for him—Russell Dean "Pipes" Johnson had contributed the soulful baritone vocals for The Coxswains, an up-and-coming R&B quintet who sang funk-laden *a cappella* in pitch perfect harmony. Initially a Temptations cover band performing at no-charge bars and low-budget weddings, within a year they had composed a dozen original tunes and began landing gigs at some of the swankier clubs throughout the Tri-State. Soon they had enough money left in their pockets (after paying off their touring expenses and incidentals such as stage costumes and Jheri curl activator) to afford finer food and even finer women. In the summer of '76, the group recorded their only single, "The Dopey Bird Stomp" with the B-side "I'll Love Ya 'Til I'm Broke." Both songs had played in rotation on a few college stations, and the vinyl was now a much sought-after collector's item, fetching better than three hundred dollars if you could find one. Not even Russ had a copy.

Not anymore.

He'd sold his for three bucks after the accident.

Russ had always been terribly afraid of heights, which was why he'd declined to join his bandmates that day they had stopped for a hot air balloon ride on their way home from a show. Russ waited behind and watched as they, along with the balloon operator, took to the sky.

Russ watched as the balloon rose higher and higher and higher, becoming a green and yellow chrysalis levitating over the verdant landscape.

Russ watched as a shard of fuselage, peeled off a 747 flying fifteen thousand feet overhead, ripped a gaping hole in the balloon's nylon fabric.

Russ watched as his friends (and the balloon operator) plummeted to the earth, their bodies smashing through the glazed atrium of a shopping pavilion.

And that was the end of The Coxswains, and Russ's career in the biz.

Seven-plus years of throwaway menial jobs later, he accepted an offer from the Aberdeen Transportation Authority to be the shuttle driver between Sulfur Springs and Laymon. Russ lapped up his role as "people-mover"—his passengers moving to the beats of his boom box while he moved them to their destinations. Over the course of the next decade, with his stardom as a local personality established, the county granted Russ carte blanche to personalize municipal property. So that's how both he *and* his Boom Boom Bus came to be the colorful, captivating characters many adored to this day, as inseparable as Gogo the Bear and her Rocket Tricycle.

Few knew of his tragic coda with the Coxswains, and that too was how Russ preferred it. Music was still in his blood, and it always would be. Sometimes, though, it only reminded him of blood spilt.

As Russ took his first sloppy bite of his chili cheese dog, he was startled by a half dozen resounding thumps in quick succession—heavy footfalls tromping along the roof—starting at the rear of the bus and pausing right over his head.

What the hell was up there?

He peered out his rain-streaked windshield. Aside from the hazy fluorescent glow of the Sha Nom Nom Mart, he could not make out anything through the blustery curtain of the night.

The footfalls resumed, banging like bowling ball fists toward the back again.

"Goddamn kids," Russ mumbled, heaving himself from his seat while throwing the door lever.

Previously those punk-ass brats had lobbed eggs at his bus, scrawled vulgarities on its windows, and once tied linked soda cans to the undercarriage, creating enough of an unholy racket to prompt Russ to evacuate his passengers. He looked a damn fool for it.

He'd have thought such tempestuous weather would have discouraged the mischief makers, but guess not. He blundered off the bus, cupping a hand over his brow to screen his eyes from the downpour.

He walked around the vehicle, squinting up at the roof. He could see nothing. Russ supposed they might have leapt off and scrammed already. Or were hunkered low enough to be out of his deficient range of vision.

"Hey! Whoever's up there, you come on down! No more monkeyin' around!"

The only response Russ received was the bone-clattering rumble of nearby thunder. In less than the minute he'd been outside, he had gotten soaked all the way through to his skivvies. He shivered. He was feeling the damn fool again, and he wasn't going to put up with it.

"I'm leaving now! If you fall off, it's your own dumb fault!"

Russ circled back to the bus doors. He set one foot onto the first step when he heard, or thought he heard, a scrape of metal directly above him.

He peered once more toward the roof, narrowing his eyes as raindrops stung them.

"Anyone there?"

A hulking shape, silhouetted by a flash of lightning, descended upon him, fast as the lightning itself. Then Russ's head was enveloped in a darkness so deep, he felt as though he were falling.

The last musical note, such as it was, he'd ever hear in this life came from his own sonorous scream, abruptly cut off an instant later when he no longer had a head to scream from.

Gulliver did not actually believe Glenn's death had been a consequence of the Giants' threat should he not massacre the Micronians as directed. But he had to acknowledge the timing was, if nothing else, coincidental. Add to that murder in Laymon being statistically an even rarer occurrence than its citizens getting mauled by a bear or sucked into a tornado, Gulliver thus could not dispel the unease dogging him since he'd learned of his mailman's delivery unto the Great P.O. Box beyond.

Gulliver wondered again how much of what the Giants' agent had communicated to him was true, or at least plausible. How much did Gulliver *really* know about the Little People? There could very well be aspects of their lives that they hid from him, or that he simply never observed.

After all, he didn't—couldn't—keep them under constant surveillance. It wasn't as if he were one of them, proximity notwithstanding.

But Gulliver was, effectively, their landlord. It was his house. Maybe it would behoove him not to be so acquiescent and to require more of them, to inquire more *about* them. He had a right to know what went on inside his own home, should they be operating a miniature meth lab or some pygmean prostitution ring under his nose, or rather, his floor.

Gulliver sat on the sofa, leaning over the coffee table. He stared at the Scrabble board with the solemnity of a chess player contemplating his next move. The falsetto jabbering of the Little People near him wasn't distracting. Instead, it was like kindling, adding more fuel to the fires of his curiosity.

"Do any of you guys ever go outside?" he finally asked. "To explore, perhaps?"

Moments later, he got his tile-written answer:

YES

This perturbed Gulliver. Not that he found it all that astonishing, but it lent credibility to the agent's affirmation that the Micronians could imperil the Giants.

"Why?"

FIND NEW THINGS

"What new things?"

An off-white piece of cottony fabric billowed down from somewhere above Gulliver, alighting atop his head like an Arab kaffiyeh. He snatched it off, identifying it as a pair of old lady's bloomers. His neighbor Mrs. Jensen's probably.

This elicited peals of raucous laughter from the Little People.

Gulliver grimaced. "I don't want any of you leaving this house anymore. It's too dangerous out there."

In response, the Micronians added "WE LIKE" before "FIND NEW THINGS".

"No," said Gulliver. Then, more adamant, "I forbid it."

A clamor of outraged squeaks, like an untuned calliope, erupted all around him.

Before Gulliver could make an attempt to placate them, the doorbell clanged. This hushed the raving brownies better than any lilting words he might otherwise have offered.

He rose from the sofa and, ignoring the stereophonic thrum of a headache, went to his front door. Opening it, he beheld a squally night. Water poured in undulating sheets off the roof, creating a boggy moat around his house, lopsiding the juniper bushes. Snails lazed on the porch levee.

Nobody was out there.

But some*thing* was.

On his doorstep, taking wonky steps toward Gulliver, was a diminutive robot, about a foot in height, fashioned from what appeared to be soldered-together scraps of tin cans. It had been painted up as a cubistic caricature of mythical colossus Paul Bunyan, complete with checkered shirt, blotchy veil of beard, and sculpted foil axe.

The automaton halted at Gulliver's feet, regarding him with soulless, coal black eyes.

From a mini-speaker inside it squawked a nasally, monotone voice: *"If you delay one more day, count one more dead. Micronians be gone, else we smash another human head."*

The speaker then clicked, and the robot spontaneously combusted.

Gulliver recoiled from the hot ice-blue flames. Its paint crackled and blistered as its thin-metalled body liquefied into a glutinous puddle. Gulliver kicked the burning mess into the moat, where it fizzled and rapidly sank out of sight. The toe of Gulliver's fuzzy green slipper had caught fire, and he stamped it out with the other, leaving scorch marks on both.

Gulliver now reconsidered the grievousness of the Giants' penalties—their so-called *"unpleasantries"*—they'd sworn for his noncompliance.

When he reentered his home, he noticed the Little People had laid out a new message on the Scrabble board, one that required neither punctuation nor gesticulation to convey its exclamation of defiance:

WE

NO ANSWER

TO YOU

PART 3

THE SINKING CITY

1

For a second, Sheriff Boone could not remember what he was supposed to be doing.

Or maybe it was longer than a second. It must have been. Time became an abstraction during these lacunal episodes of his, caroming wildly through the empty spaces.

Boone knew where he was—in his office, at his desk. He knew it was after sundown, and raining buckets outside his window. And he knew he had *something* to do. But damned if he couldn't visualize that something in his head.

He concentrated and counted. He reached twelve, then he remembered.

Twelve seconds, at least. More than that. Must have been. Over twelve seconds... had it been it twenty?... thirty?... of lost time.

It didn't matter. He *had* remembered. It just took him a little while, that's all. So what if these "little whiles" (which might be classified as "senior moments" had Boone fancied himself a senior) seemed to be stretching longer and longer. He could still do his job well enough. Better than well enough.

He only needed more time to think. Sometimes.

Goddamned Alzheimer's.

Unlike his father, who had succumbed to the disease as inexorably as sleep, Boone would fight it. Physically, mentally, he could beat it. He possessed the heart of a warrior. He had been a scrappy youth—been the provider and recipient of many a bloodied nose—who'd matured into Laymon's most respected constable. That was nothing to sneeze at. It took diligence, and mettle, and... and...

And then the sheriff realized he'd forgotten what he just remembered. Goddamn.

Once Boone re-recollected what he had re-forgotten, for which he had to credit less his warrior's heart than the paperwork fanned out before him on his desktop, he headed to the block of holding cells in the south wing of the building. On his way there he passed by Zeke Cavett, manning the phones at the front desk. The deputy's name had popped into Boone's brain with barely any effort at all. Hallelujah for that.

There were four cells in total—two more than they had ever needed—a pair on each side of an arcade-ceilinged corridor laid with lustrous "Jerusalem Jade" tiling the city had purchased drastically marked down three years ago. (This same laminate could be found throughout police headquarters, as well as in the Laymon Town Hall and the I Eye Eagle Hiking Tours ranger station.) Two of the cells were, as always, unoccupied. The rearmost had been repurposed as storage for Deputy Darkcloud's amassed tribal heirlooms: feather and leather headdresses, hand-woven blankets, hand-painted pottery, and an inoperable '50s Vespa scooter Darkcloud claimed harbored the spirit of a late great chieftain. One day, when he had raised enough capital, the deputy planned to open a museum/saloon dedicated to the Pokahawnee people, with half-price drink specials during Honor Hour, 4 to 7 p.m. Monday through Friday.

The fourth cell was where their elephantine malefactor was being held, the eight-square-foot space appearing scarcely able to contain his girth. Boone suspected if the man ate so much as another half of a Chocodoodle he might not fit through the cell door anymore. It was miraculous he'd gotten through in the first place.

The sheriff joined Deputy Eriksen inside the prisoner's cell. Boone noted it smelled, curiously, of melon, and the floor was tacky in spots.

The giant, with a contusion spanning the acreage of his forehead, sat on the beechwood bench. Or rather, leaned into it—the bench looked more a window sill under buttocks the size of a Cadillac Eldorado's bumper. His wrists and ankles had been double manacled, then tow-chained to steel eyelets embedded in the cement wall. While his rancid clothes were being boiled clean, he had been supplied a fresh pair of snug fitting XXXL boxers to wear, as well as a seafoam green California King bed sheet tailored for him with arm and head holes cut out of it. He drooled copiously onto his bosom.

The giant grinned toothlessly at Boone when he entered his cell. The sheriff found the acknowledgment unnerving.

The giant's fingerprints had yielded no results as of yet. The only clue to his identity was a long-expired club card, discovered in his pocket, to the long-closed Krumbott's Super Store. The name on the card read "Huey Lewis."

"Like the singer?" Clive had asked.

"And Huey Lewis was an actor too," Deputy McQuinn elaborated. "He's in that movie *Duets* with Gwyneth Paltrow." McQuinn was a fount of who-gives-a-crap pop trivia.

Huey had been in their custody and conscious for almost six hours, with Clive interrogating him for most of that time. Boone hoped the deputy might have learned something about him by now—who he was, where he was from, why he was in Laymon. Although he showed up in none of the criminal or traffic databases, a man as huge as a grizzly could never have gone unnoticed anywhere he went. Unless he had been raised in the wilderness. He might well have been born and bred a mountain man, uncivilized as he was, taught to live off the land and his wits. And his own people, whoever they were, might very well have exiled him because those wits of his obviously had gone scrambled.

"Get anything out of him?" Boone asked.

"I think he's mute," Clive answered.

"That must've made questioning him a mite challenging."

"I managed to establish a couple of interesting things," Clive added haughtily. "For one, he likes red licorice."

Boone arched an eyebrow. "Why is *that* interesting?"

"Watch."

Clive produced from his trouser pocket an open package of strawberry Twizzlers. He slid out three strands and dangled them before Huey, just out of his reach. The giant, eyes brightening and ballooning, stretched for the candy as far as his shackled arms would let him, moaning imploringly.

"You want this, big guy?"

Huey moaned more insistently, the cuffs digging trenches into his flesh.

Clive edged over to the corner behind him. Boone only then noticed a knee-high pyramid of cantaloupes there, which explained the melony scent in the air. The deputy picked up one of the ribbed fruits from the top of the stack and presented it to Huey.

"Trick for treat?"

Huey nodded, smiling, eager to please.

Clive tossed the cantaloupe to him. The giant caught it between the palms of his massive hands and squeezed near effortlessly. The rind burst into shards. Orange pulp splatted onto himself and the floor.

Huey laughed riotously.

"Good boy," Clive praised, again proffering the pieces of red licorice toward him, closer this time. Huey snatched them away with his beefy fingers and chomped at them greedily, the interior of his mouth churning a blood red purée.

The sheriff let out a whistle. Not so much because he was wowed by the demonstration, but rather because the deputy was so plainly proud for orchestrating it and Boone didn't want to dampen the young man's jubilation.

"I figure," expounded Clive, "if he can crush a melon like that, he's able to crush a person's head." The deputy simpered, wearing such a smug expression one would think he'd cracked the case and already written the book about it.

Boone nodded. "Mighty clever theory, Clive." The sheriff did have to commend him. The boy was thinking outside the box. Even if it were a box punched full of holes.

"But he couldn't have done it. Not with those bare hands of his."

"But look at them. They're like boat paddles!"

"Oh, they are sizable, I grant you that. But *not* quite big enough to apply the uniform pressure necessary to flatten an entire adult human skull."

The deputy frowned, almost pouting. "No?"

"'Fraid not. His hands would have to be…" The sheriff performed some rough mental arithmetic. "Oh, 'bout two to three times larger, I reckon."

Clive lowered his head, crestfallen. "I thought I nailed this one."

"There's always next crime." The sheriff patted Clive on his sagging shoulder. Poor guy, Boone thought. Still, he figured it was good for the deputy to get chafed down a few nubs. Might knock some of the cockiness out of him.

Clive sighed. "What should we do with him, Sheriff?"

"Call Bumlicker." (I.e., the Bümlichen Institute for the Cognitively Impaired, the state psychiatric hospital, founded by esteemed seafarer/trepanner/syphilitic Admiral Bümlichen) "Have somebody from there pick him up."

As Deputy Eriksen calculated how much licorice it would require to facilitate their prisoner transfer, they heard the clink of the outer jail door being unlocked and the frantic shuffling of feet approaching.

It was Deputy Cavett, his face a ghastly pale—which was not out of the ordinary for him, allergic as he was to UV rays and hence following a strict zinc oxide application regimen.

What told Boone something was seriously amiss were the tributaries of indigo veins bulging from the sides of Cavett's neck.

"Sheriff!" he gasped. "There's been another one!"

The heavy downpour of hours before had tapered off to a fine drizzle that clung to the exposed skin of Sheriff Boone's hands and face. He felt as if he were coated in a slimy film, the byproduct of whatever evil force was at work in Laymon. Or maybe it was pinesap.

Although it was late, well past last call at the local taverns, a small crowd of rain-drenched, slack-jawed spectators—one in a *Butthole Surfers* T-shirt, others with no shirts at all—had converged on the scene. Deputy McQuinn was barely keeping them behind the yellow tape with chants of "Shoo! Shoo now!" a phrase which had a far greater impact when he opted to brandish his pistol in front of them. And yet, the undaunted crowd had only stepped back a negligible distance and would not disperse, because this was an *event*. (Q: "Where were you when Mr. Russ got whacked?" A: "Shit, I was *there*, right after it went down. I saw 'im get bagged and tagged, man. See, I took a pic on my cell... An' here's another angle.")

Shockingly, Dr. Morgan Devlin, the county coroner, was already there by the time Boone, chauffeured by Clive, had arrived. When he had received the call about another possible homicide, Devlin explained to the sheriff, he had been in the Laymon area visiting a friend.

What he did not explain was that this friend was Vic the barber, his purveyor of the purest cocaine in the region. As a board-certified medical practitioner, Devlin had easy access to a candy store of painkillers: Amytal, Nembutal, Seconal, Codeine, OxyContin, Percodan, Percocet. He was even able to procure, on a more restricted basis, Adderall and Dexedrine. But none of these gave him the exhilarating rush of premium uncut Peruvian flake. Or was it Bolivian? What did it matter? It was stupendous stuff.

What did matter was Vic hadn't been open for *any* sort of business when Dr. Devlin dropped by his shuttered shop, which would explain (had Devlin explained it) why the M.E. looked rather strung out right now.

"This is one skid mark that won't come out in the wash, Sheriff." The doctor's tone was surly, bitters and bile mixed in equal parts, spoken with a fluttery snarl as if an invisible horde of angry bees were assailing his lips. Boone thought this mien suited Devlin's physical appearance much better than his usual smarminess. The M.E. bore a squat, flabby body, a porcine nose, and pigs-in-a-blanket fingers. Tufts of coarse black hair that looked pasted-on flared from his scalp. A rumpled beige blazer and crooked tie completed the picture of a displaced Middle Earth troll not yet acclimated to Upper Earth life.

"Looks like you got yourself a serial killer."

Sheriff Boone bristled. "A li'l early to be pulling that card, ain't it Morgan?"

"Just calling it as I see it. And what I'm seeing here is a replay of your mailman. Head flattened like a flapjack. Excuse the technical jargon."

The sheriff surveyed the scene. The body of Mr. Russ, née Russell Dean Johnson, lay face down in a shallow puddle—or rather chest down, or ass up, for he had no face to speak of anymore—across the street from the Sha Nom Nom Mart, right beside his funkadelicized public transport. Once again, robbery didn't appear to be a motive. The perp left Russ with eighty dollars in his wallet along with his crocodile shoes and James Brown memorial platinum pinkie ring. What the perp didn't leave was the victim's head intact. It had been reduced to a grisly burgoo of mashed tissue and pulverized bone, garnished with spirals of Russ's rufous Afro.

After Dr. Devlin finished taking his ghoulish snapshots, carping and cussing to himself all the while, Boone watched Deputy Cavett zip up Russ's body in a cadaver pouch, intoning an appropriate prayer for his dearly departed soul, then wheeling the gurney over to the waiting county meat wagon.

The sheriff could at least be thankful there weren't any media present, not even *The Regal Eagle*. As soon as he got word of another "evicted spirit," Deputy Darkcloud astutely had headed off Kris Greeley, pulling the reporter over and citing him for an inoperative brake lamp. Took up near an hour. Kris would probably scribble off an op/ed piece about violations of his First Amendment rights or some such. But hey, one can't be driving around with a broken taillight. That's dangerous.

As for material evidence, once again not a damn speck was collected except for the body itself. The torrential rains had likely rinsed away anything useful to the investigation, if there had been anything to be found to begin with.

Two murders in two days. Same exact M.O. And both victims had been municipally employed, which made Boone speculate the perp may have some gripe with Laymon's civil servants. A demographic to which, he had to note, he and his deputies belonged. So that was a concern.

Or just as possible, maybe there was another, completely unrelated connection, linking the victims by their favorite hockey team or sherbet flavor, or where their names fell in the phone directory.

For Sheriff Boone knew evil, even in its most cunning guises, had a way of not always making a whole lick of sense.

2

Gulliver stood on the road that led to Aunt Augusta's ranch.

He didn't know how he had gotten there, or why he was there, but there he was. His aunt's white two-storey farmhouse, with its gabled roof and dormer windows looking like a sad whelp's eyes, rose to his right atop a knoll sown with blue hydrangeas. The graying barn that corralled her prized herd of shaggy-fleeced goats sat at a slight slant to his left. Between the structures was a grazing field, a water well pump, and the crabapple tree Gulliver had climbed into as a boy to listen to the wind singing off its leaves.

There was no wind now, the tree branches hung silent, and while the sun shined brightly above, it radiated no heat, none that Gulliver could feel. He noticed he couldn't smell anything either, no wildflowers, no goat manure, no aroma of whatever berry pie his aunt had just baked and set out to cool on the porch rail. Perhaps he was coming down with a cold.

And then he saw her. Kat stepped from behind the trunk of the crabapple tree, a tress of her sable hair looping into the corner of her mouth, her sun-twinkled eyes catching Gulliver's. She was barefoot and wore an ivory country dress spun out of some gossamer thread, with frayed scalloped fringe and a long scrap of fabric cinched at her waist for a sash. It was totally not Kat's style, reminding Gulliver of a churchgoing gown worn on *Little House on the Prairie*, but she made it work. She made it sexy.

He didn't know how she had gotten there either, but he knew, intuitively, why she had come. She was there for him.

Plow me, she said, without having to say anything.

Kat smiled alluringly at him, then dashed for the barn.

Gulliver chased after her. He could perceive her perfect hourglass body silhouetted through the diaphanous frock. Oh, how he yearned to touch her again! Right then, he wanted Kat more than he had ever wanted anything. More than his Rollickin' Rocket Home Missile Kit, more than his gimpy dog Rondo, more than even (God forgive him) his mother and father. He would gladly trade a kidney, an arm, or an eye for her—so long as his disfigurement didn't repulse her—but not his heart, never his heart, for that was reserved for Kat alone.

She was an astoundingly fast runner, much faster than Gulliver at any rate, pulling farther ahead of him and reaching the barn well before he had even made it to the head of the road. She stopped, blew him a kiss off her ruby red lips, and disappeared behind the barn door.

When Gulliver arrived several footfalls later, he was not as out of breath as he would've expected himself to be. Yet he felt near manic, his blood coursing through him like whitewater. He yanked open the barn's door, allowing the natural daylight to repel the unnatural gloom inside. It was a battle the daylight was losing.

Something was very wrong here, thought Gulliver.

Most conspicuous, there were no goats. Their absence was not what confounded him, but rather that by all appearances they had never been there at all. There were no pens, no troughs; no shears, hay hooks, or any other ruminant-raising implements along the walls. Neither were there any smudges of shoveled dung nor clumps of matted wool to be seen anywhere on the earthen floor. The barn was a hollow wooden husk, not at all the hub of bleating billies, nannies, and kids Gulliver remembered.

Fearlessly he moved deeper within and saw the structure wasn't quite empty after all. A shaft of the afternoon sun penetrated between the rafters above, creating a dappled spotlight on a hunched figure in the rear of the barn.

As his eyes adjusted to the opium den lighting, Gulliver realized it wasn't a single figure, but two. Sitting astride a stubby-legged milking stool with his back to him was a lanky, hooded shape in a pair of farmer's overalls. The oversized hood was dusky and nigglingly familiar, but Gulliver's attention was drawn too irresistibly to the second figure to recall it to mind.

In front of the seated figure, submissively posed on her hands and knees like some four-legged beast of the field, was Kat. She was naked now. Gulliver gazed first at her profile, at her gaping mouth issuing such wondrous concupiscent moans. He then zeroed in on her tumid breasts—more like udders really—rising and falling with her breaths. The seated figure twiddled and tugged Kat's nipples with his fingers, pumping her juice from them, filling the galvanized bucket set beneath her chest.

The scene was perverse. And degrading. And arousing.

Definitely arousing.

Gulliver couldn't help himself, couldn't tear his eyes off Kat.

Then she turned her intoxicated face toward him.

"Hi Gulliver. Thirsty?"

Only at this moment did Gulliver detect there was something *off* about the seated figure's hands. The fingers were too lean, the joints too strikingly attenuated. Scrutinizing them, he saw the phalanges were indeed stripped of flesh. Skeletal.

Gulliver yelped with sudden recognition.

The figure whirled its cowled head toward him, revealing the immutable skull visage of the Grim Reaper—to be known henceforth, Gulliver supposed, as the Grim Farmhand, which had to have been a step down vocationally.

"Get out, you useless sack of meat!" it bellowed ghostily. "I'm busy here!"

Gulliver, overcome with horror, revulsion, and a hint of jealousy, fled. He ran out of the barn, toward the woodlands that demarcated Aunt Augusta's property.

Behind him, a thunderclap of violently splintering wood. Gulliver halted and peered over his shoulder.

The sky had gone gray with pregnant clouds. The roof of the barn was buckling outward like a hatching egg, giving birth to a corpulent, red-maned Giant. With mighty sweeps of its fat waggling limbs, it smashed through the barn's timber walls, its gargantuan body bulldozing over the fallen rubble. It wore only a loincloth of some unknown pelt, its blubbery gut almost concealing the garment beneath it.

The creature bore an uncanny resemblance to the man Gulliver had Heimliched in Kat's coffee shop, only now he was thirty feet tall, a terrifying ogre borne out of some medieval fable orated by Norsemen around a bonfire.

Could the likeness be a coincidence? Or had the Beanie Roast incident been staged? Had the "choking" man been, in reality, another agent for the Giants?

Perhaps it was a test for Gulliver, but for what purpose? And was Kat complicit in the ruse?

Glowering ferociously, malevolently, down at him, the Giant barreled toward Gulliver, the soles of its naked verrucose feet thwacking the ground like tandem jackhammers. Tremors rattled Gulliver's jaw and shook his bowels.

He ran like hell.

But hell, it turned out, was not quick enough. Although Gulliver possessed the gazelle-like legs of an Olympian—*where did he get those?*—the Giant had a vast enough stride to catch up with its prey in the short time it took Gulliver to breach the forest. With the creature's foul, furnace-hot exhalations gusting down his neck, Gulliver raced frantically along a rough-hewn footpath through the trees, the crepuscular light barely enough to see his way by, but plenty enough for the Giant to see him.

It reached through the canopy and plucked Gulliver up by his head between its fingertips, lifting his squirming body before its monstrous doughy face. Acne scars the size of moon craters pitted its triple chin. Its cheeks sprouted whiskers like withered vines. This close, its fetid breath stunk even worse, like an outdoor fish market during a heat wave, almost causing Gulliver to pass out.

The Giant, eyeballing Gulliver with condescendence and contempt, spoke at him in a voice so stentorian it could have done stand-in voice-over work for a wrathful God.

"I can pop your bean like bubble wrap."

The Giant squeezed Gulliver's head a nanonewton tighter to emphasize the feasibility of its statement. Gulliver winced, a typhoon of nigh unbearable pressure roaring inside his skull.

"No… please," Gulliver whimpered.

"Destroy the Micronians, or we will destroy everyone in your life," threatened the Giant. "Then you."

Gulliver trembled. The Giant regarded him scathingly, as one would study the gooey remains of a squashed bug.

"Do not cross us, Mr. Huggens. We will be watching. Always."

The Giant smiled at him with cruel relish, its teeth like dual rows of severely weathered tombstones. Gulliver spotted the prong of a deer's antler stuck between two of its premolars.

Then, with a mere flick of its thumb and index finger, it mashed Gulliver's head.

Gulliver felt his blood stream down his face—

No, that couldn't be right.

He didn't have a face anymore…

Gulliver awoke with a jerk and a shriek. Sweat, not blood, trickled down his face, leaving salty tracks.

Reorienting himself, he saw it was still dark. And cold. He was lying in his yard, under the stars, in his Halloween owl-in-witch's-hat pajamas. He had been tied down to the lawn, again, this time with dental floss strung around metal garden markers. He peeled off the floss, ripped the markers from the ground, and chucked the bunched-up tangle away from him.

"Not funny, guys," Gulliver growled at the Little People, whether they were within earshot or not. "Not funny at all."

He scampered inside his house through the kitchen door, shuffled to his bedroom, rubbing his chilled hands together. He wriggled underneath his blankets. His bioluminescent Robby the Robot alarm clock told him it was fourteen minutes after three in the morning. It should have been dead-of-night quiet, but Gulliver's body still resonated, his lungs pumping air furiously in and out, his heart lobbing grenades in his chest.

He had trouble returning to sleep. He sensed he was being watched, though he supposed this sensation was no different than usual when one shares his dwelling with a gaggle of Peeping Tom Thumbs. The dream—nightmare—had been harrowing, but that wasn't what unsettled Gulliver most.

Gulliver feared it foretold more terrible times yet to come.

The next morning, Gulliver waited for the bus to take him to work. He leaned against the signpost, a pair of bracketed beams forming an inverted L that, to him, evoked a gallows pole. To his knowledge, the post had never been used for hanging save for the bullet-riddled carcass of the man-trampling "Killer Stag" in the summer of '83. Still, the mental association did nothing to assuage the bilious pangs of foreboding now simmering in his belly.

With his gaze directed down at a caravan of carpenter ants marching by his feet, Gulliver was surprised when the bus glided up in front of him. Surprised because the Boom Boom Bus's diesel motor always sputtered, loud and unremitting, so one could hear its approach from a mile away.

Gulliver was further surprised—shocked really—when he saw that it was, in fact, not the Boom Boom Bus, but some other county public transport, a nondescript airport shuttle half the size of Mr. Russ's.

Maybe the Boom Boom Bus had broken down.

Yet another, even more disconcerting surprise greeted Gulliver when he boarded. Instead of Mr. Russ, who more than once had bragged he had never missed a day's work in all his years running the route, the operator in the driver's seat was this scrawny fellow sporting an oily Prince Valiant mullet that slithered up and down his shoulders with each spastic bob of his head, leaving an indelible yellow stain on the collar of his white guayabera shirt.

"Good morning," the driver said, not at all gaily, his head continuing to wobble as if mounted on a coil spring. He swung the doors shut, then sat there idly, anticipating Gulliver to do something. Gulliver didn't do anything.

"Pass or pay?" the driver eventually asked.

Gulliver waffled a moment before fishing his wallet from his pants. He flipped it open to show his bus pass tucked inside the clear plastic sleeve, an action he hadn't had to perform in years.

"Where's Russ?" Gulliver inquired, replacing the wallet into his pocket.

The driver gave him a discomfited sideways glance as he pulled the bus away from the curb. "He's no longer with us."

"What do you mean? What happened?"

"He was killed, sorry to tell you." Being the bearer of such bad news visibly aggravated the driver's head wobbling.

"Killed?"

"Yup. Last night."

Something snagged deep in Gulliver's throat—a reflux of trepidation. "How?"

"Murdered, from what I hear. Don't know much more than that."

"His head was torn off," interjected an elderly woman sitting beside her husband, both in matching plum-colored cardigans. The lady went on to explain she had heard the news that very morning from her cousin who runs the diner out on Route 33—the nice one, not the yucky truckers' stop—who had heard it from one of her regular customers, who had heard it from her son, who had heard it from one of his friends who'd posted an eyewitness status update on his Facebox page. ("Saw a dead body last night! Check out my pics!")

"I thought his head was smushed, dear," said the lady's spouse.

"Was it?" The woman pondered this a bit, then shook her head. "No, I'm certain it was torn off. Same as that poor mail carrier."

"Now *his* head was smushed."

"Are you sure?"

"Said so in the paper." The man appealed to Gulliver for support. "Didn't it?"

Gulliver's face blanched as the interior of the bus reeled around him like he was on some diabolical carousel. Everything about him felt sick, and he urgently needed to get off this ride and back onto terra firma.

"You okay, son?"

"Stop the bus!" Gulliver blurted, verging on hysteria.

"You're not gonna ralph, are ya?" asked the wary driver.

"Please… just stop… the bu-uh-errrrrrr." Gulliver puffed out his cheeks, damming his mouth with his fist.

"Yup. You're gonna."

The driver promptly coasted the bus into a scenic turnout overlooking the Devil's Horns, braking alongside the guardrail.

Gulliver bounded down the metal steps, staggering, nearly stumbling. Once both his feet were planted on the ground, he waved the driver on. Bobblehead seemed reluctant to leave his pallid passenger out there on his lonesome, until the stooped-over Gulliver gave him a thumbs-up. The bus rolled away.

Gulliver stood on the open roadside, distraught and disoriented. While his nausea had mostly subsided, hellish visions of Mr. Russ as a headless fountain of gore harassed his brain. Learning of the two identically unique slayings jarred Gulliver to his very core, unmooring any vestiges of well-being he had still retained, sending them careening and colliding into the darkest realms of his psyche, inexplicably accompanied by the sounds of dying chimes and faint clicks. He felt like the world's least fun pinball machine.

The Giants were true to their word, their message to him clear: *Micronians be gone, else we smash another human head.* Russ and Glenn, both guilty of nothing more than being acquainted with him, had been murdered because of him.

Because he refused to do the Giants' bidding.

Gulliver agonized over all those he knew personally in Laymon, however remotely—there were so very few of them—who might be the Giants' next victim. Mr. Knox? Captain Vic? Kat?

Oh God no. Not Kat.

She might be the most innocent of all. Kat was somebody who wanted nothing more to do with him, and yet, due solely to his unrequited longing for her, she could well be a target. If Kat were to have her head smushed betwixt titanic fingertips, Gulliver would not be able to live with himself. Nor, for that matter, would he have anything to live for.

He couldn't let it happen.

Gulliver had stranded himself midway between his home and downtown Laymon, a distance of approximately nine rural miles. He was at a loss about what he should do now, where he should go.

Should he find Kat and warn her? (And Mr. Knox, and Captain Vic, and whoever else?) Should he alert the Little People of the threat to them? Should he arm himself, buy the biggest gun available at Bucks 'n' Butts?

What *could* he do?

Gulliver looked southward down Fairview Avenue, then craned his neck to peer as best he was able around the bend doglegging north. There were no vehicles approaching, none he could see anyway. He listened. There was no wind, no rustling of foliage, no twittering of birds. Scarcely any sounds at all, save his own quavery breathing.

Again he sensed he was being watched, from somewhere within the dense woodlands flanking the road.

The Giants could be anywhere, proven masters of stealth and concealment and assassination. A formidably trained clan of ninja behemoths, ruthlessly battling for their own survival. The notion made Gulliver shudder.

He then heard the Gregorian chant-like drone of a small engine. He scanned the cloudless sky and spotted a chalky red, single-propeller plane flying from between the Devil's Horns. It soared over him, less than a thousand feet above the tree-tops, and appeared to be descending. The airfield, the aircraft's logical destination, was about a fifteen-minute jog to the east.

Gulliver had an idea.

A half-baked, half-buttered one admittedly, but one he could act upon the spur of that moment nonetheless. He trotted after the plane, which was already disappearing behind the pinery as it came in for a landing.

3

The airfield was an eighty-acre open space, cleared of timber and brush in the 1940s for use as a pauper and pet cemetery. Because its substratum was laden with breccia rock that made digging dirt-cheap graves more strenuous than practical, the site was soon scrapped. Only two inhumations had ever occurred there, a transcendentalist poet and his loyal mongrel, both buried in unmarked plots. Laymon's old-timers recall the dog's name was Princess Furdelia, while the scribe's had been lost to the dustbin of history.

In the seventies, the land had been purchased from the county by Gulliver's neighbor Mr. Jensen after he had served out his last tour of duty in the Air Force. He'd repurposed it as a chartered airfield, mostly piloting sightseeing flights over the mountains for lovey-dovey honeymooners, family vacationers, or eagle fanciers. Laymon was not much the honeymoon or vacation destination it once had been, but the *accipitridae* buffs still hired him to bring them as close as humanly possible to the noble national symbol, often scaring the crap out of the things when doing so. (The rangers managing the I Eye Eagle Hiking Tours condemned the practice, but, without it being illegal, couldn't stop Mr. Jensen from making a buck off it.)

Take Wing Air Charters comprised an unpaved runway, a transplanted barn converted into a hangar—the U.S. flag painted on its gambrel roof—and, beside it, a trailer office with a window view of a flaccid Stars and Stripes windsock. Three four-passenger Piper Cherokees, the sum of Mr. Jensen's well-kept, decades-old fleet, were moored just outside the hangar doors.

Jensen was toiling over the engine compartment of one of his planes, the same red model Gulliver had followed there, the others being blue and white to complete the patriotic theme. Perched tippy-toed on the top rung of a grease-smeared step-ladder, he gave the impression of a child playing somewhere he shouldn't be.

"Mis… ter… Jensen!" Gulliver huffed, gasping after his mad sprint.

"Gulliver?"

The old man lifted his head, eyeing Gulliver in bafflement, bordering on suspicion. He climbed down the ladder, slipping a socket wrench into the pocket of his boilersuit which, being half-unzipped, showcased a briar patch of gray chest hair.

He swaggered up to Gulliver, wiping his soiled hands with an equally soiled rag. A manly man was what Mr. Jensen came across as, the sort who chops his own firewood and wears moonshine aftershave from unlabelled apothecary bottles. That is, he came across that way now, when he wasn't sweet-talking his dahlias or zinnias.

"What brings you 'round here?"

"To ask you a favor, sir."

Gulliver had never visited Mr. Jensen's place of business. Years previously his neighbor had on a few occasions offered to take him up for a firmamental spin over Laymon. Gulliver politely declined each of the invitations, in the last instance explaining he had a delicate stomach and was susceptible to airsickness. This *may* have been untrue, but since Gulliver had never rode in an airplane, it could have as well been so. More to the point, Gulliver was just not the kind of person who went joyriding with neighbors.

"Would you take me up?" he asked.

"I thought flying made you queasy."

"M-maybe-ee not anym-m-more," Gulliver stuttered, flip-flopping not among his fortes. "Please. It's important."

"When do you want to go?"

"Now?"

Mr. Jensen squinted at him like a shit-smelling Clint Eastwood.

"What's this all about, Gulliver?"

"I need to find somebody," Gulliver answered. "In the mountains." He hoped he didn't sound too prevaricating, but as he was uncertain how Mr. Jensen would react to them going Giant hunting, Gulliver opted for circumspection.

"Why? Someone lost?"

Gulliver nodded. Lost. That worked.

"Wouldn't you be better off going to the sheriff? He can rustle up a squadron of search planes. Do that all the time for missing hikers. And they'd cover much more ground than I could myself."

"Not missing. More like hiding."

"Hiding? From what?"

"Getting caught. You know, for the murders." Gulliver's mind was spinning the threads of his impromptu story more feverishly now, though he still managed to avoid weaving outright fiction. Father never approved of fabrications, declaring they would weaken one's "verbal supremacy" in any dialogue. Truth, he'd said, was like science—incontrovertible.

Mr. Jensen snorted. "If *that's* what this is about, if you know something about what happened to Glenn and that other feller, then I really recommend you let the pros handle it."

"I think there's a reward," Gulliver continued, presuming this to be the case. "For anybody with information leading to the killers' capture."

"So go tell it to the sheriff."

"I'm not sure though… It's m-more of a hunch."

Mr. Jensen chewed this over, swishing his shoe in the dirt.

"Please, sir. I could use the money." (Nothing fallacious in that statement. Everybody could use money.) "I'll split whatever reward there is, if we find them."

"And that's a big 'if,' ain't it?"

"Well, if we do, we'd be heroes, wouldn't we?" Gulliver hoped he piqued his neighbor's interest, appealing to his manly man's appetite for action, or chance of it.

Jensen had worn a shallow furrow in the ground before stopping his pendular foot. He ran his tongue across his teeth and spat sudsy spit.

"A hunch, huh?"

Gulliver nodded, anticipating a terse refusal.

"What the hell," Jensen said. "I've bet my life on less, and I'm still here and kicking."

Within fifteen minutes, Mr. Jensen completed a maintenance check of the red Cherokee, topped off its fuel tank, and had them both buckled into the plane's springy sheepskin seats and taxiing onto the runway.

Pushing the throttle all the way in, he accelerated to thirty, forty, then fifty miles per hour. It wasn't as bumpy as Gulliver had expected, though the rumble of the plane's engine was strong enough to vibrate his neighbor's jowls like Jell-O being spanked. Mr. Jensen didn't radio the tower—there wasn't one in sight—nor anybody else. Gulliver wondered if the airfield were sanctioned by the FAA, if they even knew of its existence at all.

Once the plane hit sixty mph, Mr. Jensen pulled back on the yoke. Gulliver felt his stomach constrict as they lifted off the ground and ascended into the sky.

A cluster of jaundiced clouds hung in the distance to their right. Gulliver envisioned Giant clan elders passing around a ceremonial calumet carved out of a tree trunk, then thought more commonsensical of it. Having endured for millennia wholly under the world's radar, he very much doubted the Giants would indulge in such a conspicuous habit as smoking.

"That's smog," Jensen said. "Drifts in from the chemical factories up in Halvaport. Sometimes it collects in our valley like that and gets trapped."

"Is it dangerous?"

"I wouldn't want to breathe it too long without a mask on. But it'll clear up soon as the winds sweep through again."

For the first ten minutes of the trip, Gulliver stared out the starboard window at the monochromatic blue above and the ocean of evergreen below. The woodlands soon tailed off into an almost barren morainal scree that transitioned to the Devil's Horns, the only mountains surrounding Laymon with high enough elevations to have snow still blanketing their peaks. To Gulliver's knowledge, most of this area remained unexplored, or at least unmapped, terrain. He marveled at the topography that was, from this new vantage point of his, all at once recognizable and alien to him. He might as well have been flying over the moon.

"So where do you think this guy is?"

"Somewhere they can't be found."

"*They*? We're looking for more than one killer?"

Gulliver nodded.

"How many?"

"A *large* group of *people*, I think." Gulliver realized he was juggling semantics now, another of Father's impermissibles, but for some reason it didn't nag at his conscience so much when he was a thousand feet in the air.

He caught his neighbor eyeing him critically. Then the old man donned a smile as bright as his dentures could produce.

"That should make the bastards easier to spot!" he blurted with gung ho gusto. Military people loved a tactical advantage.

Mr. Jensen leveled off the plane, gliding it through the glen between the Horns. Soon they were on the other side of it and Jensen began to circle above another expanse of evergreen.

"This is the remotest area?" Gulliver asked.

"That's all untamed wilderness down there, my boy."

Untamed perhaps, but in Gulliver's estimation not near inhospitable enough to keep out the more intrepid human trespassers. He groaned.

"You want remote, eh?" Mr. Jensen said, taking Gulliver's disheartened sigh as a challenge demanding besting. "I'll show you remote."

Jensen banked the plane left for a short while, steering them over a broad, arid gorge piled chaotically with massive boulders, many cleaved apart by the prehistoric-looking trees that had sprouted underneath them, their trunks twisted so tortuously they should have been screaming. Gulliver couldn't imagine anyone living down there, but there were indeed plenty of unexposed spaces to hide, perhaps even vast caverns extending downward into the Earth's crust.

Now this was Giant country.

Only then did Gulliver accept the reality that creatures not wanting to be found wouldn't be. Certainly not from a plane. He chided himself for having conceived the lamebrained idea to begin with.

But what if he did, by some stroke of extraordinary luck, locate the Giants' village? Then what would he do? Curse them? Shake a fist at them? Wave hello? If he had a military-grade cluster bomb, he could drop it on their big cold-blooded heads, blowing them into a thousand tiny Giant bits. Gulliver, however, didn't have a military-grade cluster bomb. He didn't even have a water balloon. He might as well have been sight-seeing up there, for all the good it would do him.

"Who are we searching for, exactly?" Mr. Jensen must have picked up on Gulliver's frustration, or wished to allay his own germinating concerns that this might be one mission impossible to accomplish. A wild goose chase. Gulliver had been rather surprised his neighbor hadn't pressed for more details before taking off, but then the spirit of adventure, not to mention avarice, can often motivate one to blindly seek out treasure in a minefield.

"Any signs of a hidden town or city."

"You mean a campsite?"

Gulliver nodded. Sure.

Mr. Jensen clucked. "If it's hidden, how are we supposed to get a bead on it?"

Gulliver could've spouted off several reasonable responses of things to look out for—smoldering fires, felled trees, heaps of discarded animal bones—that would have forestalled setting off Mr. Jensen's Loco-Meter, but his mind wasn't thinking so incisively right then due to some lightheadedness. Perhaps he was predisposed to airsickness after all.

"Giant people live there," Gulliver answered candidly. "I guess I was hoping they'd be simpler to see."

"Giant people? Yeah. Of course." Mr. Jensen exhaled a disgruntled grunt as something deflated inside of him. "Trying to find new buddies for your little bunkmates?"

"Oh, no. They're actually mortal enemies."

"Be that as it may be, I don't think we'll be finding Paul Bunyan today."

Gulliver recalled the tin can robot self-destructing at his doorstep only the night before.

A *Paul Bunyan* robot.

Had Mr. Jensen been the shadowy figure who, disguising his face and voice, posed as the Giants' agent? Could his neighbor be one of the architects behind these nefarious machinations? Would Gulliver be their next victim?

Or was Gulliver being paranoid?

His paranoia notwithstanding, as somebody who had no friends-of-a-feather to speak of, could Gulliver really trust *anyone*? He found if one didn't—couldn't—trust a soul, the possibilities for treachery in others were limitless.

Gulliver braced himself. Any instant now his neighbor would try to force him out of the plane, sending him plunging to his death, pleading for divine intervention all the way down yet knowing the hard, heartless earth would provide no clemency when it finally met him. Jensen could then report it had been an accident, the misfortunate consequence of an unsecured seatbelt, a malfunctioning door lock, and some freak turbulence. Or maybe he wouldn't report it at all, leaving Gulliver's broken body to be devoured by wolves and cougars and bears and nature itself, his fate forevermore a mystery.

A morose Mr. Jensen arced the plane sharply around in a vertiginous roller coaster U-turn, Gulliver's palms glued to the ceiling, until they were homeward bound for the airfield.

Gulliver, still very much planted in his seat, stared at the ground beneath them. His eyes widened. He sat up, excitedly pointing out his window.

"Over there! What's that?"

Mr. Jensen craned his neck forward and peered through the window at the area where Gulliver was indicating.

"What's what?"

"That!"

His neighbor harrumphed and settled back into his seat. "That's a boulder, Gulliver."

Gulliver, his nose mashed up against the glass, studied the object of his attention, now directly below them. "Are you sure?" He sounded like a kid whose parents just told him the mall's Santa was only an actor paid by the hour.

"What did you think it was?" Jensen responded peevishly.

Gulliver sighed, leaning his forehead against the window. "Sort of looked like a huge head. Wearing a hat."

They spoke not another word for the remainder of the flight.

Their shifts at the Beanie Roast both ending at three, Kat and Becky were able to do lunch together at Roberta's Hot Pot Café. They sat in the very same booth Engelbert Humperdinck had dined a decade before, after one of his performances in Sulfur Springs. On the wall above the Formica table, his pit stop had been commemorated with an engraved silver plaque under his autographed paper placemat. Which would've been pretty cool, had either Kat or Becky known who "Dingleberry Humpindick" was. (Ditto for the Hoyt Axton wall.)

"What you need, girl, is to get drilled by some super stud. Or, this being Laymon, any regular stud will do, long as they got the tool for the job." Becky said all this while munching on a mouthful of the cheese fries they were sharing, crinkle cuts smothered in Velveeta and a generic brown gravy.

"I have no trouble getting laid when I want to."

Becky shot her friend a quizzical expression. "Don't you want to?"

"Yeah," Kat replied. "But I got standards. They may not be much, but they're mine."

"I got standards too. Guy's gotta have a thick one."

Becky chortled, displaying clods of potato caulking her wide-gapped teeth.

Kat wasn't blowing bubbles about wanting to hook up with somebody. She appreciated the restorative properties of a good screw as much as anybody. She had only become more and more discriminating over the years. The novelty of the men she'd historically dated had worn off. Always the same guys strutting through the same revolving door, with their god complexes and god's gift attitudes, swinging their manhoods around, spooging wherever they pleased—on Kat, on the car seat, on the dog. It had grown tiresome, as tedious as one's thousandth game of tic tac toe, and provided her nothing her showerhead massager couldn't achieve with much less hassle and headache.

Again her thoughts turned, rather salaciously, to Gulliver Huggens. It wasn't like her to obsess over somebody, yet the dude kept insinuating himself into her *After Midnight Ecstasy* romance novel fantasies. What was it about him that still intrigued her so, still attracted her? Was this what those super-market checkout magazines meant by a couple having "natural chemistry"? Kat wasn't sure. She hated science.

Gulliver wasn't particularly good-looking, especially when compared to some of the narcissistic Adonises she'd let sample her wares in the past, but he hadn't qualified for her reject pile either. And he probably wasn't the smartest guy in any room, though in her experience the smarter ones were also often the cruelest. And yes, he was a loony toon. While this had never been a deal breaker for Kat before, it didn't explain why she longed to see him again after the debacle of their first date.

Maybe that was it. In his way, Gulliver was as emotionally damaged as she was. The difference was Kat had developed enough armor to insulate her from the pains of life. Gulliver, despite his obvious efforts to show her he had his shit together, instead seemed so fearful and fragile, like an orphaned puppy put out in the snow. Kat wanted to take care of him. To protect him. To mother him. And to fuck his brains out.

Upon introspection, Kat supposed this was sort of messed up—the "come here, baby, and let mommy make you feel better" shtick—but she'd weathered far more warped relation-ships than that. Usually she was nothing more than the boxed-up toy, opened whenever her man wanted to have some private (and sometimes, not private at all) playtime, until he had used her up or busted her up and threw her out.

Gulliver Huggens could be a nice change of pace from that.

Gulliver was definitely late, this according to every clock in the shop. An hour at least, which was unheard of for the boy.

Mr. Knox would call him in another minute, make sure he didn't get his days off mixed up, even though he always worked the same schedule. Maybe he had drunk too much the night before. Knox knew Gulliver was a boozer—he could sometimes smell the double-digit proof liquor on him—but Huggens was also one of those closet cases who never discussed his vices. It wasn't any of Knox's business anyway. Not until it began to affect *his* business. He just hoped Gulliver wasn't drowning his sorrows so much he'd end up going under completely.

The phone rang. Knox snatched up the receiver.

"Hi, Mr. Knox," murmured the caller.

"You were supposed to be here an hour ago, Huggens."

"I know... I-I had, umm, an emergency."

"Are you okay?"

"Yes. But I won't be coming in today. Sorry I didn't call earlier."

Mr. Knox glanced at the caller ID screen on the phone's faceplate. It read "TAKE WING AIR CHARTERS."

"Are you at the airport?"

Gulliver's tentative whine took the form of a guilty "yes."

"You going someplace?"

"Just home."

That clinched it for Knox. Gulliver positively was coming off a binge. The boy must've somehow wandered onto or near the airfield last night and passed out. Knox didn't fault him much. He himself had woken up in some mighty bizarro places after partying his guts out. Once, in a Porta-Potty at a church construction site, and this other time inside the camel pen at a zoo. Hey, that shit happens.

"You gonna fly home?" Knox asked facetiously.

"No. I'll catch the bus."

"Alright. But don't be pulling this kind of stunt again, Gulliver, else I'll be giving you your walking papers. Y'hear?"

"Yes, sir. I'm sorry."

"Apology accepted. Now go grab yourself some shut-eye and a shower. Pop some Tylenols. Maybe crank one off. That'll do ya a world of good."

"Thanks, Mr. Knox."

"Yeah, yeah. See ya Friday."

Mr. Knox hung up the phone, rubbed his hands on his dungarees, and plonked himself down onto the stool at the counter.

He considered he might've been harder on Gulliver than necessary—too much Mr. T, not enough Mr. Brady. Then again, some tough love might do that boy a world of good too.

Knox heard the tinny ding of the bell over the entrance door, but did not glance up from the batch of invoices he'd started riffling through, trying to find the one for the stair machine that made you lurch like a ballet dancer with a head wound.

"G'mornin'," he said to the customer entering. "Be right with ya."

The scent wafted over him, a heady blend of incense and flowers and feminine pheromones that brought to Knox's mind the time, long ago, he had enacted the steamiest sections of the Kama Sutra with this Asian girl inside a Buddhist temple in northern Cali.

He raised his eyes from the sheaf of papers, the missing invoice still unaccounted for, but that could wait. A customer, especially *this* customer, should not have to wait, and she probably seldom did. She embodied what he and his MC crew once termed a "buttered muffin" (the inverse being the "puke pie"). Knox didn't normally go for goth types, but this chick wore the look well enough to cause a pileup on a country road. She had on skimpy nurse's rags, dyed puce and embellished with bands of safety pins and light gauge chains. Green hosiery, perforated in spots, clung to sinewy legs ending in a pair of Doc Martens boots.

Knox was amazed he had never noticed her before. Maybe he needed to get out of the shop more.

He grinned at her. "What can I help you with, miss?"

"Hi. Is Gulliver around?"

I'll be damned, Mr. Knox thought. This must be the gal from the coffee shop, the one Huggens had been chasing after. He had to give the kid kudos. Gulliver had first-class taste in tail, even if he was too deluded to recognize she was way out of his league.

And yet, she *had* agreed to go out with him, and that was a helluva impressive feat in itself. Sure, Gulv struck out, but at least he got to step up to the plate and bat.

"He called out today," Knox informed her. "You're Kat, from the Beanie Roast, ain't ya?"

"Gulliver told you about me?"

Knox folded his arms, striking an accusatory posture. "If you're the one who romper-stomped all over his heart, then yeah, he told me about you."

Kat groaned, slouching her shoulders, bearing the weight of penitence. "I guess I was pretty bitchy. I was just trying to, y'know, not lead him on."

"I'd say ya nailed that coffin shut."

Kat pouted, flecks of face powder clumping on her upper lip. Knox's expression softened. He had a weak spot for sad ladies.

"Should I tell him you dropped by?"

"No. I'll come back another time when he's here. Thanks, Mister—"

"Knox. But you can call me Reggie. This here's my store."

Kat's eyes swept the premises, as if taking inventory of every out-of-order appliance there, how many dollars each was worth. Then she smiled coquettishly, or maybe it was more of a smirk. Knox couldn't tell if she was impressed with his empire, or scoffing at it.

"Nice place," she said.

"Drop by anytime," Knox drawled, "if ya ever need something serviced." He sounded like a dirty old man, but so what? Whatever kept his blood a-flowing these days.

Kat nodded, turned, and headed for the exit.

Knox couldn't help leering at the sensuous swing of her hindquarters, an ass as pinuppable as Bettie Page's outlined beneath that polyester skirt, its material stretched so taut it could've generated another Big Bang had the seams burst. If that happened, Knox envisioned the new universe it'd create would be hotter, wetter, and wilder than this one.

His kind of universe.

Kat and her righteous ass went out the door. Damn, that girl was a buttered muffin, fresh from the oven. With some sizzling fatback and two eggs, sunny-side up.

She made Knox hungry.

4

It was Wednesday according to Deputy Cavett's desk calendar, which he reliably flipped daily. Wednesdays are, typically, the least eventful day of the week for law enforcement. This is because most lawbreakers have by then made their peace with God for whatever transgressions they'd perpetrated the weekend before, and they had not yet geared themselves up to do whatever Devil's work they were scheming for the weekend to come.

This Wednesday, however, was proving to be abuzz with constabulary-centric happenings, even when one excluded all matters pertaining to the homicide investigations.

At 12:17 a.m., Kris Greeley, co-publisher of/reporter for *The Regal Eagle*, was arrested for domestic battery, after having clobbered his housemate Anthony with a half-eaten roasted shank of lamb during a heated cohabitants' quarrel. Although Anthony declined to press charges, upon his release Kris drove to Wisconsin to stay with his mother indefinitely. As such, the future of their newspaper was unknown, but circumstances had certainly put the brakes on it for now, which would spare the Laymon PD Kris's barrage of needling inquiries into the killings.

At approximately 9:00 a.m., Huey Lewis—the supersized vandal, not the '80s singer—had escaped during his transfer to Bumlicker. Upon their arrival at the mental institution, the attendants opened the rear doors of the transport van, only to discover their passenger had broken out of his restraints and, like a rogue rhinoceros, charged berserkly at them, over them, and into the woods. A district-wide manhunt, consisting of over a hundred Rackham County law enforcement personnel, had been convened. Thus far, hours later, the posse's efforts yielded nothing. One would presuppose spotting a mastodonic madman would be a walk in the park, but when the park is thousands of acres of mostly uncharted wilderness, the odds are stacked in the fugitive's favor.

Sheriff Boone had entertained the possibility that Huey Lewis might be the still-at-large Potato Sack Rapist. The repeat predator, however, had reportedly struck again the night before—this time seventy-five miles away in Bellaire Parish, attacking a 26-year-old librarian out for a late-evening jog—while Huey was still in custody at the sheriff's headquarters, crushing melons for strawberry licorice.

To top off that Wednesday's out-of-the-ordinary agenda, the sheriff had been summoned by Ms. Fairview, aka the Wheezing Widow, for a tête-à-tête that morning.

He was not looking forward to it.

Ms. Fairview owned half of downtown Laymon, primarily food establishments like the Beanie Roast and Roberta's Hot Pot Café, as well as the preponderance of now vacant business spaces and, before it had shut down, the Fairview Lumber Mill, on which the entrepreneurial Fairviews had built their fortune. She thus wielded significant influence over municipal affairs, becoming Laymon's de facto (albeit nonelected) mayor ever since the city could no longer afford the salary for a proper one.

Fairview lived on the family estate by Lowlands Lake that she, due to failing health, hadn't left for well over a year. The sheriff requested Deputy Eriksen chauffeur him to the widow's residence. Clive all too ecstatically agreed. Boone reckoned the deputy hoped he'd put in a good word for him with Fairview, endorsing Eriksen as his successor when Boone hung up his holster for the last time.

Which hopefully wouldn't be today, the way today was going.

They arrived at the tall wrought iron gates ten minutes before noon. The gates, modeled after those in *Citizen Kane* but with a calligraphic "F" instead of a "K" at its pinnacle, were being virulently eaten away by rust.

Clive rolled down his window and reached his hand out to push the square red button on an antiquated two-way call box. The speaker on the box squelched, then crackled off into silence. They waited several seconds. That was all it did.

"Hello?" Clive said into it.

They heard the hollow clank of a lock disengaging. The gates began to part slowly, creakily, on cantilever rollers, one side halting prematurely before the other.

Clive eased the squad car through the almost too narrow gap. They cruised up the serpentine pebble driveway, passing an arboretum of doomed trees—centuries old sugar maples and bur oaks and the odd sad sycamore—the sparse foliage already withering on their boughs.

Life was draining out of this place, Boone thought, Death staking eminent domain to the property.

The Fairview Manor house sprawled ahead of them. What once could have been described as stately had now fallen into a state of disrepair. Whole sections of the brick and stone façade were chipped and crumbling. Dirt, pollen, and webs scabbed over the many double windows. The chimney tilted toward the sun, as if craving the warmth it had long been deprived of from the forsaken hearth below.

Clive parked beside the Weeping Midwife fountain, its rectangular basin clotted with natural detritus and a maggoty duck carcass, the tip of an arrow poking from its breast. Years before, a lightning bolt had obliterated the statuary's "weeping" head, so now the water percolated from the scorched nub of her neck.

"Wait here," Boone said to Clive as he stepped out of the car. "I shouldn't be too long."

"Put in a good word for me," the deputy bullishly replied.

Sheriff Boone strode up to the imposing copper entry door, with intricate bas-relief Oriental dragons coiling around each other in some sort of dance, or perhaps copulating.

He rang the doorbell, dislodging sooty flakes that peppered his right shoe. He had shaken off most of it when a middle-aged woman answered the door. She was attired in a white caregiver's uniform so anachronistic it could have been handed down to her by Florence Nightingale herself. The stout woman's frizzy brown hair was done up in a complex bun, her flinty countenance betraying no emotion whatsoever. She instantly gave Sheriff Boone the heebie-jeebies.

Boone removed his white Stetson hat, an accessory he only wore on formal occasions requiring him to look his most official. Ms. Fairview admired a sharp-dressed lawman.

"Please come in, Sheriff," the nurse said. "Lady Fairview is expecting you."

Setting the hat back on his head, the sheriff followed the woman inside. She escorted him along a master corridor, its opulent décor showing varying degrees of dilapidation—the wilting blades of potted plants, the opaque layers of dust blearing all the paintings and mirrors, the threadbare center of the once well-trafficked carpet. A palatial glass chandelier dangled precariously above. They passed an abundance of hallways branching from the corridor, leading to the various rooms in the home, but each so bereft of light they might as well have led nowhere, an eccentric labyrinth of dead ends. They took none of these passages, and Boone soon found himself climbing a grand spiral staircase.

The staircase wound up to another long corridor, lower in height than its downstairs counterpart, windowless and dimly lit by half-moon wall sconces. Dark-stained teak doors, all shut, broke up the beadboard wainscoting lining each side, nearly indistinguishable from the rich mahogany walls. Fusty, sepulchral air pervaded.

They walked to the end of the hallway, halting before a pair of sturdy swinging doors outfitted with crystal knobs. A white keypad with three unmarked black keys was installed on the jamb. The nurse pushed the middle key. They waited several seconds before a diamond-shaped green light blinked at the top of the keypad. The nurse grasped both glassware handles and drew the doors open.

She ushered Boone inside. Ahead of them was what Boone reckoned to be the room's singular window, blocked by brocaded drapery flowing from ceiling to floor. A few feet in, the chamber forked into two facing alcoves. To the left, on a large screen television—the room's sole source of luminescence—was a financial news program, its sound muted, a stock ticker running along the bottom of the screen. Mounted on the walls around the TV was a gallery of, presumably, family photographs that must have spanned many generations of Fairviews. No matter how old or faded the photo, each of the stiff-spined subjects exhibited the distinctive Fairview mien, one of privilege and puissance, the type who mustered pride even in their own flatulence.

In the right alcove lay the beshawled Wheezing Widow. She was propped upright on plush pillows in an immense four-poster bed which lacked its canopy, this due to every inch of useable space surrounding her being occupied by a staggering array of medical apparatus—intravenous drips and infusion pumps, respirators and aspirators and analyzers, and separate monitors for every vital sign a human can have monitored. And those were just the gadgets Boone recognized. Or sort of did. There were other contraptions attached to her that may well have been acquired at a science fiction convention.

In the wan lighting, Ms. Fairview most resembled a gangly marionette with its strings severed. Her flesh looked like chicken jerky shrinkwrapping her osteoporotic bones. What remained of her thin-as-cobweb hair was matted in knotty clumps, conjuring a picture in Boone's mind of a senescent Medusa, in a saggy harlequin green nightgown, whose scalp of snakes had died and shriveled up there.

Fairview, well into her nineties, looked much worse than she had the last time the sheriff, or anybody else, had seen her. For her final public appearance, she had attended the grand opening of Blair's Beauty Barracks, which she half-owned, rolling up in her motorized wheelchair. She had contracted emphysema by then—hence the Wheezing Widow epithet—but she must've aggregated a medical encyclopedia's glossary of other debilitating maladies since. Without these machines doing all the breathing and pumping and painkilling for her, she'd no doubt be reposing in a sumptuous casket within the family crypt by now. This was no way to live. Boone couldn't help feeling sorry for the ol' gal.

"Don't you goddamn look at me that way," she croaked, her eyes still blazing with characteristic fire.

Boone ceased pitying her. This slight, sickly dame nevertheless retained the ability to intimidate the hell out of anyone in her presence. As long as Ms. Fairview's brain was saber sharp, she could cut you down into a thousand bouillon cubes. The sheriff braced himself for the vitriolic thrusts to come.

"Sorry, ma'am."

"Address me as Ms. Fairview." She coughed stridently, making no effort to shield her mouth. "'Ma'am' is for those being coddled. Do I look like I need coddling to you, Sheriff?"

"No, ma—," Boone caught himself, "Ms. Fairview... You look good."

"Save the platitudes too. I look like shit." She regarded him, smacking her blue-tinged lips. "Unless you think I still look good enough to ride, in which case hop aboard, lover."

Boone reined in his disgust. "No, thank you," he answered coolly, casting a glance at Fairview's nurse standing sentinel by the doorway, impassive as ever. "I'm on duty."

"Just as well," Fairview snuffled. "You'd break me like I was a candy cane." She sniggered to herself. "Wasn't always like that. Used to be able to take it every which way for hours, and then keep begging Kip for more."

(Kipper Fairview had been Ms. Fairview's husband for some fifty years, until the day he'd tripped into his mill's buzz saw, which didn't kill him, and then, being a staunch do-it-yourselfer, sewed himself up with an unsanitized needle and thread, which put him into septic shock, which did kill him. The locals joked afterwards that Kipper's biggest regret had been he couldn't box up and bury himself.)

"Godfucking tit itches like a sonuvabitch," Ms. Fairview grumbled, her wizened fingers immodestly scratching the mummified mamma.

Boone averted his eyes, but could still hear her scraping away at herself, like a quill doodling on ancient papyrus. Only then did he notice the eagle, stuffed and suspended by wires from the tooth-and-flower cornice in the far corner. Its frozen pose was the antithesis of noble—the bird hung upside down, its wings gracelessly askew, beak agape in a petrified squawk. As if it were tumbling from the sky, Boone concluded, not at all amused by it.

"You do know those birds are endangered?"

Ms. Fairview sneered at him. "Going to arrest me, are ya Sheriff?"

Boone didn't answer that.

"If I had my druthers," the widow declared, "I'd shoot the glorified buzzards out of their nests. Wipe out every last one of them. Then we can put this town back to work."

"Except for the eagle tour guides."

Ms. Fairview shrugged, her tongue skating figure-eights on the inside of her cheek. "Sacrificing a half dozen of those feather-strokers," she said priggishly, "in favor of putting saws back into the hands of three hundred loggers. I'll sleep fine on that. Hell, I'd even give them ranger boys jobs picking up trash for me, so they would still be doing their bit to conserve the environment. Everybody's happy."

Boone was tempted to comment on how happy the eagles would be about being sniped from their aeries, but he kept this flippant remark to himself. A part of him, he was ashamed to admit, agreed with her.

"So how's your murder investigation coming along?"

The sheriff was prepared for this line of inquiry and had already rehearsed his authoritative, if equivocal, response over and over in his mind, since he couldn't very well read from the case file right there in front of her.

"The medical examiner from Sulfur Springs has supplied us with some valuable insights. We're now pursuing several possible leads based on what—"

"Oh, don't crap in my oatmeal, Boone," Ms. Fairview interjected, flapping her cadaverous hand at him. "I know you got bupkes."

Boone wondered if there was a mole in his department—Deputy Eriksen?—feeding her information on unpublicized police matters. Kissing up to her. Maybe doing even more than that, if the crone had her prurient way.

"I know this damned town is sinking like a rotting dinghy, but let's not row her into a brewing shitstorm."

"It's still a very young investigation," protested the sheriff.

"Two killings in two days. In Laymon, for fuck's sake!" Ms. Fairview's breathing grew wheezier the more flustered she got. "We don't do no first-degree murders here, much less multiple ones. If you don't draw a lariat around this quick, the state Feds might butt into our business, and you know how much I abhor those government dicks poking in my hole."

Sheriff Boone, to his consternation, found he also shared the widow's sentiment. Ms. Fairview took justifiable exception to any out-of-town bureaucrats undermining local interests by imposing their own, especially when it negatively impacted revenues from her many investments in the city.

With Sheriff Boone, it was simply a matter of honor. He reckoned any federal agent would regard him as some small-town rube who was in way above his badge, accustomed only to collaring drunk drivers, rounding up juvenile delinquents, or tracking down lost hikers. He didn't relish the prospect of any Bureau guys, in their snazzy suits and designer sunglasses, waltzing in onto *his* turf and cavalierly commandeering *his* investigation. It was downright disrespectful.

"Folks don't want to visit, much less live in, a place that stinks of death." She coughed again, ejecting flecks of spittle (or perhaps it was dust). "I want you to get a handle on this hubbub before it becomes national news. Else when you're up for re-election, I'll see to it you'll be making your concession speech."

While the soupy pall creeping over his mind made him question if he should even run for re-election next year, Boone still resented the threat. He would bow out of his post on his own terms, damn it, not because this noisome, near skeleton of a woman plied her clout to ruin him. After seventeen years on the job, he deserved better than that.

But Boone, wisely, said nothing in response. No point bringing a simmer to a boil if it were only going to get you more burnt.

"Do we understand each other, Sheriff?"

Boone nodded.

The gaunt woman harrumphed, dismissing him with a feeble flick of her wrist. She then shut her weary eyes, lulling herself to sleep to the whooshes and beeps of the machines she relied upon to keep her alive well past her expiration date.

Sheriff Boone exited her chamber trailed by the nurse-warden, much as if he were a paroled convict being marshaled out of the prison. While Fairview Manor was not a prison—not for Boone anyway, though he couldn't speak for the widow—he welcomed his release from its confines all the same, hastily returning to the relative comforts of the squad car.

"How'd it go?" Deputy What's-His-Name asked.

"Just drive," Boone mumbled.

"What?"

"Drive, goddamn ya!"

The deputy drove.

Gulliver chose to walk the entire 3.2 miles home from Take Wing Air Charters, ignoring his stinging sore feet and the passing bus going his direction. He had a load of heavy matters on his mind, and he'd hoped he could sweat off some of their weight by hoofing it. Yet by the time he reached his front door late in the afternoon, he was still encumbered by the same dismaying thoughts, unresolved.

He shambled into his house, shutting the door behind him. The instant the door's dead latch clicked into the jamb's strike plate, he was showered with color—ragged flakes of blue and red and green and white. Confetti. Accompanying this deluge were the screechy cheers of the Little People.

As he brushed away the rainbow bits clinging to his face, Gulliver remembered that today was his birthday. How could he have forgotten? He had his reasons, of course. The Little People, though, were sticklers for marking special dates. Three of them anyway, to Gulliver's knowledge, these being his birthday, Christmas (they loved to parody the Nativity beneath the tree), and this esoteric Micronian jamboree every October which climaxed in the formation of an impressive Little People pyramid in Gulliver's kitchen.

Across the living room ceiling drooped a glittery purple "Happy Birthday" banner, creased and torn and taped in spots, that had been dug out from the crawlspace. On the dining table sat a chocolate bundt cake, decorated with nine skinny candles and frosted in vanilla buttercream, Gulliver's favorite. Beside the cake was a pressed glass bowl of pink fruit punch, spiked with Rhum Barbancourt judging by the empty bottle beside it. Also resting on the tabletop, a conical papier-mâché party hat for Gulliver, painted with capering lizards, if he had to hazard a guess what the crudely rendered figures were.

The Micronians all wore their own party hats of festively dyed whirlybird maple seeds.

"This is all very sweet," commented Gulliver, genuinely touched by their benevolence. "You didn't have to do this."

He was answered with some gay Micronian exclamations, which Gulliver interpreted to mean *"It was no bother at all! We wanted to do it!"*

"Thanks, guys."

Gulliver gravitated to the dining room table, onto which the Little People had congregated. He soon surmised they were already rapturously inebriated on their own punch, some sort of wobble-dancing, some sort of warble-singing, the others goading Gulliver through exuberant arm gestures. Smiling, he stooped over the cake and blew out the candles in a single puff. They applauded and squealed.

For two hours, Gulliver celebrated the anniversary of his birth with those who hadn't been present at it.

They played a series of party games. First, a hybrid of Hide-and-Seek and Three-Card Monte, wherein a Micronian hid inside one of three toilet roll tubes, Gulliver then having to guess which contained the homunculus. Next came several rounds of *Primetime Charades*, Gulliver versus the Micronians, each taking turns pantomiming a TV show's title or character until the other solved it or gave up. Finally, a variation of musical chairs called Extinction. Gulliver and the Little People lined up single file to walk through a hula hoop-sized circle drawn in gold crayon on the living room's hardwood floor while a blindfolded Micronian operated the stereo, randomly switching it on and off. Whoever was inside the circle when the music stopped was disqualified, that is, considered extinct.

Gulliver won this game every time. The irony—or was it augury?—was not lost on him.

After the festivities wound down, Gulliver sat on the sofa, the Micronian-made party hat still strapped upon his head. Nursing the last of the fruit punch in a Hamburglar mug, he once again contemplated his and the Little People's quandary, tossing out any course of action he deemed impracticable or unethical. Within minutes, that rubbish bin was close to overflowing.

Gulliver observed the Little People sweeping up the confetti and erasing the crayon circle from the floor, collecting the dishes from the table and fighting over the remaining crumbs of bundt cake. Despite himself (or rather, despite their sometimes rascally selves), Gulliver loved them. They were his family now, which made it all the more difficult to decide what to do next. Gulliver, of course, didn't want anybody else he knew snuffed on account of his inaction. Yet, the wholesale extermination of the Micronians because they allegedly posed an infectious threat to an underground civilization of colossi was hardly an appealing alternative. The Little People were defenseless, pacific beings who had no idea a hit had been put out on them. They trusted Gulliver implicitly. To betray that trust was unconscionable.

Perhaps it needn't be so much an issue of the peril confronting the Giants, but the proximity of that peril to them. In which case, the solution was glaringly obvious.

"You need to move out. Far away from here."

The Micronians rebuked him with ululant cries of such unmistakable indignation that Gulliver did not require the Scrabble board to translate them.

"I know what I'd said. But things have changed. You're not safe here anymore." He made emphatic stabbing motions with his arm into the air. "You gotta go. All of you."

This elicited more dissenting shouts, sounding like a tumultuous covey of partridges in a burning pear tree.

"I wish there was another way," Gulliver said. "But there just isn't."

Then, a moment later, his tone buoyed with an amended proposition: "I can come with you. We can all go together. Wherever we want. We'll have our very own adventure. We'll find someplace new. Someplace even better than here. And we'll be even happier... What do you say?"

The Micronians' response was not quite immediate, but it was decisive—a crescendoing cacophony of crashing objects reverberated all around him. Silver and brass bric-a-brac banged, ceramic vases smashed, and wood picture frames cracked as they tumbled from the shelves and tabletops onto the floor.

"Stop it!" Gulliver commanded.

The salvo of noise ceased.

Gulliver stepped toward the hutch, bending over to pick up the walnut-framed photograph lying facedown by it. Its gold leaf molding was intact, but the glass had been shattered in the fall, marring the image underneath a brittle asymmetric web. It was his family's Christmas portrait, their last family portrait, now with slivers of broken glass slicing through them. Cutting through Father's head and legs, Mother's neck, Dale's torso. Only Gulliver, being the smallest figure in the photo, was spared. Again.

Gulliver delicately re-set the frame on the hutch's shelf, managing not to knock out any of the shards.

A vortex of unpleasant feelings—fear and anger, sadness and despair—curdled within him, coalescing into an acerbic porridge he wanted to, but couldn't, expel. He couldn't even dry heave for the therapeutic benefit.

"Why can't you understand?" Gulliver bawled. "Why can't you trust me? After all these years!"

He cupped his palms over his eyes, blocking tears that never come.

"Stubborn! Little! Bastards!"

The Little People never answered him, leaving Gulliver to palliate his inner turmoil himself and to finish cleaning up the mess they'd made for him.

Mr. Jensen knew Gulliver Huggens was crazy, though it spoke to a certain extent of sanity that the young man generally acted very low-key about it.

Gulliver's neighbor had suspected there was something off about him the first instance Jensen caught him late one night fastened to a tree with an extension cord. Jensen later confirmed this suspicion when Gulliver implausibly pinned such deeds on a community of tiny folk living in his house. And now Huggens professed there were bloodthirsty giants hiding out in the mountains, swinging into town once in a while to slay a Laymon citizen.

Yeah, Gulliver was demonstrably bonkers. But then, Mr. Jensen didn't hold that against him.

Since the Incident, who was he to judge?

While Martin "Marty" Jensen ultimately had not been discharged from the Air Force for impaired mental acuity, he might as well of been stamped with a Section 8 after he'd recounted the Incident to a few fellow jockeys in his squadron. From then on, until the very last day of his tour of duty, he was the butt of umpteen bad jokes and silly nicknames. All in good fun, they had assured him. Yet Marty Jensen couldn't refrain from wondering if everybody, behind his back, impugned his capability to remain clearheaded under stress, a denigration to any proudly serving USAF pilot.

He'd questioned it himself sometimes, although he *knew* what he saw. And it was no hallucination. Neither his eyes nor his mind had been playing tricks on him. It was as real as anything he had ever experienced in his fifty years of flying.

May 8, 1966. Airman Jensen, twenty-two years old, was serving his second year stationed at Da Nang Air Base in South Vietnam. At 2300 hours, as part of a four sortie night op, he took off in his O-1 Bird Dog in advance of three F-111 Aardvark fighter bombers, dropping flares to illumine their target areas near Hà Tinh. After deploying the flares, and before the bombers had reached the targets, Jensen's aircraft came under heavy ground fire, impelling him to divert from his flight plan and return to base via an alternate route.

Within minutes—a duration that had felt like an eternity to him—Jensen had gained enough altitude to cloak himself above some low-lying cloudbanks. Safe from the scopes of enemy artillery, he radioed in his OK status and exhaled the breath he'd been holding since the last shell exploded mere meters away from his lightweight monoplane.

Up there at ten thousand feet, it was like a whole other world. A world between worlds, glorious and idyllic. A lolling crescent moon smiled down on him. Jensen could discern in its silvery glow the cottony carpet of clouds below him. Stars, many as bright as his lambent cockpit panel lights, stippled the sky around him, clustered into constellations he could identify by name: Andromeda, Pegasus, Ursa Major—

Then he saw it.

The object materialized, innocuously enough, as this distant, radiant splotch outside his portside window, rather small yet too large to be a star or planet. Jensen presumed it to be a comet, though he could make out no luminous tail of gas and dust following in its wake. But that in itself wasn't unusual. What was unusual was the splotch was rapidly growing in size. Getting closer. Taking shape.

Within seconds, it was soaring alongside his plane, only a hundred or so meters away, pacing him. The object was oblong, elliptical, and, to Jensen's estimation, about ten times the size of his own aircraft. Black hexagonal tiles interspersed with phosphorescent pustules covered its surface, giving it the vague appearance of a partially deflated soccer ball. It emitted no visible exhaust, no detectable noise. Its light-globs pulsated subtly.

Jensen would evermore assert the object was not of this Earth. Not a weather balloon, not space junk, not some anomalous natural phenomenon, but an honest-to-God UF'inO.

He tried calling in the sighting to base, but discovered the radio was dead. All his flight instruments were going haywire, fluctuating erratically.

The object sidled up nearer his plane, aiming perhaps to blast him, or to sideswipe him, or to swallow him.

Taking evasive action, Jensen decelerated and dived.

The alien—yes, dang it, alien!—ship performed the same maneuver in exact unison. It then mirrored every move, every velocity of Jensen's plane. He couldn't shake it. On top of that, without his gauges to help guide him, he was now disoriented, in all probability still over enemy territory, though he wasn't too worried about the Cong at that very moment.

What the hell did the damned thing want from him?

Unexpectedly, the ship ascended a couple of hundred feet, floating to the right until it was positioned directly above him. Then one of its lower light-globs distended, like a prolapsed sphincter, and began jettisoning some sort of dark, viscous substance. A profuse quantity of the brown-green sludge splattered his plane, causing it to rock. Jensen tightened his grip on the yoke, his knuckles whitening, complementing his face's pallor.

Dirty veins streaked across the plane's windows. He could smell the stuff, a vile, distinctly fecal odor, and Jensen realized this: the spaceship was sousing him with its raw sewage. Biological waste. Extraterrestrial excretions.

Poop from another planet.

Perhaps Uranus.

Jensen tittered nervously through his clenched teeth. It was all he could do to not totally freak out.

Having done its business, the ship veered upward and shot into the cosmos, vanishing somewhere beneath Orion's belt.

His instruments functioning as normal again, thirty-six minutes later Jensen arrived back at Da Nang Air Base. By that time, a rain shower had sluiced away all the ordure from his plane. The dearth of substantiation notwithstanding, like any dedicated serviceman he promptly reported the Incident to his commanding officer, who promptly ordered him to undergo psychiatric evaluation.

The rest was regrettable history in the airman's otherwise exemplary military career.

Once his tour had ended, Jensen, by then feeling like an embarrassing chancre on the U.S. Armed Forces' privates, elected not to re-enlist. Instead he returned to his hometown, Laymon, and took a job doing maintenance at a cargo airport in Sulfur Springs.

Less than a year later, he met Babs, a cocktail waitress at Po' Pappy's Bar & Grill, to whom, in a drunken bout of candor, he'd related his close encounter of the effluent kind. As fate would have it, as a child Babs herself had—to her very patchy recollection—been abducted from the family camper by Greys. Eight months following their first date, the two were married. Three years later, Jensen bought the land that would become Take Wing Air Charters. Since then, Marty and Babs had led a blithe, E.T.-free life together.

So, considering all the skepticism and scoffing he'd been subjected to in the past, Jensen thought it a tad hypocritical of himself to criticize Gulliver now for his own flights into the fantastical... even if it was plain as day Huggens, unlike Mr. Jensen, had joined the batshit brigade.

Little people. Giants. Next up, mermaids, or unicorns, or dragons, or centaurs. Whatever Gulliver's fertile imagination could manifest. The guy must be desperate for friends. Unless he didn't need any because he already had plenty in his head.

Then all Gulliver really needed, Jensen supposed, was some professional help.

Since business was dead, Mr. Jensen had made it home from work by mid-afternoon. The very moment he entered his house, he sensed something was not copacetic.

"Babs?" he called out.

Babs wasn't there.

Ordinarily, when he got in, his wife would be cooking them supper in their Provençal kitchen, setting the Castilian table in the dining room, or watching *Wheel of Fortune* on the rear-projection TV in their "getaway grotto." Yet Jensen found both the television and the stove turned off, neither even warm to the touch.

On the dining table sat a porcelain cup, the chipped one, with the cold dregs of Babs's sencha tea stagnating on the bottom. Beside the teacup lay her imported crosswords book, translated into English from its original Japanese. (His wife had become an avid Japanophile.) It appeared she was stuck on a puzzle: a seven-letter word for "Vomiting the pond, or crap biscuits." Jensen wrote "LOZENGE" in the last of the empty boxes and moved on.

He next checked the master bedroom, sewing room, and bathroom—no Babs. While rinsing his gritty hands in the bathroom sink, he peered out the casement window. All he could see was part of the patio deck. No Babs there either.

Maybe she was in the yard, watering the flowers.

Jensen tugged open the French doors in the drawing room and stepped out onto the terrace.

There were three things he noticed, in this sequence: the deck needing a fresh coat of sealer, the hose uncoiled across his lawn, and his wife lying on the ground.

"Babs!" He dashed over to her.

Her liver-spotted hand still clutched the spouting nozzle of the hose, its spray having saturated much of the lawn. It had also thoroughly soaked Babs's cherry blossom kimono so it was swathing her petite frame like a shroud. From a distance, her husband presumed the dark lunula fanning from the robe's collar was merely her sopping brunette-dyed hair.

He was wrong.

Up close, Mr. Jensen realized his wife's head was virtually gone. Blood dribbled from the stump of her neck. Only these gory lumps lay there, squished blends of Babs's flesh and Babs's brain and Babs's bone and Babs's hair, looking as if Babs's head had imploded.

Now it looked nothing like her at all.

As a veteran wartime pilot, successful business owner, and always faithful husband, Jensen was tough enough to stifle the scream that came lunging halfway up his gullet.

Instead, he crumpled to his knees, onto the swampy grass, and wet himself.

5

Sheriff Boone didn't have to look, knowing full well what he would see, but procedure prescribed he must inspect the body. Kneeling down, he raised the sheet, nodded solemnly, lowered it again.

It was as he'd expected—a third identical homicide in as many days. And still no leads, no clues. Only the bodies, and none of them were talking.

Boone rose and surveyed the cordoned-off yard. Well-manicured lawn, shrubs, lots of flowers. A hardwood deck with all the accoutrements: propane grill, teakwood table and chairs, patio umbrella, chaise lounges, tiki torches. The home was a standard cottage with several Tudorbethan enhancements to its exterior, making the residence appear much pricier than similar model homes in the area. The couple's dream house, turned now into a nightmare.

Clive exited from the back of the home, having completed his questioning of the victim's husband, Marty Jensen. The deputy approached Boone.

"Darkcloud and Cavett are about wrapped up inside, Sheriff."

"Anything?"

The deputy shook his head. "No signs of the perp having entered the house. He probably waited for the victim to come out here, then attacked her."

"Husband say much?"

"Just that he wasn't home when it happened, and he has no idea who might've done this. We'll check out his alibi, but I don't think he's a suspect."

"Your job ain't to think, Deputy," Boone snapped. "It's to get me the facts."

"Yes, Sheriff." The deputy eyed him sheepishly, looking to be on the verge of sniveling. Clive was the sensitive type; a Magic 8 Ball could hurt his feelings.

Sheriff Boone, of course, had disremembered this.

He sighed inwardly, softening. "Pardon my guff. I'm a mite frustrated."

Before Eriksen could reply with any words of cunning sycophancy, Deputy Cavett ran up to them, excited as a lame man miraculously healed.

"Sheriff! We found a partial footprint on the side of the house. Appears to be from a boot. Got some caked mud off it too."

"Make sure you get a cast of the print," Boone ordered. "And send the mud over to the lab in Wexler."

"Yes, sir."

"And Deputy—"

"Yes, Sheriff?"

"Best bag those shoes of yours as well, now that you've got evidence stuck to the bottoms of 'em."

The deputy knitted his brow, perplexed.

Sheriff Boone gestured at the shorter man's feet. Cavett gazed down at his black Oxfords. It took him a moment to suss out he was standing on a mushy morsel of poor Mrs. Jensen.

"Oh, my Lord—" Cavett crimped his lips in mortification. "Sorry, sir."

He stepped aside, stripped off his shoes, and carried them away, his stocking feet sloshing through the waterlogged grass.

Sheriff Boone paid the deputy's walk of shame no mind as his attention had been drawn elsewhere, toward the house next door. He'd glimpsed somebody peeking through the curtains of one of its rear windows, but the individual had shrunk back out of sight before the sheriff could lock onto his face.

Boone turned to Clive.

"Why don't you go question the neighbors? See if anybody saw something."

"On it, Sheriff."

As Deputy Eriksen hustled off, Boone's eyes roved the crime scene yet again. It might as well have been a set, everything there a prop for a movie he'd never seen.

Another nonsensical murder, committed on his watch.

He was doing all he could do, but he wasn't doing near enough. Citizens he had sworn to serve and protect were still dying.

The sheriff felt wrung out, useless, about fit for that pasture on the road ahead of him, with all its amenities—unlimited R and R, early bird buffets, marathon naps. Each day much the same as the one before it. The life of somebody who has pretty much quit living.

Or, in Boone's case, of somebody who will have forgotten what to live for.

He beheld the victim's husband through the patio door glass. He sat at the dining room table—a table the couple must've shared for countless meals—hunched forward, his face buried in his hands. The posture of a man who had lost the most irreplaceable thing in his world.

Sheriff Boone slipped away toward the loamy-smelling vermicomposting bin, the spot in the yard farthest from both the victim and her spouse. He dug his cell phone out of his pocket, flipped it open, and dialed a number.

"Hi, hon," Boone said when his wife answered. "No, I'm going to be late again... Very late."

His eyes fixed on a flaxen-crested wrentit perched on a branch, calling to its mate.

"I just wanted to hear your voice."

Gulliver was almost certain the sheriff had caught him spying out his parent's bedroom window. Now he fretted over how he might, through the lawman's eyes, appear culpable.

An hour prior to this, he had heard the sirens approach, saw the white squad cars line up at the curb in front of his neighbor's home. He'd moved into Mother and Father's room, which offered him the best view of the Jensens' yard. From there, he could identify the contorted form of Mrs. Jensen, resembling some large, spindly, floral-plumed bird that had been shot out of the sky.

He hadn't known his neighbor—the victim—at all well. In fact, he had never even spoken to the woman. In double fact, in all the time he'd lived adjacent to her, Gulliver didn't believe she had ever ventured off her property, and only then had braved the world outside to perform yard chores or to retrieve the mail. It wasn't that she was unfriendly. She had smiled at him on those rare instances when they spotted each other simultaneously. Gulliver theorized Mrs. Jensen may have been an agoraphobe, or a mysophobe, or even a coulrophobe (not so preposterous, as Laymon had once been voted number one in the region for rent-a-clowns per capita).

Now, at least, she was free of whichever neuroses had tormented her, and of any other earthly woes she may have endured. Yet, what a whopping price she had paid for this freedom.

And Gulliver, by his own default, had been the one to levy that dreadful price, on all of them, Glenn and Mr. Russ and Mrs. Jensen…

He had to lay down. Had to devise some means to end the slayings without acceding to the Giants' demands.

Without having to slaughter his little friends.

Gulliver scooted across the top of the linens, careful not to rumple them, to the middle of his parents' bed. He stared wistfully at the whirring ceiling fan above, much as he had done as a child, nestled between Father and Mother when the dark shades of night made his own room too baleful to sleep in.

He imagined they were once again there beside him, Father to his right, Mother to his left. Could almost feel the comforting warmth of their bodies, their voices whispering into his ears, advising him what to do—

Father told him to employ cogent, tenable arguments to persuade the Giants to renounce their fiendish plot. Mother, rather callously, told him he must kill the Micronians, for their blood was surely less precious than that of his fellow Man. Like pesky bugs, they were.

Neither option struck Gulliver as practical, nor attractive.

He was jarred out of his semiconscious state by the waning chimes of his Westminster doorbell, followed by assertive knocks at his front door.

Gulliver gingerly slid off the bed, smoothing out any wrinkles or dimples his body had created on the blankets. He then went into the living room. Answered the door.

Gulliver kept his face as stoic as he was able upon seeing the immaculately groomed constable standing before him, grinning, his teeth looking to him like sharpened knives ready to cut.

"Good afternoon, sir. I'm Deputy Eriksen, Laymon PD. May I come in, ask you a few questions?"

Gulliver nodded and stepped aside to allow the deputy into his home. What else could he do, without arousing more suspicion?

But you're not a murderer, Gulliver! Relax....

The deputy halted in the middle of the living room. Gulliver, his legs jittering, flopped down on the sofa, clutching one of Aunt Augusta's candlewick-stitch pillows in his lap.

"Won't you have a seat, officer?" Gulliver pointed at the Bauhaus club chair across the room, between the bookcase and the television. It had been Father's imbibing seat, the old man's favorite place in the house.

"That's alright," the deputy responded. "I won't be taking up much of your time."

Clive surveyed the room, noted the sparkly banner overhead, the remnants of rainbow confetti on the floor.

"Had a party?"

"Yes," Gulliver replied. "It's my birthday."

"Hope you had fun."

Gulliver shrugged. "It wasn't much of a party."

The deputy produced a small, ruled notepad from his breast pocket, along with a blue rollerball pen.

"May I have your full name and occupation?" he asked, clicking the pen.

"Gulliver Huggens. Repairman at Knox Electronix."

"That's on Fairview Avenue?"

"Yes. At Stagg Street."

The deputy jotted down the information.

"Were you aware your neighbor, Babette Jensen, had been attacked earlier today?"

Gulliver nodded. "I s-s-saw you out there. In the yard."

A bead of sweat trickled from Gulliver's temple down to his jaw. He wiped it away with the heel of his hand. Why was he so nervous?

He hadn't murdered anybody. Not really.

"She's dead, isn't she?"

"By any chance, did you see anything unusual, anything suspicious, over the last few hours, or even days? Unfamiliar vehicles in the neighborhood, strangers loitering nearby?"

Gulliver shook his head.

"Nothing out of the ordinary at all? Even the most trivial-seeming detail might turn out to aid our investigation."

"I don't pay that much attention to those things."

"I would like to speak to your party guests. Maybe they witnessed someth—"

"I was the only one here," Gulliver interjected.

The deputy regarded him, nonplussed.

"As I said, it wasn't much of a party."

Deputy Eriksen clucked his tongue and clicked his pen, sliding it and the notepad back into his pocket.

"I think we're done here. Thank you for your time, Mr. Huggens. If you happen to recall anything that might be useful, you can call the station." The lawman turned to exit. "Enjoy the remainder of your birthday."

An idea struck Gulliver like a Brobdingnagian's cudgel. There *was* another option besides those proposed by the specters of Father and Mother.

Law enforcement agencies boasted a myriad of networked resources to which Gulliver himself did not have access: personnel, transportation, computers, weapons. They were, in essence, an army, expertly trained to do battle with evildoers of all stripes and, presumably, of all sizes.

"I-I know who did it," Gulliver averred.

The deputy stopped, faced him. "Pardon?"

"I know who murdered them all."

The deputy stiffened, appraising him soberly. "You do?"

"It was the Giant People."

The deputy would have shrugged off such a farcical claim as the blabber of somebody psychologically challenged, had it not reminded Clive of the grand piano-proportioned, violently unbalanced Huey Lewis.

"What makes you say that, Mr. Huggens?"

"I rode on Mr. Russ's bus. And Glenn delivered my mail."

"And Mrs. Jenson was your neighbor. Are you saying the victims are all associated with you?"

Gulliver nodded. "And their skulls were crushed, right?"

"I cannot comment on that."

"I think they want to scare me. Show me they mean business."

"The giants?"

Gulliver nodded again. "They'd probably pinched their heads between their fingertips. Or maybe they clap their hands together. Depending on how big they are. I've never seen them. But they want me to, umm…" Gulliver leaned within tongue's length of the deputy's ear, lowering his voice. "Get rid of the Little People."

Eriksen adjusted his stance, putting a more comfortable distance between his ear and Huggens's lips.

"The little people?"

"I suppose they'll keep killing folks until I do what they want."

"Which is to get rid of these litt—"

"Shhhh," Gulliver hushed. "They might hear you."

"The little people? They're here?"

"Yes. Somewhere."

The deputy's investigative inquisitiveness, along with his patience, evaporated. He thanked Gulliver for the information, assuring him they'd be in touch should they require additional information, and that, yes, they would act on his information, as appropriate.

Then the deputy departed.

And Gulliver, as he shut his door, felt he made a wise decision.

Now the Giants would incur all the crime-fighting prowess of the Laymon Township Police Department.

It was half past nine in the evening, several hours beyond when his shift regularly ended in less eventful times. Sheriff Boone sat at his desk. After skimming over the latest intra-regional police memos (hulking escapee Huey Lewis was still on the lam, the Potato Sack Rapist was still no closer to being apprehended, and the juvenile pastime of "Bambi Bombing" had spread to Gabriel Ridge), he perused compilings relating to his own jurisdiction's scourge: inconclusive coroner reports, paltry evidence breakdowns, redundant crime scene photos, fruitless witness testimonials. None of it was coming together. Nothing was drawing him closer to the perpetrator, or to a motive, or to any speculation who might be targeted next.

Boone felt, more than ever, that he was combating an infinitely superior foe, one who might've already dug his grave, figuratively speaking. Literally speaking, who knew?

But that wasn't what disconcerted him most.

A lady had dropped by to visit him a little before eight. She had brought with her a dish of her three-bean casserole, assuming correctly he'd not yet had any supper, aside from a Chocodoodle from the vending machine. She told him about the male gold-breasted nuthatch she'd spotted that morning in the honeysuckle bush, what a beautiful voice it had, and how she wished he could have heard it himself.

At this point in their conversation, Boone's impaired lucidity whipped back into focus. Before that, the sheriff could not recollect who this kindly woman in his office was.

For about three minutes, he couldn't recognize his own wife of thirty years.

Granted, the sheriff was both mentally and physically exhausted. Yet he would be remiss to discount the signs of his brain's deterioration steadily worsening. These cracks in his mind—a mind once as solid as the Hockensmith Dam—were undeniably spreading, leaking memories in intensifying surges. How long would it be before nothing and nobody appeared familiar to him anymore, before he would become a man without any history he could recall, without any cognizance of his own identity? When would he become an emptied vessel, biding his time observing things he could no longer name, until the day he gave up the ghost? And then would even his ghost remember the life of Sheriff Cyrus Roy Boone?

Boone smiled at his wife. Lorna. Wearing that lacy ecru dress he liked so much on her.

"Are you alright, Cy?" she asked, sympathetic, concerned.

Boone nodded, assuaging her worry. "Just tired, hon." He blotted his tearing eye with his knuckle. "Seems all I've been hearing lately are sirens, phones ringing, and body bags being zipped up."

"You'll get to the bottom of things. I know you will."

"If I don't soon, the Feds will be sticking their big noses all 'round here." Sheriff Boone flumped backward into his chair, looking more haggard than Lorna had ever seen him. "Hell," he sighed. "They're welcome to it."

"None of that talk," Lorna, hands on hips, admonished her husband. "You're not one who moves aside for anybody."

Boone grumbled to himself. Only a couple of years ago that would have been true. The Sheriff Boone of today, though, was just so... what was the word?...

Mercifully, Deputy Eriksen stepped into the office bearing more probably nugatory paperwork.

"Evening, Mrs. Boone."

"Hello, Clive."

"Witness transcripts, Sheriff, for the Jensen case." The deputy proffered the documents to his superior. Boone took them.

"I'll let you work, dear," Lorna said, mellow as a lullaby, as she sauntered toward the door. "Make sure you rinse out the casserole dish and bring it home."

Sheriff Boone nodded, his wife once again inspiring a smile, however faint, on his face. Somehow only Lorna could make a murder spree seem equivalent to, say, a rash of garden gnome thefts.

If only it was.

"G'bye, Clive."

"Goodnight, Mrs. Boone." The deputy mimed doffing an invisible hat.

After Lorna left, Boone flipped through the pages his deputy had furnished him. Too much to read. "Summarize it for me, Clive."

"Of the three neighbors I spoke with, one was at his job in Sulfur Springs at the time of the murder. Another was out shopping at Eagle Market. The other was home, but didn't see anything. Though he did spin a doozy of a yarn for me."

The sheriff raised an eyebrow at him.

"He says the giants did it."

Boone's eyebrow went squiggly. "The football team?"

"No, sir. Real live giants. Like Paul Bunyan, Jack up the Beanstalk."

Boone ruminated on this. "You don't suppose he's talking about that big crazy fellow? Hugo, was it?"

"Huey. Huey Lewis. I thought of that too, but we'd ruled him out for the bus driver killing, remember?"

Sheriff Boone hmm'd. "Who was this person who told you it were giants?"

"Gulliver Huggens. Resides at 16 Klunghoffer Street, right next door to the Jensens. He's employed at Knox Electronix downtown, lives alone... except for a group of little people he says he's protecting."

"Little people? Like dwarves?"

"I'm not sure. I didn't pursue the topic all that in-depthly. Should I re-interview him for more specifics?"

Boone shook his head. "Nah. Don't bother. Sounds like the guy's a few lily pads short of a pond."

"He seemed harmless enough."

The sheriff whisked his tongue back and forth across his teeth. "Just to be on the safe side though," he drawled, "check into his background, see what you turn up."

"Okay, Sheriff. You got a notion about him?"

"Not particularly. But you know it wouldn't be the first time nobody suspected the sweet-as-pie, never-would-hurt-a-fly homicidal maniac next door."

Kat retched.

"Oh, he was cute," Becky countered, chewing her cherry-flavored bubblegum, which smelled to Kat like cough syrup.

"He was a pompous jackass with way too much hair."

"But he was pretty funny."

"True," Kat conceded. "I laughed at his hair."

Becky was driving Kat home after Wednesday's "Hump Night" at the Stinkpit Club in the S.S. Becky chugged around in an '82 Toyota Corolla that was half falling apart and half fallen apart, many parts jury-rigged together with duct tape. She told people the car was haunted by the original owner, who one day had been found in it dead from a heart attack. Since then, the horn would intermittently beep itself, the radio tuned itself, and the headlights flashed on and off on their own accord. Of course, these all might have been symptoms of the aging vehicle's own gradual demise. But "ghost car" sounded far cooler.

It was two hours past the curfew mandated by Laymon's sheriff because of a couple of recent killings. Seemed like over-reacting to Kat. She had lived in cities that had better than a dozen murders a day year round, and they didn't shut the place down at nine. Becky wasn't too worried about being caught though. Laymon only had, like, five cops. And if by chance they were pulled over, they could play the "ignorant slut" role. That would get them off... with a warning, that is.

"Shit, Kat. It's the same every week. Any guy shows an interest in you, you shoot down."

"Do you mean the stalkers, or the losers?"

"Everybody. You have such impossibly high standards."

"If you like 'em, you can have 'em."

Becky snorted. "But they like *you*, Kat."

Becky was transparently jealous of all the attention Kat received at the bar (though Becky's ginormous hooters drew many a hooched-up admirer). After only a month of hanging out together, their conversation had already become routine.

"What about that short dude with the nose ring? He seemed into you."

"He was just using me to get to you. Classic Fat Friend strategy." Becky swatted the beefcake air freshener dangling from the rearview mirror. "I want a guy like *that*. Rock-hard Latino with those 'I'm-gonna-fuck-the-shit-out-of-you' eyes."

"Want him to smell like piña colada too?"

"He could smell like rotten skunk ass if he looks like that."

Kat commiserated with Becky, even if the sympathy was not reciprocal. Admittedly, Kat still enjoyed all the wooing and wanking over her—and the free drinks that went along with it—but ever since coming to Laymon, she chose to give much more evaluative weight to a guy's quality of character over his money, power, or prestige. No more douchebags, dirtbags, or scumbags for her, she'd pledged herself. She had even resorted to wearing an Egyptian cartouche pendant, bought from a palm reader off the interstate, which was guaranteed to ward off assholes. It didn't work.

Becky pulled up outside Kat's place and dropped her off. Kat waved at her friend as she drove away, tooting her horn thrice in valediction.

Once the taillights of Becky's jalopy disappeared out of sight, Kat turned from the deserted street and walked toward her home, a bland two-storey duplex in a neighborhood assembled from other cookie-cutter domiciles. She rented the building's top floor. The bottom half was occupied by Mr. Lansdale, an ex-logger who mostly kept to himself—i.e., he talked to himself, laughed with himself, yelled at himself. He was a veritable one-man family of four.

Kat was drunker than she thought. She wobbled toward the front door, which opened into a foyer beelining to her neighbor's home entrance and, to the right, a stairway leading up to her own. She was already dreading the climb. It would suit her just as well to lie down on the lawn and crash there until dawn. No biggie. She'd done it before.

"*I love you.*"

That was a child's voice, Kat thought.

Coming from somewhere nearby.

Kat stopped and waited, swaying slightly on her feet. The night was quiet as a morgue. All she could hear was the choppy rolls of her own breaths.

And then, there it was again: "*I love you.*"

Same cadence, or rather the lack of it. More like somebody mimicking a child's voice. Or a sped-up recording.

"Who's that?" Kat called out impulsively.

A single porchlight barely illuminated the front of the house, its brightness bleared by the ossuary of dead insects layered within the sconce.

Kat should have felt more trepidatious, or at least wary, but the night's lavish consumption of alcohol and several tokes off Becky's marijuana chillum had blunted the edge off any flight instinct she might've normally had.

"*I love you.*"

Kat advanced toward the source of the voice, along the side of the house. A wide, rooty dirt passage, flanked on the left by a copse of arching trees, ran to the overgrown backyard of the property. Whenever she expected to be home late, Kat always left on her kitchen light, which now casted a candescent trapezoid from the window above onto the ground below.

In the center of this lit area was a teddy bear.

Kat smiled.

She stooped to pick up the toy, appraising it. It was medium-sized, ideal for snuggling, and looked brand new, but with a few alterations. The synthetic brindle fur at the crown of its head had been spiked up with gel. Safety pins were attached to each of its cheeks, connected by a silver rolo chain looping under its snout. Affixed to its paw with beading wire was a long-stemmed black rose.

"*I love you,*" it said.

A talking punk rock bear. How awesome.

"Who left you here, furry man? Where's your mommy? Or daddy?"

Kat entertained the possibility that the guy from the electronic store—Gulliver—might have planted it there for her, a gift to re-pique her interest, to entice her to take him out for another test ride...

A damp sheet of thick cloth stretched over her face, so taut against her mouth she couldn't scream, only gargle air. It stank like cleaning fluid, or maybe tequila.

Dropping the teddy, she scratched at the coarse fabric with her fingernails. She flailed her arms and kicked wildly, trying to fight off whoever had snuck up on her and seized her from behind. But he was strong. Stronger than her.

"Oh my god," Kat thought, "He's killing me!"

In her head came flickers of a recent newspaper article she had read... sound bites of people she'd overheard talking at the Bean... something about a rapist who, when he attacked somebody, put a sack over their heads.

"Oh my god," Kat rethought, "I'm being raped."

A moment later, Kat's thinking grew misty, then murky. The moment after that, she plunged into a dreamless sleep.

PART 4

THE UGLY TRUTHS

1

When Kat regained consciousness, around her all she could see was blackness, absolute and impenetrable.

She logically figured she'd somehow gone blind. She then, also logically, freaked out, wailing like a banshee in a Spanish soap opera. She soon ceased this histrionic caterwauling, as it only aggravated her skull-splitting headache and, evidently, was not aiding her predicament. Nobody had answered her cries, which was just as well. At that moment, she was in no mood to make any conversation, even if it meant her rescue.

Rescue from what?, she wondered tepidly, clamping her head between her knees, her mind pleading for the unrelenting pain within it to subside.

Minutes passed. Maybe hours. Her migraine mitigated to a dull pinching of her sinuses.

Now at least she could think. Figure out what the hell had happened to her.

Kat patted herself down, checking herself over. Everything, aside from her vision, seemed okay. She could tell she still wore the same clingy club dress from the night—nights?—before. Her feet were bare, her chunky heeled Mary Janes God knows where, and her hair was a brambly tousle.

She didn't feel beaten up or bruised. More importantly, she didn't feel like she'd been violated; there was no soreness, no man-manufactured stickiness or crustiness down there.

So, if this wasn't rape, what was it all about? Why would somebody knock her out? Unless... Had Vladamir found her? Or Takeshi? Or even Brent? But how? She had always covered her tracks so scrupulously when she had to. Moreover, she didn't think any of her exes, as deranged as some of them may have been, possessed enough perseverance to chase her all the way to this bumblefuck town.

Kat concentrated on determining where she was. She ran her hands across the hard ground upon which she sat. Cold, compact earth strewn with leaves and stones. Could she still be outside, beside or behind her house?

"Hello!" She called out. "Mr. Lansdale! Can you hear me?"

Something wasn't right. Something deadened her voice.

Only then did she notice how fusty the air smelt around her. There was no wind, no drafts at all.

As if she were confined in an enclosed space.

Still too helium-headed to stand up, Kat crawled in one direction until her fingertips grazed something blocking her path. A wall? Using solely her sense of touch, she examined the barrier. It hadn't been fabricated, was not made of concrete or brick or metal. It was rough and chinked, more of a natural rock face. While her hands probed up the slick vertical surface, she caught sight of furcated shafts of the breaking dawn above her.

She could see!

She could see she was in a fucking hole.

A fucking ravine, to be more precise. Once her eyes had adjusted to the dark, she judged the area encompassing her to be even smaller than her apartment's bedroom. Its sides were much too steep and slippery to climb, lacking serviceable handgrips or footholds. And with the lone apparent egress, the opening through which the daylight seeped, being twenty or thirty feet above her, she had no chance of freeing herself from this dank and dismal dungeon.

Somebody had put her down here.

Somebody who must have plans for her.

"Help!" she yelled heavenward. "Somebody! Help me!"

That is, somebody besides the mystery dude who dumped her down there.

Kat continued to scream, more and more despondently, until her lungs tired out and her throat burned raw. She crumbled again to the ground, folded herself up, and sobbed.

Nobody was coming for her.

Not until *somebody* wanted to.

Gulliver loafed on his sofa, nursing a glass of Irish cream, reassuring himself he took the most pragmatic and proper course.

If you were confronting a bigger enemy, you needed bigger guns. He didn't expect the Laymon Police Department to wage combat with a battalion of Giants by itself. They would likely mobilize one of the branches of the military: the Army, Air Force, or the National Guard, who'd deploy their heaviest ordnance to vanquish their folkloric foe.

Gulliver imagined the engagement would resemble something out of a Japanese creature feature, but with more mortal monsters.

Or so he hoped.

Gulliver had done his duty. People would hail him a hero. He might even earn a civilian's medal, conferred to him by the President of the United States personally.

So why was he nagged by such remorse?

Perhaps because the Giants probably weren't, strictly speaking, monsters. Although he had never seen one, Gulliver very much doubted they possessed serrated horns or spiked tails, taloned fingers or membranous wings. They surely didn't breathe radioactive fire or shoot venomous quills from their bodies. Apart from their size, Gulliver pictured them as archetypal humanoids, not differing much in appearance from his own. Evolutionarily, he might well be more closely related to them than to the Micronians.

Gulliver couldn't even perceive the Giants as monstrously evil. They were, in his estimation, a peaceable race that only wanted to be left alone, yet had been incited to violence to stave off their impending extinction. Self-preservation being the most powerful motivator of any living thing, Gulliver could not arraign the Giants for their will to live, even if the avoidance of their end, from Gulliver's perspective, did not justify the means.

From the Giants' point of view, Gulliver was their best hope for salvation. How ironic was it then that he may have instigated their holocaust.

The telephone rang.

Gulliver, partially tranquilized by the liqueur, debated with himself whether or not to answer it while he reflexively picked up the receiver. Committed now, he put it to his ear.

"'Ello?"

"We have Miss Katrina."

Gulliver immediately recognized the gruff, sinister, almost robotic voice on the line. It was the Giants' little agent.

Gulliver gulped. "W-wha?"

"We have your girl, Mister Huggens."

The Giants had kidnapped Kat? Why?

For leverage, of course.

The bile burbling in Gulliver's belly instantly solidified into a jagged nugget, scratching and scraping the tender tissues around it. He sat up, the receiver nearly slipping out of his sweaty hand. What should he do? What *could* he do? Think, Gulliver, think! He hastily formulated a strategy to remove Kat from the Giants' bargaining table.

"B-but, uhh… she's not my girl."

"Eliminate all the Micronians by midnight," the caller continued, undeterred. "Or we will kill her. If you speak to the police or anyone else about this, she will likewise be killed. Are we understood?"

"No… please," Gulliver began to implore.

The agent had already hung up. Gulliver, shaken to his core, did not. The phone's connection clicked over to a dial tone, reminding him of a flatlining cardio monitor... the future of Kat's heart in—Gulliver consulted the gilded majorette clock on the mantel—fourteen hours, thirty-two minutes.

Three frantic minutes later, Gulliver was out the door.

Gulliver had neither the time nor the patience to wait for the bus. He sprinted madly all the way downtown, legs pumping like tortured pistons, lungs gasping like ancient bellows. Twenty-nine minutes later, he reached the corner of Fairview and Hoggath Road. He plopped down onto a park bench, beneath the stone effigy of city founder Jebediah Laymon. There Gulliver recuperated for five minutes (during which time his bus had driven past him), his calves aching like they'd been battered and deep-fried. He then rose and speed-limped from the town plaza toward the Beanie Roast.

First order of business: verify the Giants weren't bluffing.

Gulliver propelled himself into the coffee shop. He spotted Becky, Kat's buxom co-worker, slaving away behind the counter, attending to the half dozen customers in queue all by herself. She appeared frazzled, scarcely able to keep up with taking, preparing, and serving the orders. Her last customer, a Boss Hogg lookalike in a grubby John Deere cap, chastised the overworked gal for not ladling enough foam onto his latte. Losing her already tenuous composure, she asked him if he wanted her to hock a loogie in it. No, missy, he responded, the regular foamy stuff will do.

Meanwhile, Gulliver had craned his neck to peer into the café's backroom, praying he would find Kat there on a break or occupied with some café-oriented task.

No Kat.

Becky, finished now with the late-morning rush, slumped against the sink, her chin practically resting on her bosom.

Gulliver approached her. "Excuse me."

She eyeballed him as if he were a dish of her daddy's dirty undies.

"What?" she said tetchily.

"Is Kat here?"

"Nope. She was a no-show today."

"A no-show?"

"She didn't call. Doesn't answer her phone either. She's probably still zonked out. Too many Long Islands last night." Becky tsk'ed. "Bitch left me here to run the opening shift by myself. She owes me big time."

Gulliver's baseless optimism was diminishing exponentially. Still, he had to be sure.

"Can you tell me where she lives?"

Despite her Kat-bashing diatribe, the question prompted Becky to look askance at him.

"Who the hell are you?"

"Gulliver… I work at the electronics repair place down the street."

"Oh, yeah." Becky nodded, eyes widening in recognition. "Kat told me about you."

"I really need to find her."

"Since I don't think she'd appreciate me giving out her personal info like that, I can't tell you. But I'll tell you where *I* live if you want to pick me up later."

"Please," Gulliver exhorted, "this is urgent—"

"Forget about her. Kat's just not into you. Me, I like weird guys."

His defensive mechanism activated. "I'm not weird."

"I know," Becky responded consolingly. "And I'm not busy tonight. Why don't you come over and play with my toys? On me." She bit her bottom lip seductively.

"C-can't," Gulliver stammered. "S-s-sorry." Then he made like Road Runner out of the shop.

Gulliver paused outside on the sidewalk, anxious and aimless. He knew it did not matter where Kat lived. She wouldn't be there. The Giants were not ones to pose idle scenarios to scare him, to goad him into action.

The Giants had Kat.

Now Gulliver had to do something about it.

He scrolled through his options—

Dissuade the Giants. As Gulliver didn't know the Giants' whereabouts, he didn't know how to contact them. Even if he did, what could he say to compel them to renege on their plot?

Eliminate the Micronians. No… he couldn't…

Do nothing. And true to the Giants' word, Kat would most certainly be executed. Gulliver could envision finding her headless body dumped on his doorstep. Implicatively, Kat's blood would be on his unraised hands, hands already stained with the ichors of Glenn, Mr. Russ, and Mrs. Jensen.

Gulliver's eyes drifted over to the vacant retail space where he had been introduced to the Giants, or rather, their midget messenger, mere days before. The entrance door was shut now, but without a handle, obviously unlocked. Maybe, just maybe, the agent had left behind something that might indicate how Gulliver could locate the Giants. He recognized it wouldn't be something as conspicuous or as explicit as a AAA TripTik or a phone number (Giants wouldn't have telephones anyway), but Father taught him even the measliest of twigs could be traced to a specific region, and that region might be Giant country. While such a serendipitous discovery was improbable, and Gulliver hardly the horticulturist his father was, at that moment it was the best—and only—plan he had.

He pushed open the warping wood door and went inside.

The dryrot reeking interior was as dingy and lugubrious as his previous occasion there. Stepping out of the glaringly bright sun, Gulliver had even more difficulty discerning anything between the solid blackness of the rear and the muted daylight filtered through the papered windowfront.

He heard susurrant drones whizzing all about him, crisscrossing waves of near subsonic static. Yet the noise was not electronic in origin. It was buzzing with life.

Something brushed against his hand. Then his cheek. The same something, he realized, that emitted these strange zigzagging streaks of sound.

He turned his attention to the windows.

Silhouetted winged critters flitted across the glass panes plastered over with blanched holiday wrap. The tableau looked much to Gulliver like an aerial view of pixies skating at Santa's Village.

But they weren't pixies... more like...

A needle-prick stuck the nape of his neck. Followed a second later by one to his left temple. Then his right wrist. The bridge of his nose. His upper lip.

Gulliver was under attack.

Twirling his arms about him, he fled the space. It had become a haven for yellow jackets—honeybee-impersonating hornets—volatile creatures that possessed zero tolerance for intruders.

Gulliver slammed the door behind him. He swatted away a few of the sting-happy beasties that had chased after him, sending them skyward. A few more flew out of the round hole where the doorknob should have been, but just as swiftly retreated back to the security of their nest within. They had made their point. Several times, in fact.

Gulliver inspected the wounds on his arms. Angry red welts, swelling and sore. Nothing, though, that wouldn't heal over time.

He recalled his phantasmal mother's words:

Like pesky bugs, they are.

The Micronians. The Little People.

Yet they weren't "people," were they? Not really, Gulliver mused. Not like him. Or Kat.

Kat who was going to die if he didn't do something.

He had to save her!

Like pesky bugs, they are. Or, more aptly, vermin. Furry, four-fingered, bipedal vermin, and impudent trespassers in his home. They had torpedoed his date with Kat, provoked the Giants to kill, and, truth be told, were by and large a thorny nuisance in Gulliver's life. And if they refused to see reason, they were giving him no choice, were they?

He peered down the street at the hardware store. A handwritten sign on its boarded-up façade read: OPEN FOR BUSINESS DURING RENOVATION.

Gulliver rallied his resolve and marched toward it.

He had to load up for his final solution.

Deputy McQuinn sat slouched at his desk in his squeaky swivel chair, fielding phone calls all morning. Most came from worried citizens, some offering unproductive leads, while a growing number came from inquisitive journalists from as far away as LaForde.

All the calls, unsurprisingly, were about the Crusher.

The Crusher was the lurid sobriquet for Laymon's serial killer, slapped onto the perp by a newspaper in Mooseneck City that very day. The name was catching on fast, judging from the callers' liberal use of it.

"I'm sorry, Mr. Wopner," apologized Deputy McQuinn disingenuously. "As I told you, it's an ongoing investigation. We can't comment any more than that."

The deputy listened and stared at his *Holidays Across the Globe* desktop calendar. Today, he noted, was Bounty Day on Norfolk Island.

"I have nothing more to add," he huffed. "I have to go."

McQuinn listened some more.

"I've already answered that. Twice. C'mon, Mr. Wopner. Really. I have work to do here."

The hinges of his jaw twitched in exasperation.

"Because it's an ongoing investi—"

Sheriff Boone depressed the phone's switch hook, cutting the call.

"Just hang up on 'em. Don't have to be so damned polite about it."

"Yes, sir." The deputy cowered a little under the sheriff's scowl.

Boone was ornerier than a mountain lion wearing an E-collar. Folks from all over had been hounding his office nonstop the past twenty-four hours. And he knew it was only going to get worse.

Already a couple of cable news vans were camped across the street, broadcasting live updates on Laymon's menace—they, too, had started calling him the Crusher, a sensationalist title that the sheriff refused to legitimatize by referring to him likewise—and this would soon snowball into a bona fide media circus, a who's who of talking heads acting as ringmasters, proclaiming Laymon a cauldron of spilt blood and brains, with a sheriff who didn't know how to turn off the heat and rinse out the pot.

Boone found himself missing the comparatively under-stated reporting of *The Regal Eagle*.

The Feds would be bulling their way into town any time now, relieving the sheriff of his responsibility, his life's duty, to protect his people. He'd be their lapdog at most, telling him to go curl up in a corner somewhere when he wasn't playing fetch or rolling over for them.

Finally, making good on her threat, the Wheezing Widow would oust the sheriff, this done without her ever having to set so much as a toe off her hospice bed.

Boone did not want to cap off his career this way. Not as an ignominious failure. The lone shiny speck on this dunghill was that, eventually, he would remember none of it.

The sheriff heard Deputy Eriksen bustling up behind him.

"Sheriff, I completed the background check on Gulliver Huggens."

"Who?"

"The giants guy."

"Oh. Right."

Clive read from a manila file folder, exhibiting far more zest than Boone could muster even on a much less beleaguered day. "Huggens had been diagnosed with mild, nonviolent delusional disorders since he was thirteen. He was also labeled antisocial, possessing a fantasy-prone personality.

"His parents died in an automobile accident when he was nine. Afterward, he'd moved in with his aunt and uncle in the N.P. until he was twenty-five, at which time he had inherited the family home here in Laymon. He's lived there ever since. Reggie Knox, his boss, thinks quite highly of him, although he did corroborate Huggens having no friends, or none that he talks about."

"Not real ones, at any rate," Boone added.

"Yes, sir. Guess you'd call him a loner."

"Did you speak to the aunt and uncle?"

"Yesterday," the deputy nodded. "I questioned the aunt, Augusta Mayhew. She resides on a farm in Sawquelle. Insists Gulliver would never harm a soul. No sadistic behaviors. Never abused the animals. Never raised a hand to anybody. Kind of a pantywaist, she said."

Boone plodded into his office and sank down into his desk chair.

Clive followed him inside, but did not take a seat.

"So the guy's wholesome as nuts 'n' berries," the sheriff groaned. "And probably not a killer."

"Doesn't appear to be, sir."

Sheriff Boone rested his stress-stiff muscles. Everything on him hurt, right down to the marrow in his bones. It hurt just to think. He let his eyelids slide south for a spell. He fantasized about nothing.

He didn't know how long he sat there, eyes closed, before his senses re-registered his deputy was still standing in front of him. Awaiting his marching orders, Boone reckoned.

"There anything else?"

"No, sir. Here's the file on Mr. Huggens." Clive proffered the folder, setting it down onto the sheriff's desk. "All of my interview notes are there, and a copy of the accident report from '85, and Huggens's single traffic citation for reckless driving of a motorcyc—"

"I'm sure it's very thorough, Clive," Boone cut him off. *Thoroughly a dead end.* "Why don't you call what's-his-face?... The coroner. See if he's gotten anything off the Jasper lady."

"You mean Jensen."

"You know what I mean," Boone growled, glowering at the deputy.

"Yes, Sheriff." Clive, cowed, turned to exit, then turned back to Boone. "Oh, sir. The mud analysis off that footprint from the Jensens' came in from Wexler. It was bear feces."

"Pardon?"

"Bear pooh, sir. Probably black bear. Maybe our perp's a hunter?"

"Or he spends time in the woods now and then, like most everybody 'round here."

The sheriff rotated his chair so he could look out his window, with a painter's view of the Devil's Horns Mountains in the distance...

Something was eluding him.

"Do you want a copy of the report?" Clive asked.

Boone didn't respond. He was thinking.

Or rather, excavating. Dredging through all the muck and morass clogging his diseased mind, scrabbling to unearth a memory he instinctively knew to be buried within. Something pertinent... or maybe it would be nothing at all. His first stuffed bear... his last bowel movement... his favorite fishing hole, on that lake east of here, where he rented a cabin every summer—

The sheriff snapped his fingers and would have shouted "Eureka!" had the word also come to him.

"Clive, you recall that fellow who'd stumbled upon some cabin, way deep in the pines. When was that? Three, four years ago?"

The deputy gave a measured nod. "Yes, sir. Name was Les... Lester Krabbock. Lived somewhere off Hardware Road, I believe."

"Find out where," the sheriff directed, rising from his chair. "Then let's go for a drive."

Gulliver plunked the four plastic Hap's Hardware bags onto his dining table. All had been triple-bagged, as the seams on each were liable to split apart if so much as a gnat alighted upon it.

Shouldn't a hardware store use heavy-duty bags, Gulliver thought, to reflect the reliability of their merchandise? It was akin to a doctor checking your heartbeat with a tin can telephone... as a tyke Gulliver had assembled one of those with Father... he and Dale used it to communicate with one another from different hiding places... one time, he'd sliced open his knuckle on the wire... took three stitches to sew him up...

Gulliver was distracting himself, diverting his thoughts away from the task at hand.

He emptied the bags, setting twelve boxes into three neat rows. He had bought out Hap's entire inventory. Opening all the boxes, he removed the three canisters contained in each, lining them up. Thirty-six canisters. Gulliver hoped it would suffice, as he had never done this sort of thing before. Never thought he could do it.

Was he really doing it?

Yes, he was. He had to. For Kat.

Gulliver read the instructions on a canister:

"Kills mites, fleas, ticks, ants, spiders, and silverfish for up to 180 days. One unit treats 5,500 cubic feet. DO NOT use more than one CHIGGER CHOKER PLUS fogger per room. DO NOT use in small enclosed spaces such as closets, cabinets, or under counters."

Since Gulliver hadn't the foggiest what a lethal dose for a Micronian would be, he wasn't taking any chances. After shutting off the stove's pilot light, unplugging the appliances, and stopping up the rear door jamb and all the window frames with double layers of duct tape, he planted five bug bombs each in both bedrooms, the living room, dining room, and kitchen. He placed three in the bathroom and two in the crawl-space. Every closet got one. He set up the last three in the garage, still housing all the undisturbed artifacts from his father's cucumber-fungi hybridization experiments. With one of Father's kerchiefs tied over his nose and mouth, it was the work of five minutes to trigger the lot and flee the toxic gas permeating his home.

Once outside, Gulliver shut the front door behind him, duct taping the gaps around it.

Sealing the Micronians' doom.

On impulse, he had grabbed the two remaining bottles of Fizzy Navel wine coolers, still sitting on the kitchen countertop from the night Kat came over, and took them out with him. He walked a few paces across his lawn before easing himself down onto a section of grass grown long and lush.

Gulliver tugged the kerchief down beneath his chin and uncapped one of the bottles. Guzzled it. He then leant back, imagined he was floating on a placid green sea, gazing up at a blue sky garnished with puffy white clouds.

Clouds far less deadly than those filling his home now.

He opened the other bottle, swigged that one too. After a while, he dared to regard his house, its curtained windows seeming to regard him in return.

To his surprise, Gulliver felt no anvils of guilt hanging off him, no twangs of conscience jabbing him. His soul held fast, unrepentant.

He felt righteous.

For this was but the natural order of an ecosystem, the cycle of life on our planet. Survival of the fittest, the fastest, the smartest. The biggest. The prioritizing of all living beings on Earth, as it has unfolded for eons. This was not cause for contrition. The spider did not apologize to the fly, the cat did not apologize to the mouse, the tiger did not apologize to the antelope.

Yet these slurred words spilled from Gulliver's mouth: "Sorry it had to be like this, guys. Wish things could've gone different."

Then he wept.

2

The sheriff expected Lester Krabbock's way-out-of-the-way domicile, a relic of the abandoned Blessed Acres housing project, to be far more ramshackle than it was. Yet Krabbock obviously kept up the quarried stone homestead with a proud homeowner's pride. Roof reshingled, windows washed, weeds weeded. In the gravel driveway, there was only one wheelless car—a Peugeot—propped up on cinder blocks. Out here, that said something.

The interior of the home, however, was saying something else, and Boone reckoned he might have to hire a translator to interpret it. The masonry fireplace featured a disco-mirrored hearth, rope lights spiraled around the timber beams and joists, and a kidney-shaped Jacuzzi bubbling in the center of the capacious den. The room was reigned over by a pack of big game animal heads mounted along the walls, trophies from Krabbock's many Northern Peninsula hunting expeditions. They all wore different types of hats.

The sheriff sat back in a pink vinyl Barcalounger. Deputy Eriksen leaned forward uncomfortably in an even pinker arm shell chair. Lobster-red Lester lazed in his hot tub, silver corkscrew chest hair and his Marv Albert-y toupee dripping with condensing steam. He seemed mighty content being cooked alive there, Boone thought.

Both lawmen made concerted efforts to pay no attention to Krabbock's wormish winky squirming beneath the roiling surface.

"Place was strange, damned it was," Les assured them. "Sure neither of you want a nip? Got a full bar over there."

"No, thank you, Mr. Krabbock," Clive answered. "We're on duty."

"Gotcha."

Not very much was known about Lester Krabbock other than he was rich, Jewish (the town's only), and had moved to Laymon from Southern California to be "closer to nature." That was knowledge enough for most locals, who generally gave hedonists like him a wide berth.

The moist air in the den stank of rotten eggs. The stink emanated from the hot tub. Lester had aquifer water from Sulfur Springs shipped to his home for his own personal daily soak sessions. Along with the medicinal benefits, he believed the odor aided one's ability to meditate.

Sheriff Boone didn't buy into any of that malarkey. If something smelled like crap, count him out.

"Please, go on," the sheriff said, almost beseechingly, breathing through his mouth.

"This was what, three winters ago? I was solo hunting for buck—I only go for eight points or better—east of the Horns, I think. It'd snowed, so the trackin' was good. I was followin' a huge sonuvabitch. Hooves wider than my paw."

To illustrate, Lester lifted a pruney hand from the water. Boone agreed with a curt nod those were sizeable hands of his, though the fact that he'd seen a *much* larger set only a few days before he kept to himself.

"I came upon this cabin, smack in the middle of nothin'," Lester continued. "Nothin' but wildwood for miles all around. A Davy Crockett condo, y'know. Figured it was a hunters' rest, so I go on towards it. It didn't have any windows. What it did have, I shit you not, was a satellite dish on the roof. Struck me as peculiar, way out there in Grizzly Adams country, someone watchin' TV. People livin' that kind of life usually don't care much for MTV, or the Food Network, or *MacGyver* reruns. I mean, these're people who wanna get away from civilization, right?"

Clive glimpsed the derby-sporting deer head across from him winking, then another head, a black bear in a porkpie, stretching its lower jaw in a mock roar.

"Animatronic," Krabbock explained, noting the deputy's flummoxed expression. "It's an extra service my taxidermist down in Cohamango offers. I think it spices up the place."

For the sake of being polite, both lawmen concurred.

"You were saying," Boone prodded.

"Yeah, so, here's this cabin. In hindsight, it could've been some mobster's hideout, and I could've gotten my head blown off just for knowin' where they was hidden. But as I said, at the time, I was thinkin' it was a hunters' hideaway. Hunters who couldn't let go of their ESPN for a weekend. So, comrade huntsman that I am, I go up to the door 'n' knock. Nobody home. Least that's what I thought. Door was locked too. So I decide to circle around.

"Now out front there was a stripped sawlog with a splittin' axe planted in it. And on the side was this monster of a gas generator, which they must've used to power that TV of theirs. And it was runnin'. In back, weren't much but your ordinary shithouse. Looked inside it. Smelled like shit. A fresh coat of it, is what I'm sayin'. So I figured, with that and the generator rumblin' away, whoever had been there hadn't been gone long, and was likely comin' back.

"I figure my sixth or seventh sense must've kicked in then. I got spooked. Something weren't kosher, know what I mean? Even with me having my A-Bolt locked and loaded, I still felt like a rabbit sittin' in an open field in hawk territory. So I make to skedaddle.

"I head 'round to the front of the cabin, aimin' to go out how I came in. That's when I spied the sawlog again. Only now there weren't any axe in it. Then I see another pair of footprints in the snow alongside mine, going 'round the back same way I had gone. Somebody was trackin' *me*, and they were wieldin' that mean-lookin' chopper.

"Well, rifle or not, I wasn't about to play hide 'n seek with any psycho on his home turf. So I hotfooted it through them woods, peeking over my shoulder every few heartbeats to make sure he wasn't gainin' on me. But I guess he weren't followin' me at all. After I covered 'bout a mile, I slowed up a bit without lettin' my guard down none. Soon as I got back to town, I reported what I just told you fellas to you fellas. Though you didn't seem to take the matter with much magnitude."

"Since you hadn't been assaulted," Clive explained, "we couldn't really act."

"So if I'd staggered into your station with my skull filleted, that would've earned me your due diligence?"

"That would have been cause for official concern, yes," Boone retorted.

"So why the concern now?"

"We think it might be connected to a case—"

"The Crusher! You thinkin' my guy's the Crusher, ain't ya?"

The sheriff grimaced. "It's only a theory we're working on." Their *only* theory.

Lester grinned. "Dang, if I helped catch the Crusher, that would be somethin', wouldn't it? I might get to be on *Regis*. And it'd be one heckuva mitzvah."

"So you can take us to that cabin?" the deputy asked.

Krabbock nodded after a beat. "I remember my bearings pretty well. Should be able to find it again. But it's at least a three or four hour hike from here. You sure can't fly or drive in."

Boone checked his Timex. Almost eleven. If they left by noon, they would reach the cabin well before dark.

"Better get moving then," he said, rising inelegantly from the recliner. Clive likewise stood. Lester Krabbock climbed out of the Jacuzzi, raring to go.

The sheriff averted his eyes.

"Sir, uh… clothes are mandatory for this sort of business."

"Not a problem," Les replied. "Just lemme throw some-thin' on."

"Please do," Clive said, staring down at the floor. "Throw on as much as you can."

After two hours, as per the insecticide's directions, Gulliver was able to re-enter his home. Again donning his train robber kerchief to protect himself from the acrid vapors, he rushed in to open all the windows, then exited once more to let the rooms air out for another thirty minutes.

Upon his return inside, he surveyed the aftermath. His house still reeked as if it had been submerged in isopropyl alcohol, and everything appeared to be coated in an oleaginous residue, as though somebody had peppered the whole place with furniture polish. All the depleted foggers sat right where he'd set them.

What Gulliver did not see were any fallen Micronian bodies strewn across his floor. Neither was there a single little pilous corpse to be found under the sofa, or the beds, or the tables. Nor were there any in the closets or cabinets or drawers (though he swept out from behind the curtain hem a belly-up black beetle, its legs folded in upon itself in arthropodal prayer). Perhaps, he surmised, the Micronians had all expired in their nests beneath the floorboards or beyond the walls, these hollows now serving forevermore as their catacombs.

This thought brought on another tsunami of melancholia in him, analogous to what one might feel after euthanizing a baby carriage full of kittens. Gulliver was all cried out, so he crumpled onto the sofa, unscrewing the cap off a bottle of Rasputin Vodka he had fetched to salve his sorrows while he waited for the Giants to make good on their end of their agreement.

He wondered if—when—they released Kat, would she thank him… her hero… her man?

Gulliver heard the muffled yet identifiable clink of shifting dinnerware.

He rose from the sofa and raced into the kitchen. Steeling himself, he cautiously opened the leftmost cupboard over the counter. It revealed only its assortment of glasses, cups, saucers, and a mug with a crackled decal of Mickey Mouse waving its leprous gloved hand at him.

Nothing to see there. How could there be?

The next cupboard held his plates and bowls. Gulliver, less leery now, opened it.

Peering over the lip of a soup crock were five Micronians, each with a drinking straw pressed to its mouth. They blew forth a volley of toothpicks, riddling Gulliver's face, narrowly missing his eyes.

He backpedalled from the cabinet, more stunned than injured. He swept his face with his hand, knocking the largely ineffectual darts to the floor.

So the resilient buggers hadn't perished. They were like cockroaches after all, surviving their pyrethroid apocalypse.

Except cockroaches didn't retaliate with blowpipes.

Gulliver had only a millisecond to ruminate on this before pain stabbed his right ankle. He howled, springing his foot off the floor and seeing the tip of a steak knife shallowly driven into his Achilles tendon.

Two Micronians in cardboard battle armor fled from him, ducking around the corner into the hallway.

Gulliver plucked the knife from his flesh and chucked it into the sink. He inspected the wound, which, though it had broken the skin, wasn't bleeding.

Distracted, he barely caught the glimpse of the second brigade of tiny soldiers charging his left ankle, wielding a chef's knife like a battering ram. Gulliver, still balanced on one foot, hopped out of the path of their attack.

The thwarted miniature militiamen squealed in terror, tossed aside the blade, and ran for the refuge of the pantry.

The bastards were aiming to hurt him. Perhaps even kill him. The audacity!

Admittedly, Gulliver had been the aggressor, but it was Micronian obstinacy that had impelled him to resort to such extreme measures. They could have relinquished their cubby-hovels in his home—*HIS* home!—and resettled someplace else, anyplace else, so long as it was far enough from the Giants' colony. And Gulliver would have been more than amenable to helping broker their move. Together they could've gone southward, laying new stakes in the safer, sunnier climates of Florida, or Mississippi, or Mexico.

Instead, the Micronians chose to ignore his pleas, to defy his command. And defiance had its repercussions.

Now that they were out for his blood, Gulliver's lone recourse was to tap theirs—one by one if necessary.

Gulliver needed a weapon of his own.

He ran to the hallway closet, standing aside when opening it in case another Micronian ambush lay in wait within for him. None did. He looked above the rack of hanging coats and scarves and the orange life vest with its yard sale tag still attached. Up there, a shelf stacked with the dusty leisure antiquities of his childhood: games like Clue, Jenga, and Trivial Pursuit Earth Sciences Edition; chemistry, astronomy, and electromagnet learning kits; and three shoeboxes storing die-cast toy soldiers, which on principle Father would've banned from their household as frivolous and war glorifying, but because they depicted in historically accurate detail the regalia of a miscellany of military—from Roman Legionnaires to Civil War Confederates to Japanese Samurai—they just barely qualified as educational aids.

Behind all these items was what Gulliver had been rummaging for—the air rifle his brother had, at ten years of age, assembled himself from some PVC pipe, a wood block, a toilet lever, and a nine-ounce CO_2 tank, bound together with coils of copper wire. Dale used this homemade peashooter to pop balloons taped to a sheet of particleboard in the yard, until Father confiscated it after an errant "pea" punched through the kitchen window and into Mother's clavicle. There on the shelf it would remain, Father dictated, until Dale turned thirteen. And there on the shelf it had remained ever since, since Dale never saw his thirteenth birthday.

Gulliver took down the rifle and the plastic box of BB ammunition beside it. He poured the silver pellets into the drilled-out chamber. Once fully loaded, he checked the CO_2 tank, hoping it was still usable. He pulled the toilet lever trigger, grinned when a pellet launched from the barrel and pinwheeled the soapstone crucifix on the wall.

He combed the living room first, pivoting the rifle back and forth as if it were a dowsing rod set for Micronian blood. He spied no hint of them, not even when he laid on the floor flat on his stomach, the best vantage from which to view underneath the furnishings.

He rose to a squatting position and froze, breath bated. He waited, listened. The silence was pervasive, an inside-the-eye-of-a-hurricane kind of silence.

And then, behind him, the patter of their feet scurrying across the floor. Gulliver, whirling around, indiscriminately aimed and fired, the shot achieving nothing but gouging out a groove in the wall paneling.

He heard a *whoosh* of something to his left—a rustled curtain, or perhaps a Tyrolean-traversing Micronian. He spun and squeezed off another shot, which only served to fracture one of the ornate floral handles off the Capodimonte vase on the credenza.

So firing willy-nilly was not the most effective tactic to employ. He opted for one less precipitous. Eagle-eyed and owl-eared, Gulliver patrolled his living room, rigorously inspecting every square inch for the minutest sign of movement.

Something small and swift scampered past his feet, drumming the hardwood floor like a summer shower on a beach boardwalk. Gulliver glimpsed a pair of Micronian soldiers dashing into the dining room. He raised his rifle, but they had taken cover beneath the table before he could center them in his sights.

He slinked into the room, peered under the table and, beyond it, the liquor cabinet. At first glance, he saw nothing to target. Then, shifting his line of vision, he spotted behind one of the cabinet's Chippendale legs what appeared to be a coffee bean—traditional Micronian clogs—with, yes, a little trousered leg jutting from it.

Gulliver started to tiptoe around the table to get a better shooting angle. He hadn't even negotiated the nearest corner when his sneakers slid out from under him, plopping him onto his derrière in a classic comic pratfall. He smacked his head against the Shaker buffet, momentarily blurring his vision.

Gulliver rubbed his smarting crown with one hand while lifting the other before his face to examine, having laid it in the greasy puddle on the floor in which he had slipped. He smelled his fingers. Cooking oil. Some sort of booby trap, was this?

He then watched as the head of John Bartram toppled over toward him... or rather, the bronze bust of the pioneering botanist, shoved off the summit of the buffet where it had been perched for as long as Gulliver could remember. In that sliver of a second before the plummeting sculpture would've caved in his cranium, he rolled aside with the kind of amazing agility made possible by such "oh, shit!" instances as this. Bartram's weighty head impacted the floor with a resounding thunk, creating an unsightly crater in the wood—which was better than one in Gulliver's skull.

From his prostrate perspective, Gulliver now had a clear panorama of all the action happening below ankle level. Single and multiple detachments of Micronian infantrymen, armed with sewing needle lances, sprinted from covert to covert.

Gulliver popped off a succession of exactingly aimed—but every one still a hair's breadth belated—pellets: one bore into the baseboard, another gave a mastectomy to the majorette clock, and the last penetrated a slot of an electrical wall outlet, generating whorls of hissing smoke and spitting sparks.

He zeroed in on a contingent of commando sprites, four or five of them, scrambling down the hallway and disappearing into his bedroom.

Gulliver flipped over and onto his feet. After making a pit stop in the kitchen to snatch a package of Decadent Darla's snack cakes, he went in pursuit of his quarry.

Gulliver stopped just inside the threshold of his room upon stepping into something squishy. He reached over and tugged on the hanging pull chain. The overhead Gutesjahr Blimp light came on.

Gunking up the floor was a nauseating mixture of, from what he could identify, broken raw eggs, coffee grounds, liquid hand soap, wheat flour, dishwashing detergent, Dijon mustard, ketchup, and mayonnaise. Gulliver's clothes from his closet and chiffonier drawers—all his shirts, pants, underwear, and socks—lay in disarray in the slurry.

He began to pick up the articles, realizing at once his Vander Hutton dress shirt and his best pair of corduroys were soiled beyond salvaging.

But this was no time to brood over ineradicable stains. It was a diversion, undoubtedly.

Or a defilement.

Gulliver's steely eyes scanned his bedroom.

Where are you sick bastards?

He produced the chocolate-covered snack cakes, crinkling the wrapper.

"Hey, guys. Got a treat for you. Come come, yum yum!"

Gulliver slogged through the Micronian-made mire that encrusted his shoes like wet cement. Reaching the halfway point between his door and the closet, he pocketed the cakes and deigned to kneel one knee into some ketchup and coffee paste. He peered beneath his bed, seeing nothing but a landscape of dust and shadow. Sticking the air rifle under there, Gulliver waved it around, banging it against the bedframe's legs, trying to draw out any Micronians that might be hiding in the murk.

One bolted from behind the nightstand, making a break for the closet along the room's unobstructed perimeter.

Gulliver blocked its path with the rifle, bringing it down like a parking lot barrier gate. The Micronian skidded to a halt before it, then reversed its fleet-footed retreat. But Gulliver was quicker. He thrust his left arm out toward the wall, impeding the tiny soldier's course yet again, boxing it in.

The Micronian backed away from Gulliver, pressing itself into the corner. Its body trembled like an insect beating its wings, its eyes bulging in comprehension of its predicament. Furry hands clasped supplicatingly. It chirped at him, perhaps groveling for its life, perhaps summoning for help, or perhaps it was only the gibbering squeak of a creature too terrified to speak intelligibly.

Gulliver struck with murderous-minded precision. He swung the solid wood butt of the rifle at the Micronian, smashing it against the wall. Heard the revolting, satisfying crunch of little brittle bones.

Oh God, he killed it. He killed one of his Little People. Like it was a cockroach.

No.

Like it was the enemy.

This was war. And, naturally, a war begat fatalities. Death. By his hand.

What was he doing?

They were his friends. They'd cooked countless meals for him. They'd shined his shoes, folded his laundry, ironed his shirts. Scrubbed his floors, dusted his furniture. They'd read together, watched TV together, played Scrabble together. They made him laugh. They made him happy.

Most of the time, anyway.

Enough of the time.

What kind of person wages war with friends?

What kind of person was he now?

Gulliver eased the rifle away from the wall, bracing himself for the sight of mangled Micronian remains.

To his stupefaction, there were none. The corner was bare save for the fresh indentation made by the weapon's butt and the silty brown trail left from the once leaky roof.

Where did the Micronian go?

Where had they all gone?

A sensation of rippling warmth wafted around Gulliver. He sniffed. The air in the room had assumed the scent of charred car upholstery, calling up that dreadful, deep-rooted memory, a replay of his brother's last desperate entreaty to him—

"Help me, Gulliver! Please!"

—which almost made him wail in anguish. He jammed his fists over his ears, clenched his eyes shut, stifled his breath, and shook his head vigorously. Trying to exorcise that ageless moment from his brain, to quell the wrenching pain it again wrought.

Could this be some form of psychological warfare the Micronians had adopted?

No. The smoke Gulliver saw pouring into the hallway was very real.

"What have you devils done?" he shouted as he rushed out to investigate.

Fissioning tongues of flame licked the living room. The curtains had been reduced to ash, the television melted into bubbling black lava, and the bookcase was now receiving the *Fahrenheit 451* treatment.

Its intense heat thrashed Gulliver, driving him into the kitchen. After some lightning-round deliberating, he got down onto his haunches and opened the cabinet beneath the sink, removing Mother's eight-quart stockpot stored therein. He set it under the faucet, filled it to the brim. Gulliver lifted the sloshing pot from the basin and hefted it to the entry of the living room. He slung the water into the inferno. It only laughed at him.

The fire advanced and conquered.

Gulliver coughed, choking and tearing on the dense sooty smoke storming his home. He crouched low and scuffled out the rear door, blundering into the yard.

The blaze raged.

After hacking up a lungful of slag-gray sputum, Gulliver slumped onto his lawn. He watched with rheumy eyes the destruction of his house.

Less than five minutes ago, the glow through the kitchen transom was almost as inviting as that of a crackling fireplace. Now, with the flames having punched through all the windows and Stygian smoke eddying out of them, 16 Klunghoffer Street—the Huggens family residence for better than four decades—had become a hellish tempest.

Gulliver thought he had won.

Then it'd occurred to him, with his home razed to embers, the Micronians might be the posthumous victors.

But it had been their home too.

Perhaps there were no winners. The canons of war could be so abstruse.

And what if some of them had managed to escape?

What if Micronians were, right now, journeying into the mountains, back to their nether hills?

Toward the Giants.

Even one mini wayfarer might be a breach of the Giants' iniquitous terms. If Gulliver had failed at his assigned task, then Kat may well pay for his failure, and this forced march into the maelstrom would have been for naught. He had failed everyone. How many, be they Man or Micronian, would die because of him?

Gulliver heard something.

A pulsing *thp-thp-thp* noise, growing louder, nearer. It sounded like a lawn sprinkler, except it originated from the sky. He squinted into the late afternoon sun.

In the distance, a helicopter approached. At least it had appeared to be much farther away than it really was. As it cut through the ribbons of rising smoke, Gulliver saw the aircraft was quite small, about the length of a baseball bat. A remote-controlled toy, he realized. It descended and hovered a mere meter before Gulliver's face. Its framework had been plainly assembled from pieces of metal and wire, soldered together then painted jet black. An antenna resembling the Eiffel Tower protruded from its tail boom.

Gulliver considered running away, but scrotum-gripping fear and funereal-grave logic had paralyzed him. If the black chopper were one of the Giants' inventions—which it most certainly was—fleeing from it would be futile. In all likelihood it was outfitted with a machine gun, or a missile launcher, or a phosgene dispenser. He would be bumped off before he'd even unbent his knees.

So there Gulliver stayed, eyes locked on the contraption's dark-tinted convex windshield. It seemed to be observing him. Judging him. He waited for it to pass sentence.

A tubular chute—much like a derringer's muzzle—telescoped out of the helicopter's underbelly. Aimed squarely at Gulliver's heart.

Gulliver anticipated the flash that would put out his lights forever...

The tube instead ejected a scroll of parchment. It landed harmlessly in Gulliver's lap.

The model helicopter ascended into the sky at an oblique angle, attaining heights of twenty feet, fifty feet, one hundred feet. It then exploded in a varicolored pyrotechnic display, with arcing branches of twinkling whites, blues, reds, and purples.

Gulliver gaped at the spectacular disintegration for several seconds, causing him to miss witnessing his house collapse in on itself. He had heard it, though, all its lumber bones breaking at once, and that was devastating enough.

With some apprehension he slipped the rubber band off the scroll, unrolled it.

The Giants had at last delivered their pronouncement for Gulliver.

It was an acquittal.

It was a map to Kat.

3

Almost four hours had elapsed since they had set out into the wilderness, led by the nattily outfitted Lester Krabbock. For the occasion, Les had "thrown on" a hardwoods orange parka bedazzled with autumnal-hued gemstones, an ostrich-down insulated pair of matching trousers, a red fox-fur cap with authentic scrimshaw visor, and Prada Italian leather hiking boots. The others, in their regulation police uniforms, felt understandably underdressed.

In addition to himself and Clive, the sheriff had called upon McQuinn for backup, entrusting Darkcloud and Cavett to hold down the fort in town. Boone now questioned the wisdom behind choosing the young deputy to accompany them. While he was a more than competent officer, on this expedition he demonstrated a not-so-commendable proclivity for whining. Specifically, about his feet. After trekking their first mile, Quinn had alluded to his interminable discomfort every five minutes or so, as well as straggling a good fifteen to twenty paces behind the group.

"Is it much farther, y'think?" McQuinn moaned again, limping along.

"We follow the river 'nother coupla miles or so, maybe," Krabbock answered—again—scarcely exhibiting any irritation at all. (The patience of a parson, Boone thought to himself.) "Then we'll veer east. Should make it there before nightfall. Maybe."

McQuinn whimpered in response. He didn't like Les's maybes.

"You need a rest, Deputy?" the sheriff inquired brusquely.

"No, sir." Whimper. "I'm good." Grunt. Whimper.

Good as annoying, Boone thought.

The sheriff spotted a long-tailed, red-billed black bird; its ornithological name, at that moment, evaded him. This didn't trouble him. His mind was honed on their mission.

Another hour and three-quarters passed and even Boone had to confess his own dogs had begun barking fiercely at him. They'd hiked across at least twenty miles of evergreen. All around them, forever green, as far as Boone could see. He had no damned clue where they were. He couldn't even make out the mountains through the mantle of dense foliage above them, allowing barely a sliver of sunlight to pierce it.

Boone wondered if Les had gotten them hopelessly lost.

Sure, they'd brought along some basic survival supplies—canteens of water, trail mix, first-aid kit. But this was supposed to be a day trip, and the day would be waning soon. They had packed no overnight gear. No tents, no sleeping bags, not even a lantern. In a few short hours, they would be enclosed and exposed within the darkest wilds of this nameless country. This land wouldn't care a tick's toot if the lot of them gave up and died in its belly. They'd just become more food for the forest denizens.

And then, well before death greeted them, they reached it.

It was pretty much as Krabbock described. A windowless log cabin. More of a shack, really.

To Boone, a cabin denoted a vacation retreat. This was obviously a residence and, yes, a hideout. For somebody who didn't want to be found, didn't want to be seen.

Somebody who, since Les Krabbock had been here years before, had upgraded to a second, larger satellite dish installed onto the level rooftop. Both dishes faced east, toward Laymon.

Boone glanced up. Most of the branches of the tall trees surrounding the dwelling had been sawn off, ostensibly to optimize communications reception, sparing only the highest boughs to keep the property below concealed.

From their position ten yards away, however, the sheriff could hear no blaring televisions or stereos or radios within. The gas generator beside the cabin, similar to the type that powered Captain Calico's Carnivals, was not in operation. The entrance door was shut.

Nobody home. Maybe.

"Looks quiet," Clive whispered.

Boone deliberated a moment. "Clive, you come with me. Quinn, stay here with Mister Krabbock. Keep a sharp lookout. Watch our backs. And yours."

Deputy McQuinn nodded. He had forgotten all about his aching feet.

Much as Boone had forgotten how forgetful he could be. This was no time for that.

Sheriff Boone drew his Smith & Wesson, Deputy Eriksen his Beretta, each thumbing off their safeties. They approached the cabin as stealthily as possible across the unavoidable floor of crunchy coniferous needles.

Arriving at the front entry, Boone signaled Clive to hold back.

The cabin's construction was simple, but not shoddy. The logs had been skillfully notched together and mortared with cement. The sheriff appraised the door. It was hand-hewn, the pinewood pocked with chisel marks, with an oxidized double-helical iron handle with fleur-de-lis backplate.

Boone tested it. Locked.

Why would somebody need to lock up his place way out here?

Maybe somebody who wanted to hide something besides himself.

The sheriff considered he didn't have a search warrant, but he wasn't about to waste time sending one of his deputies into Sulfur Springs to get one. He formulated an alternative.

"You hear screams in there, Clive?"

Clive listened intently. Shook his head.

"Well, I do."

With that, Boone raised his foot and, with as much force as he could muster, kicked his heel against the sweet spot underneath the handle. The door burst inward, splintering the right side jamb from top to bottom.

Deputy Eriksen's eyes widened a bit, but he didn't protest the sheriff's action.

Boone nodded at him. Ready?

Clive nodded in response. Ready.

They went in.

For the habitat of a troglodyte, it smelled mighty pleasant to Sheriff Boone. He had anticipated the cabin's interior to reek of feces (human or otherwise), or body odor, or putrid meat, or something equally repellent. Instead, the air was imbued with lavender. And apple strudel. If he'd closed his eyes, Boone could have believed he was entering his own home, his wife baking one of her delicious desserts in their kitchen.

Yet the visual, as lit from the domed skylight above, belied these fragrant evocations of domestic bliss. The cabin's single room bore the busy fingerprints of a mad inventor's workshop. A welter of mechanical and electronic apparatus, in apparent varying stages of progress or dismantling, dominated the space on multiple surfaces. Tubes and wires and switches, monitors and boxes and circuit boards. Parts attached to other parts, often forming unrecognizable wholes, though Boone could tell everything there had a purpose, or would have a purpose, even if only in the creator's manic mind.

In the corner there was a cot, its polar fleece blankets neatly tucked under the thin mattress. Opposite this, a meager but orderly food preparation area—a baker's rack with shelves of canned staples and a few jars of beans and oatmeal.

They combed the premises, Boone taking one side, Clive the other. A couple of minutes was all that was needed to scope the cabin out and assure themselves it was, at the moment, unoccupied. Boone holstered his pistol. Though Clive lowered his weapon, he opted not to stow it right then.

"What is all this stuff, sir?"

Boone, of course, hadn't the remotest idea about any of it either. Still, he was flattered his deputy would ask him, deferring to the superior officer's vaster vista of experience.

"Looks like our hermit is the tinkering type—"

"Sheriff."

Boone, examining a thingamajig resembling a medieval marital aid, turned his head. His deputy stood by a partially slashed, yet still quite serviceable Shinto screen, the lone divider in the domicile.

"Over here."

The sheriff came up beside the deputy, saw what he was seeing behind the screen.

A wall of photographs, printed on photo paper. There were dozens push-pinned in the rough wood, overlapping one another. The subject of every image was the same: this unexceptional man in his mid twenties to early thirties, going about his unexceptional business—walking down Fairview Avenue, entering the coffee shop, exiting the electronics store, etcetera, by all appearances unaware he was focused in a camera's frame.

Even more curious, several of the pictures seemed to feature this same oblivious individual *inside* a home: a kitchen, a living room, a bedroom. Just sitting or standing there; watching television, cooking, eating, sleeping. Boone noted these particular shots were all taken from a high angle, with a wide-angle lens.

"That's Gulliver Huggens," Clive stated, pointing at the wall. "They're all him."

Boone arched an eyebrow. Who?

"Babette Jensen's neighbor," clarified the deputy. Then added, "the one who believes in giants and elves."

Oh, yes. Boone remembered now. He nodded.

"Appears Mr. Huggens has an admirer. Or a stalker."

"It's like a shrine," commented the deputy.

The sheriff clucked in agreement.

He continued to appraise the photos a while longer before directing his scrutiny to the workbench before them.

To the right was a CCTV monitor. Next to it, a custom-built computer, a digital printer, a reel-to-reel tape recorder, a dynamic microphone with table tripod, and an RF transceiver, with a pair of padded headphones plugged into it.

Deputy Eriksen's eyes took everything in, making sense of none of it. "Think this is related to the Crusher?" he asked.

Sheriff Boone didn't know what to think of this, and that made him very uneasy.

Gulliver ran, the scroll clenched in his fist.

He sprinted the length of Klunghoffer Street, then raced southward along Fairview Avenue, away from downtown Laymon. His quest, however, was not leading him to Sulfur Springs. The road he sought didn't even officially have a name. Some locals long ago had dubbed it Loki Lane, though "lane" implies a semblance of a road. Loki Lane was in actuality a stone-strewn gully, once having been a spring-fed brook before the construction of Fairview Avenue had diverted its waters to the Fairview Mill.

Even at full-steam stride, it would take Gulliver half an hour to reach his destination. Only from there could he begin to follow the map.

The Giants had hand-drawn it in the style of a pirates-of-yore treasure map. The paper had even been made to be stiff and fulvous, simulating old parchment, as if dunked in weak tea then left to dry out in the sun (the "50% Recycled" watermark revealing the ruse). Next to a cardinal rose, they had sketched a familiar landmark—Loki's Rock—designating it as the starting point. A dotted line indicated the direction and number of paces to get to the iconic capital X, the spot labeled "Here There Be Kat."

Gulliver had to keep running. Kat needed him.

And he needed Kat. Needed to know she was safe. Needed just to see her again.

So he ran. Ran until his legs, his lungs, his heart felt on the brink of surrender. And still he ran farther, because he feared Kat's time might be running out. The map, after all, did not say "Here There Be Kat, Alive and Kicking." It may as well have ambiguously stated "Here There Be Kat's Body."

A procession of disturbing images streaked through Gulliver's mind: Kat burnt over a sacrificial pyre, or skinned and salted like cured venison, or the victim of the Giants' preferred mode of dispatch, her head crushed between their gigantic fingertips.

He hoped he wasn't already too late.

Behind him, catching up fast, came the distinctive growl of a two-cylinder, V-twin engine. Gulliver slacked up to a staggering trot as Mr. Knox, decked out in his usual cuff-to-cuff denim, pulled in front of him on his Harley-Davidson Panhead. Gulliver, swabbing rivulets of sweat from his brow with his sleeve, trudged toward his boss.

Mr. Knox eyed him. "Feeling better, Huggens?"

Gulliver halted. He bent over, palms on his kneecaps, recouping his spent breath.

"Can you... <gasp> ... do me a... <gasp> ... favor, sir?"

"You gonna puke, son?"

Gulliver shook his head. "I need a ride... to Loki's Rock."

Gulliver explained to Mr. Knox that he'd lost something near there. No, he couldn't say what it was. It was personal. But it was absolutely, astronomically crucial he find it, because if he didn't he might lose it forever.

And he couldn't live with himself if that happened.

They rode.

Straddling the seat behind Mr. Knox, Gulliver fused his arms around his boss's butt-log of a waist and clamped his thighs against the quaking, thundering machine, half praying for the old man to slow down, half wishing he'd speed up.

Less than ten minutes after Gulliver had hopped on, Knox had negotiated the bumps and clefts of Loki Lane. The forest throughway terminated at the mammoth limestone formation Loki's Rock, which many thought resembled a cresting tidal wave that had instantaneously calcified. Now a popular teen lovers' hangout—evidenced by all the etchings of "4eva" endearments across the rock's face—it had once served as a shelter for the indigenous Pokahawnees centuries before, until the colonists raided their hunting parties.

Mr. Knox idled his bike, letting his passenger dismount.

Gulliver teetered upon the bone-dry earth, his feet numb from paresthesia. He hobbled around in a circle, restoring circulation to them.

"Sure you don't want me to tag along and help you look?" Knox asked once more. "It gets dark as a bear's asshole in those woods."

"No thanks," Gulliver answered. According to the Giants' instructions—*if you speak to the police or anyone else about this, she will likewise be killed*—he had to go at this alone. Gulliver had even secreted away the map down his pants. He wouldn't need to consult it again until he was out of eyeshot of his boss.

"Well, at least take a flashlight."

Knox unbelted his studded Viking leather saddlebag, pulling a black 3-D Maglite from it. He tossed it to Gulliver.

"How far you gotta go?"

"As far as I have to."

"Alright then. Best of luck."

Gulliver nodded at his boss. Then, upon orienting himself by the location of the pre-gloaming sun in the sky, he sallied forth into the woody depths.

Deputy Eriksen found the metal box underneath the workbench, covered by a sheet of primrose-colored oilcloth with strawberry asteroids on it. Boone thought he might have had a tablecloth just like it at home. Or perhaps that had pears on it. Or bananas. Some fruit, definitely.

"What is it?" asked the deputy, rotating the ice chest-sized box in his hands.

How in hell would I know?, Boone thought. "Don't know," was what he said.

Undeniably, it was one peculiar object, yet another device whose function was not immediately determinable. Six two-foot by two-foot plates of stainless steel, sand-papered to a matte finish, had been masterfully welded together into a very durable cube. A pair of ergonomic handgrips jutted from opposite sides of it. Most perplexing of all, a perfect inscribed circle had been cut out of one of the planes, creating a hole large enough to fit a—

"Best not do that, Carl," the sheriff warned.

Clive. He meant Clive. But Clive didn't catch his gaffe.

The deputy, quite impetuously, had been about to insert his hand into the box's dark hollow before even getting a peek inside. He froze, then, grasping the sagacity of Boone's directive, withdrew his fingers.

Boone fished a silver penlight attached to his jangly key chain from his trouser pocket. He switched it on, aimed the beam into the hole.

Embedded within the box, marginally smaller than it, was a metal hemisphere resembling a flower with the reproductive parts scooped out. It was fabricated from an identical alloy whose segments, dissimilar from its housing, were not bonded together in any way; the "petals" appeared to have been installed independent of each other, the minutest of gaps detectable between them. Why?

Maybe they worked as individual components, Boone hypothesized.

But it was his final observation that startled him most. While it was obvious the inventor kept the device fastidiously clean, Boone's penlight illuminated some residue he must have missed—in one corner, a tiny clump of hoary hairs, some strands stained brown.

Dried blood, was it? Could be some sort of animal trap, Boone supposed.

"Let me have it."

Deputy Eriksen passed the device to the sheriff. As Boone clutched the handgrips, he noted the box was weighted about five pounds heavier on the end with the opening, so one would be most inclined to hold it with that side down. He inspected the finger-molded handles. They weren't fixed in place; rather, each was attached to an inflexible metal rod extending into the box through a vertical slot. Like a lever.

The sheriff countertwisted his wrists, jerking the handles downward with relative ease. This triggered some internal mechanism. Boone felt elements collide powerfully inside, heard the jarring peal of metal smacking metal—indeed much like the sound of a bear trap tripping. He then snapped the handles back into their upright position. The box made an abrasive noise of slowly torquing gears.

"What the hell?" Clive muttered.

Boone now had a very good notion what its function was.

"Bring that lamp over here," he instructed his deputy, pointing to a gooseneck desk lamp sitting on the workbench.

Clive fetched the lamp, but found its cord didn't quite reach where the sheriff stood.

"You can unplug it," Boone said, a bit testily, his coiled nerves getting to him.

Clive brought the unplugged lamp over to him.

"Put the top of it in the hole. And watch your hands."

Gripping the lamp by its rounded base, the deputy obediently inserted the bulb and shade section into the device's opening. Again, Boone flipped the handgrips down. Again, the metal box produced its mechanical clap, accompanied by the resounding crunch of brass and glass.

Deputy Eriksen tried to yank the lamp out. "It's stuck."

The sheriff retracted the handles and the box released its captive. The lamp's head, now mashed and mangled beyond recognition, might pass for a modern art piece in some hoity-toity museum.

"Damn," Clive uttered.

Here it was, their perp's murder weapon—it had to be—way out here in the middle of nothing but miles of godless, or goddamned, hinterland.

Sheriff Boone began to question how sensible it had been to come blindly traipsing into the native territory of a serial killer. Sure, they were four ably armed men against only one demented Thoreauvian tinkerer. Yet Boone still couldn't shake his gut instinct telling him they were at the substantial strategic disadvantage, for this individual possessed a demonstrably above-average intelligence, and a lawman could not under-estimate any adversary with an IQ to be reckoned with.

Boone proffered the death box to his deputy. "Why don't you put this down where you got it. Then go out and tell Quinn to take what's-his-name—Lester—back into town, and to call for reinforcements as soon as he's within radio range.

I want everybody out here full force pronto, including the forensics team from Sulfur Springs. Tell 'em we're gonna need all the evidence kits they got."

Deputy Eriksen nodded, blurting a duteous "Yes, sir!" before volte-facing to carry out the sheriff's bidding. Upon returning the device to its place beneath the workbench, he headed for the door. Opened it.

In a fraction of an instant, affording himself no time to react, Clive saw the tall, square-shouldered figure poised right outside the cabin's threshold. He saw it was attired in forest green military fatigues. And, lastly, he saw its face, a face like that of somebody who didn't know how to wear it properly.

A face that could hardly be described as human.

What Clive did not see was the blade puncturing his stomach, slicing upward, eviscerating him.

Boone, however, witnessed everything in its near totality, a hell-spawned nightmare that unspooled in the blink of his eyes. He'd been far too late drawing his pistol. Deputy Eriksen was already crumpled on the concrete floor, his shirt sopping with the gore gushing from him.

The sheriff aimed his gun at the figure, still wielding the six-inch Buck knife, its whetted steel beaded with Eriksen's blood.

"Drop the knife!"

With the deftest of reflexes, the figure hurled his weapon at Boone. The lawman dodged it by a shaved whisker, the blade sinking into the wooden support beam behind him almost up to its cocobola hilt.

Boone squeezed off a haphazard shot at his would-be assassin, splintering the lintel above the door. The figure fled.

Keeping his gun raised, Sheriff Boone dashed over to his deputy, kneeling down beside him. Blood gurgled from the young man's mouth like an uncorked champagne bottle. His life had drained out of him too, his eyes having gone glazed and dilated.

Damn it, Clive.

As ambitious (and arrogant) as the boy was, he'd never be filling the sheriff's shoes now. Boone considered bestowing his own uniform Oxfords upon the senior deputy to wear when laid to rest. Reckoned that seemed a meaningful thing to do.

Damn you, Crusher.

With white-hot desire for retribution coursing through his veins, Sheriff Boone rose from his crouch and gave chase.

4

Gulliver had walked some thirty-odd minutes at a brisk yet deliberate stride, assiduously counting each step he took.

From Loki's Rock, it had been 147 paces northeast to "Buccaneer's Brook," then 81 paces west to "Dead Deer Reef" (the location literally marked with a decomposing stag carcass) before he steered north 205 paces toward the "Isle of Crossed Swords." Kat was 313 paces northwest of the Crossed Swords, which Gulliver puzzled out to be two top-heavy trees that had toppled into one another.

Not much farther now. He prayed once again he wasn't too late, that he would find Kat un-burnt, un-cured, and un-crushed. That is to say, very much alive.

Turned out Mr. Knox's flashlight came in quite handy. With the sun now abutting the horizon, it had dipped below the tree line, casting the dense woodlands into even denser murk. It'd be night soon, and Gulliver shuddered to imagine how bumbling his quest would have been without the Maglite to read the map by in the all-encompassing dark.

Still, the flashlight's beam was not enough to dispel the pall of fear overshadowing him. The fear of what he would find. Or what he wouldn't find. Or what would find him.

Only 40 more paces to go.

His quickening heart was spurring him to break into a mad, desperate sprint, but he couldn't risk compromising his count lest he might miss the denoted spot and miss finding Kat. So Gulliver did not deviate from his steady, purposeful gait.

295… 296… 297… 298… 299…

Gulliver halted at the three hundredth step.

Sprawled before him was a rugged expanse of golden-brown gneissic rock, what appeared to be an extremely eroded dissected plateau with the dimensions of a hockey rink. Fractured prolifically throughout its surface area, it resembled a swath of dry, cracked skin. Coniferous trees, stunted and malformed, grew from some of the fissures, like a graveyard of wild cancerous bonsai.

Gulliver stepped up onto this natural stone platform and completed his paces. It led him to a canted, almost recumbent spruce, gaping down the middle from its uppermost crook to its bared roots, as if having been slit open centuries ago and left there to very slowly die. A hank of thick, knotted climber's rope hung from a gnarled branch.

Gulliver peered into the five-foot-wide crevasse from which the tree sprouted. Its roots clung to both sides of the rock face, stretching downward into a mysterious black void—the only place where Kat could be concealed and confined.

"Hello?" he called, aiming the flashlight into the chasm. The ray only illuminated more of the ravine's ogeed sides.

"Kat! Are you down there?"

"Yes," answered a hoarse, quivery voice. "I'm down here! Help me!"

Gulliver gulped, overcome with a combination of relief and concern. "Are you hurt?"

"No," came Kat's muffled reply. "Just really c-cold."

"Hold on, Kat! I'm going to get you out!"

Kat didn't respond.

Gulliver did not hesitate to act. He reached above him and snatched the looped climber's rope from the tree limb, then unwound it into the crevasse until he felt it slacken. About thirty feet deep, he estimated.

"I tossed you a rope. Did you get it?"

Again, he heard no response.

"Kat? Did you—"

"Got it!" she finally shouted.

"That's good. Grab on as tight as you can. I'll pull you up as soon as you're ready."

Gulliver felt the rope tauten from her weight. "Okay. I'm ready!"

The torrents of adrenaline hurtling through him enabled Gulliver to hoist Kat up near effortlessly. She materialized from the darkness of the crevasse, using her legs to help ascend Batman-fashion up the side while Gulliver continued hauling her out.

"Take my hand!" he urged.

She gripped his proffered hand, and he lifted her towards him. She planted both feet onto the rock ledge and ensured her balance by grasping Gulliver's shoulders. She was free!

And exhausted. Kat leaned against Gulliver's chest. Her eyes were sunken and crusty from jags of crying, her cheeks smudged with muddy mascara. The strapless red cocktail dress she wore was damp to the touch, her purple and white striped tights soiled and torn at the knees. No shoes sheathed her feet.

Gulliver wrapped his arms around her waist. She shivered.

"Everything's going to be fine," Gulliver soothed her. "You're safe now."

I saved you, he thought.

"Thank you," Kat said.

"You're welcome, Kat."

Her distress ebbing, only now did she regard him as someone she recognized.

"Gulliver?"

"Yes. It's me."

"How… how did you find me?"

"I'll explain later." How would he explain how he had found her? Her kidnapper furnished him with a map, simple enough. He would not mention the Giants though. And he'd just feign ignorance as to why *he* had been the one chosen to liberate her, so she wouldn't think him crazy (again).

"How about we get you away from here first?"

Kat nodded. She took his hand.

Gulliver smiled at her, then turned to lead them the way back—

"Well, looky here," boomed a familiar voice. "Now ain't this a surprise?"

Sheriff Boone crept from the cabin, his pistol cocked, swiveling it in his trembling hand. His heart hammered, his breaths expelled in droughty gusts.

He was not afraid of death. Only the causes of it. Some causes more so than others.

Such as at the whim of a cold-blooded lunatic.

Night had settled over the forest. A waxing gibbous moon emitted barely enough light to see by, while also accentuating all the amorphous patches of blackness among the trees, beyond any of which might be lurking the evildoer.

Boone flicked on his flashlight and vigilantly scanned the surrounding woods with its beam. It caught two figures lying motionless on the ground twenty feet to his right.

He approached the bodies of Deputy McQuinn and Mr. Krabbock. Their limbs overlapped like macabre fiddlesticks, their mouths yawning in silenced screams.

The sheriff inspected them long enough to determine they were both quite dead, marinating in their own blood-soaked clothes. McQuinn looked to have been stabbed through the intestines, Krabbock in the throat.

Expert kills. This was not good.

Boone hastily assessed his situation and weighed his options—dire and few, respectively. While the perp no longer had his Buck knife, no doubt he must have other weapons at his immediate disposal, or he could as easily improvise one from nature's bounty of lethal objects. Boone could hightail it the hell out of there, but he suspected the woodlands-savvy perp would hunt him down, the sheriff providing all the challenge of a myopic deer in a House of Mirrors.

The alternative would be for Boone to go on the offensive, track the perp down like any seasoned lawman would. This had much the same drawbacks as running away, although Boone reckoned he'd at least stand a more fighting chance to dodge any deathblows thrust, swung, or slung at him.

Or he could stay put and wait for the perp to come to him. Boone froze and listened, only hearing the rustling of the trees and his own clipped breaths.

He considered the villain might have already made good his escape, vanishing into No Man's Land, hereafter banished to the sheriff's Unsolved Case file. It would be the lone such blemish in Boone's illustrious, evanescing career.

Screw this waiting.

The sheriff circumambulated the exterior of the cabin to reconnoiter the rear. (A textbook precaution he had neglected to perform when they had arrived at the scene; an inexcusable oversight, for which he'd later reprimand himself. Memory permitting.)

Right now, he was eyeing the outhouse.

He closed in on the setback structure. It had been cobbled together with handcut pinewood planks, with a corrugated sheet of rusted metal for a roof. Its unpainted plywood door, with a hoop of twine serving as a handle, was shut.

Boone positioned himself five feet from the door, his gun trained on it at about somebody's stomach level. Or head level, if they were seated.

"If you're in there, come out slow, with your hands raised high."

Something thumped inside.

Every muscle in Boone's body snapped rigid, electrified with alarm.

"I won't hesitate to shoot if you give me reason to."

No response issued from the crapper.

The sheriff inhaled, filling his diaphragm with the crisp night air, then exhaled through his pursed lips, trying to purge himself of the stark fear infecting him. In all his years in law enforcement, he had never shot anybody. Nothing had ever transpired in Laymon that called for so drastic a measure as discharging a firearm at a person.

This perp wasn't a person, Boone reminded himself. He was a monster. A man-hunter.

"I'll give ya to the count of three to show yourself, before I start express-mailing bullets your way. There's ONE."

The outhouse stood quiet.

"There's TWO."

Despite the chill, a trickle of sweat skied down the bridge of the sheriff's nose. He clasped his finger around the pistol's trigger. Girded himself.

"And there's THREE!"

Sheriff Boone lunged forward, gripping the outhouse door's crude rope handle and jerking it open. (He couldn't countenance shooting a potentially unarmed man, monster though he may be.)

A feculent stench assaulted the lawman instead, the bench within unoccupied except for a rowdy wingding of bottle flies.

Boone heard a *whoosh* and a *thud* behind him.

Damn! The perp had gotten the drop on him.

His survival instinct kicking in, the sheriff flung himself behind the latrine's flimsy door, shielding his body from a billowing jet of orange heat rushing at him.

After ten seconds, like the spent breath of a fire-breathing dragon, the geyser of flames receded. The side of the wood door facing away from Boone smoldered and crackled.

Sensing his opportunity, the sheriff poked his upper body out from behind the scorched door, aimed his pistol at his attacker, and returned fire of his own.

The perp stood in a shallow dug bunker braced with logs, which had been hidden beneath a hinged panel of particleboard, well disguised with forest soil and detritus epoxied to it. He wielded a homemade flame-cannon, assembled from metal plumbing pipes, a fire extinguisher's tank, and the bell of a trombone.

The sheriff's bullet punctured the cannon's tank, igniting the leaking fuel. The ensuing blast, in turn, ignited the perp's clothing.

The perp screamed, or rather, shrieked in unmitigated terror. He hurled the flamethrower away from himself, leapt out of the bunker, and dove onto the ground, rolling around until all the flames swimming on him had been smothered.

The perp then sprang to his feet and, without faltering a step, began running away.

"Stop!" Boone barked.

The perp ignored him.

Boone at that moment cast off any qualms he had about shooting an unarmed individual. Not one this disturbed and dangerous. The sheriff popped off a couple of rapid shots at better than twenty feet. The first hit the retreating perp in the left shoulder, twirling him clockwise. The next demolished his right kneecap. He toppled sideways, striking the ground with a pained "*oof.*" He groaned through gritted teeth, incapable of moving lest brutal jolts of agony wrack his damaged joints.

The sheriff eased toward his wounded foe, his pistol unwavering. He hovered over him. Flicked on his penlight.

"What in God's name are you?" the sheriff muttered.

The perp's entire head, this being the sole part of him that was not garbed in hunting apparel, was horribly disfigured, mottled with striated layers of scar tissue, as if all the flesh had once melted off it and was amateurishly reshaped with a putty spatula. No hair sprouted from his skin, not even eyelashes. Nor did he—presuming it was a "he"—possess a recognizable nose, lips, or ears, only the cranial vents indicating where they should have been. This was one ugly bastard, Boone ruled, a verdict that perfectly correlated with its hideous deeds.

"Who are you?" the sheriff asked.

The perp croaked a name, then sobbed pitifully.

His tears were wasted on Boone.

"Pardon me for followin' ya out here," said Mr. Knox, "but you stoked my curiosity."

"I found her," Gulliver trumpeted, pointing out Kat there beside him.

"I see that alright," Knox answered, clucking his tongue appreciatively. "And what a fine find she is."

Knox moseyed up to them. "I knew you were a little briny in the brainpan, Huggens," he said, shaking his head, "but I never would've pegged you for *this* sort of thing."

Gulliver had no idea what his boss was talking about, but he was glad to see him all the same. It had gotten dark—indeed, dark as a "bear's asshole"—and Knox could lend able assistance guiding them out of the woods.

"She was taken," Gulliver explained. "I rescued her."

"You don't have to bullshit me. I understand *everything*." He gave Gulliver a conspiratorial nod. "And it's okay."

Knox's bolstering words bemused Gulliver. Even Kat, with a tilt of her head, appeared confused. Suspicious.

"Can you help me out, Mr. Knox?"

"It'll be my pleasure." He winked at Gulliver.

Knox circumnavigated Kat, appraising her lecherously. "You done shanghaied yourself a hot piece of ass, Gulv."

"Wha-huh-ah?" Gulliver gabbled. Mr. Knox believed *he* had kidnapped Kat? How could he? "No, s-sir. It wasn't me. I didn't take her." Then, to the muddled Kat, to pacify her: "I swear I didn't."

"Hey, I don't blame you one bit for wanting to bang this."

Knox grabbed the gluteal fold of Kat's right buttock and squeezed. Kat gasped, startled.

What was happening here?

"Mr. Knox! Stop it!"

"What's wrong, son?" His large, strong, ass-pawing hand clasped Gulliver's shoulder—a fatherly gesture. "Oh, you done wanted her all to yourself, did ya?"

Gulliver's head reeled with stupefaction. "I j-just want to g-g-get her home."

"Too late for that. She's seen you. That's why I throw a bag over their heads when I go log-jamming."

Bag?... Log-jamming?... Gulliver recalled hearing about the Potato Sack Rapist in the newspaper and on TV.

He gawked at his boss, speechless.

Thinking, oh God no God no.

"You're in the soup, Gulliver, but I'm gonna get you out of this, don't you worry. You and me, we share the same tastes in pussycats. How we like to play with them. All I want is, 'fore we bundle her up and put her where no one's gonna find her, is to have me a tumble with her myself. Deal?"

"No. You can't—"

Knox was already panting down Kat's neck like a horny bull who would not be denied its heifer.

"Let me at those suckalicious titties," he growled, reaching around and cupping one of her breasts. Twisting it. Kat yelped.

"Don't touch her!" Gulliver seized Knox's offending arm and wrenched it off Kat.

With his free hand, his boss clamped Gulliver's wrist and bent it backwards. Pain launched up Gulliver's arm, causing him to wince and whimper.

"Don't be selfish, boy. And don't be stupid."

Gathering her wits, Kat made her break, dashing for the trees.

"Aw, hell!" Knox exclaimed. "She's gettin' away!"

He was smiling.

Knox caught up with her in half a dozen strides, latching onto a tress of her bedraggled hair and yanking her down onto all fours, hardly exerting himself at all. Like tackling a sex doll, Knox thought as he peeled up her skirt. He knelt behind her and gleefully ripped her blue thong at the crotch.

Knox unbuckled his snakeskin belt, breathing bestially.

Kat spat out a preemptive anguished bawl, clutching her fingers around a tree root so tightly her knuckles split.

Before Knox could ravish her, Gulliver skulked up from behind and bashed him upside the skull with a chunk of gray basalt he had picked up. Knox's head fulcrummed to the left, a runnel of blood seeping from his temple. The blow, though, hadn't fazed the thewy biker much; rather it seemed merely to irritate him. Gulliver may as well have been a mosquito.

With a forcible swipe of his arm, Knox swatted the rock out of Gulliver's hands. He rose to his full, imposing height and spun around, nostrils flaring, a blizzard of anger raging in his eyes.

Gulliver took several stumbling steps back away from him, this maybe a hundred steps too few.

Mr. Knox catapulted himself the distance separating him and Gulliver, slamming the younger man in the jaw with a fist approximating a cannonball. Gulliver heard something crack, possibly a tooth, followed by a shrill chiming in his skull.

Sometime between the landing of the punch and the realignment of his sight, Gulliver had somehow gotten laid out on the rock deck near the crevasse where he'd extracted Kat. He hurt all over.

Knox barreled toward him, snagging him by the collar and heaving him up against the leaning spruce tree.

"Guess I was too quick in figuring you, Huggens. That's my mistake, and I'm gonna have to live with it."

Gulliver gazed into his boss's gristly moonlit face. It had become unrecognizable, degenerating into something atavistic, savage. Behind those maniacal eyes, Gulliver could now see Knox's innermost demons cavorting with depraved abandon.

"I promise I'll bury you and your bitch in the same hole. Nice and romantic like."

Mr. Knox's fingers interlocked around Gulliver's throat and began strangling the life out of him.

Gulliver writhed, trying vainly to pry off Knox's hands with his own while his lungs pleaded for oxygen. He grew more and more faint with each passing second. Pixels of light burst in his brain, then faded. Thousands of them at first, then scarcely any at all.

Gulliver realized he was dying.

He shut his eyes, not wishing his old friend's merciless visage to be the final image he witnessed in this world. Instead, he thought of Kat... she would be the most beautiful angel in all of paradise hereafter... she would forgive him for failing her... they would love each other for eternity... they would... he hoped... was there... sex in... heaven?...

And then Mr. Knox's iron grip loosened, the pressure on Gulliver's trachea lessened. He gulped down snatches of sweet, resuscitating air.

Gulliver opened his eyes again. Wide.

His boss's head was being squeezed, vise-like, between a pair of colossal hands twice the size of Mr. Knox's (which, by further comparison, were almost twice the size of Gulliver's). Knox's eyes bulged grotesquely from their sockets, his teeth clenched with such suffering force his gums bled. He produced a sound through them best described as a mix of air raid siren and an out-of-tune bagpipe. Blood dribbled from his nostrils. Then his head caved in like an imploding basketball. Pulpy gore and gray matter oozed between those humongous fingers.

Knox's sadistic grin had been turned sideways.

The biker's hands fell away from Gulliver's neck, and his body fell into the slick-walled rift beside them. The last orifice the Potato Sack Rapist would ever penetrate.

Gulliver cowered against the tree before the *lusus naturae* that'd fortuitously intervened in his demise-in-progress. From its abominably massive size, to its abominably unruly hair, to its abominably tattered red tracksuit, this was a man-creature the likes of which Gulliver had never encountered outside of storybooks or bad dreams.

Which, in Gulliver's mind, could mean only one thing.

"Are y-you a—" he stammered.

"Cannndeee," the he-beast interjected.

"Uh… What?"

"Caaandy!" it bellowed, taking a menacing step toward Gulliver, wriggling its porky fingers at him like mutant nine-inch long larvae.

Candy? It wanted candy?

"Candy! Candy! Candy!"

Yes, it did.

Gulliver geared up to run, a doubtlessly futile, probably fatal recourse. Then he remembered the Decadent Darla's he still had on him from his clash with the Micronians. He reached into his pocket, fished the squashed snack cakes out. Offered them to the ogre.

"H-how about this? You like chocolate cake?"

It moaned voraciously, drooling.

Rather than allowing it to get any closer, Gulliver tossed the cakes to the tremendous brute. It caught the package in its skillet-sized mitts, tore off the plastic wrap, and gobbled up the twin Swiss rolls in one gluttonous bite.

It then smiled at him.

Gulliver interpreted this as gratitude. He smiled in return, as he was equally grateful to still be alive.

"Are you a Giant?" Gulliver asked.

"Hu-eeeee," it answered.

Gulliver knitted his brow. "U-E?"

"Huey," it repeated, patting its boat's-hull chest.

Okay. The Giant's name must be Huey. Sure. Why not?

"I'm Gulliver."

"Guh-ivver," the Giant enunciated, attempting to duplicate the spoken syllables.

"That's right." Gulliver paused, not really knowing how to carry on a conversation with a heretofore purely mythological being, and one not very communicative at that, nor, seemingly, very bright.

"Well… umm… Thank you for helping me. Huey."

Huey the Giant simpered gauchely.

For several moments they regarded one another like two actors who had forgotten whose line came next.

"Gotta go now!" Huey blurted.

Gulliver nodded, though he didn't think it was asking for his permission.

The Giant then bobble-bounded off into the forest with all the determination of somebody with somewhere to go and something to do. Perhaps to report back to his clan, informing them that their territory has been secured, that the Micronian threat had been neutralized.

Gulliver re-found Kat a few feet away from where Knox had assaulted her. She sat on the ground, hunched against a tree, her eyes closed.

"Kat?"

He stooped down in front of her. She opened her eyes and stared lazily at him.

"Gulliver," she murmured. "Your town sucks."

"I know. Sorry."

"It's alright. I'm used to it."

"Come on. Let's go."

Kat nodded wearily. Gulliver slipped his arm beneath hers, elevating her to her feet.

He then began walking her home.

5

Kat had not stopped shivering. It was getting worse, almost convulsive.

Gulliver fretted she might be going into shock. Other credible infirmities also occurred to him: dehydration, hypothermia, poisoning, trauma either physical or emotional. At the very least, she'd been bruised, abraded, and manhandled. She required medical attention, stat.

He had planned to flag down a vehicle once they had reached the main road, hitching them a ride to the 24-hour urgent care clinic located on the town line between Laymon and Sulfur Springs. Problem was, the "main road" was actually a minor one. More of a detour, really, off Route 33, and thus not much travelled. Finding transportation might prove to be an unrealistic goal, and hiking all the way to the clinic in Kat's uncertain condition was inadvisable.

Still in possession of the Giants' map and Knox's Maglite, Gulliver had been able to retrace his paces back to Loki's Rock without much difficulty.

Mr. Knox had left his Harley parked there in the clearing, but not his keys.

Gulliver could run back, climb down into that hole, and find the keys on Knox's corpse. While that endeavor would be disagreeable enough, he'd also have to leave Kat out there in the open by herself, in the dark, in the cold.

Gulliver had a better idea. Rooting through Knox's leather saddlebag, he uncovered a Phillips screwdriver and a torque wrench. After exposing the bike's switch wires, in five minutes he figured out how to bypass the ignition and start it up.

He mounted the Harley, helped Kat on board the seat behind him, and off they went.

Sort of.

Gulliver had never been the consummate student when Mr. Knox had given him a few riding lessons years before, and his lackluster skills then were that much rustier now. Under his control, the bike pitched and yawed along Loki Lane, like riding a pony with a bum fore and hind leg.

Once they turned onto the service road (which no longer had any services on it), he was able to open up the throttle—to about forty-five mph. Still, it was over forty miles better than if they had walked it, and without the physical exertion.

Gulliver tried not to dwell on Kat's arms hugging his abdomen, her thighs straddling his trunk, her cheek nuzzled between his shoulder blades. Oh, how he tried! It made operating the motorcycle not only considerably more awkward than he remembered, but also his fear of crashing not near as intense.

Within twenty minutes, they had arrived at the clinic. Gulliver drove the bike up to the automatic entrance doors, parking it in the No Parking zone. He assisted Kat off the seat and shepherded her into the building.

The fluorescent-lit reception area was so bright, both of them squinted upon entering, the "Arctic Ozone" scent of Sgt. Sparkles Industrial Floor Wax overpowering enough to make the woozy Kat wobbly again. Gulliver, supporting her by the arm, steered her toward the nurse's desk.

Instead of an orthodox RN uniform, the young woman behind the desk wore a decidedly unorthodox Sexy Marie Antoinette costume. A mini corset dress with gold satin ruche and flared filigreed sleeves constricted her already svelte figure, thigh-high stockings with purple bows enwrapped her legs, and a rosette headpiece for the queen's signature piled coif topped off the flamboyant ensemble.

"I went to a masquerade party tonight," she explained, giggling. "Didn't have time to change before starting my shift here."

Gulliver hadn't asked.

He did convey the details of their harrowing experience, then enumerated all of the potential injuries and afflictions Kat may have sustained as a consequence, however trifling (up to and including forest lice).

Nurse Marie—that *was* her legal given name, she had told them, *hee hee*—sprang into action with bureaucratic efficiency and regal poise. She handed Kat a clipboard of paperwork to fill out, then bustled off to consult with the MD on duty.

Gulliver escorted Kat gently by the elbow to one of the modular fiberglass chairs in the waiting room. They sat down together. Kat loosely held the pen, attached to the clipboard by a metal beaded chain, flittering the nib above the personal info section.

"Want me to do that for you?" Gulliver asked.

Kat nodded and passed him the clipboard. Gulliver cycled through the questions on the forms—name and address, phone and email, insurance carrier, preexisting medical conditions, drug allergies, et al—and recorded her answers on the blank lines or in the empty boxes. When he got to her emergency contact, she shrugged.

"I don't got nobody here," she said. "I guess there's Becky, but I don't have her number on me." Kat looked at Gulliver with her glassy, yet still so sensuous, eyes. "Why don't you put yourself down?"

"Okay." Gulliver blushed a bit as he wrote down his name, address, and phone number on Kat's medical form, a gesture tantamount, he felt, to a ratification of their friendship.

And maybe more than that, he wished.

A short while after Gulliver had handed off the completed forms to Nurse Marie, a matronly woman emerged from a side door, robed in a white lab coat at least one size too large for her, the earbuds of a stethoscope poking out of its pocket. She appeared to be makeup-less, with a Joan of Arc haircut. She introduced herself as Doctor Brock.

"Miss Klugerschmidt?" she addressed Kat.

Kat nodded. Gulliver noticed Nurse Marie talking on the phone behind the desk, reading from Kat's paperwork.

"If you come along with me," invited the doctor, "I can have a look at you."

Kat rose from her chair, Gulliver mirroring her.

The doctor regarded him. "Sir, do you need somebody to examine you?" She pointed toward his bruised jaw. "Looks like you dinged your fender."

"No, thank you, ma'am. I'm okay. I'm just... with her. We're together."

Doctor Brock smiled at him. "I see. Well, feel free to stick around. Nurse Marie will notify you as soon as I've checked her over, alright?"

"Alright." Gulliver rubbed Kat's shoulder. "I'll wait here for you." He uttered this with an inflection that made it sound more like a question.

"I'd like that," Kat responded, and he could tell she meant it.

Doctor Brock led her away through the side door into the clinic's exam rooms.

Gulliver, much too anxious to sit back down, explored the antiseptic space around him, appraising everything from the pearl-speckled floor tiles, to the potted ferns, to the Bob Ross-inspired Happy Little Mountain landscapes adorning the walls. Only as he stared at his own reflection in the glass pane of the clinic's windowfront did Gulliver ruminate over how he had lost everything this day—his home, his job, all his personal effects and family possessions.

All his little friends.

Yet he had not been reduced to some miserable wretch, bemoaning his plight.

Because he had found Kat.

Life could be like that, Gulliver waxed philosophical. Lots of ruined bits and pieces. Then, in the rubble, you uncover an untarnished article of incontestable beauty, of priceless value, of sentimental import. We are all the archaeologists of our own lives, always seeking out those artifacts that give our life worth.

That make us happy to be alive at all.

After the sheriff had taken the perp out of commission, getting away from that far-flung charnel house proved surprisingly easy.

Inside the cabin, Boone had learned (as its inhabitant had become quite cooperative, even docile, upon his incapacitation and capture), was a souped-up ham radio capable of receiving and transmitting frequencies up to a hundred miles away. With it, the sheriff was able to contact not only his men at the station, but also the state police headquarters in Gabriel Ridge, which maintained one of the few helicopters in the region equipped for rescue operations. Boone apprised them of the situation and did his best to describe his whereabouts, using general compass directions and natural landmark positions— i.e., the Devil's Horns—which he had shrewdly jotted down in a notepad on their journey to the location.

Within an hour, the helicopter's thirty million-candle searchlight illuminated the cabin like a nuclear blast. Sheriff Boone and the perp were airlifted via basket stretcher into the craft. Two Gabriel Ridge officers remained behind to secure the crime scene. The victims would be removed later, after the forensic team did its job.

While he had been waiting for assistance to come, Boone covered Deputy McQuinn and Lester Krabbock's bodies with blankets from the cabin, Deputy Eriksen's with a sheet of white muslin off the Shinto screen. Their first-aid kit missing, he had to bandage up the perp's bloody wounds with bath towels and masking tape.

The killer had become increasingly loquacious, so much so Boone had to interrupt to Mirandize him. The perp then resumed his confession, unburdening himself of his sins, his diabolical secrets revealed like they were game show prizes. It was all very enlightening, though it changed nothing. Six people died by his hand, and he would have to answer for all of them. Answers that would not bring anybody back.

The helicopter landed on the rooftop helipad of Saint Wilhelmina Hospital in Harbor Heights. The perp's gunshot wounds were treated, and he was assigned a windowless room in the cloister ward with an armed guard posted at the door.

After he had called his wife to tell her he was okay, Sheriff Boone gave his official chronicle of events to the Gabriel Ridge chief of police, some of the finer details requiring almost Aristotelian mental effort on his part to recount. Boone didn't relish passing the reins of the investigation over to the Staties, and maybe even to the Feds, but this was standard operating procedure in higher-profile homicide cases. Little guys fought in the trenches, the big boys got the glory of winning the war.

As a professional courtesy, they had not cut him out entirely. The Gabriel Ridge chief did toss Boone some scraps to chew on: compile all witness and evidence materials thus far gathered by the Laymon PD for delivery to state and federal investigators, contact the families of Deputies Eriksen and McQuinn to notify them the men had been killed in the line of duty, and hereafter report any new relevant information he might obtain to the honchos who had hijacked his case.

And that, aside from any court appearances he'd be called upon to make, would be the end of Boone's involvement in the

Crusher case, and with it, his career.

He was done. He knew it. Besides possessing neither the physical stamina nor the mnemonic retention for the job anymore, he realized he no longer had the stomach for it either. Maybe he never had it for this degree of atrocity. Sleuthing gruesome murders committed by a monstrous modern-day Thomas Edison—would any lawman consider this a high water mark in his crime-fighting compendium? Probably, yes.

Right now, though, all Cyrus Roy Boone looked forward to was sitting out the rest of his time here on this Earth, drinking his wife's lemonade while watching the birds frolic in the trees. Even if he couldn't remember any of their names, Lorna would be there to remind him. And they would both be happy, and that'd be all that mattered.

That'd be enough for him.

One of the Gabriel Ridge troopers drove Sheriff Boone back to Laymon in a shiny black Ford Explorer, unmarked except for the stroboscopic light bar that could turn any nighttime traffic stop into a roadside discothèque. During the trip, Boone reviewed his notes, going over everything the perp had disclosed to him.

At some point he must have dozed off, for he was abruptly awakened by the yips of the SUV's siren and the trooper's yells of "git outta mah way!"

They were outside the Laymon police station, where more minions of the press had congregated. Six network news vans were parked at the curbs—one national, two local, and three cable (including UHN☹, the Unhappy Ending Network, producers of the hit reality show "Yow! That's Gotta Hurt"). A couple of pretty-faced reporters relayed with dramatic panache this story of small-town ugliness. The nondescript Explorer passed them by unmolested up until it had turned into the fenced-in lot behind the sheriff's building. One plucky young newslady dashed toward the vehicle, shouting out questions and thunking her handheld microphone against the smoke-tinted window where Boone sat. He had no comments to make, so instead waved at her in respectful acknowledgment, until the remote-controlled gate shut her out.

Inside the station it was, as expected, frenetic in activity and, just as expected, somber in mood. Darkcloud and Cavett watched Sheriff Boone enter, their doleful eyes expressing all that needn't be said. Both deputies were fielding the unceasing telephone calls from journalists, citizens, and the occasional psychic marketing their paranormal detective services. By happenstance, on this day, as permitted by the Freedom of Faith Observance clause in his contract, Darkcloud was attired in full ceremonial sachem regalia to commemorate some Pokahawnee holiday. Something to do with the Great Beaver Spirit, Boone vaguely remembered. Paying no mind to all the feathers, furs, and bones bedecking the man, the sheriff gave the deputy a list of instructions: to solicit auxiliary manpower from the Sulfur Springs PD, to verify some facts he had acquired from the perp, and to bring in a person of interest for questioning.

With that done, Boone retired to his office. He flopped down into his chair and, wrangling the last of his fortitude, made the two most difficult phone calls of his life, those to the families of Deputies Eriksen and McQuinn. How do you tell somebody their son, husband, or brother is dead? Boone didn't know, yet he did it anyway. As their superior, Eriksen and McQuinn's blood was on his hands too.

Afterward, the sheriff shut the ringer off and closed his eyes, falling asleep to the languid beat of his own tired heart.

"Mister Huggens?"

Gulliver turned away from the window. The orotund voice behind him had come from a policeman who resembled

Burt Reynolds from his *Smokey and the Bandit* days. He wasn't wearing the sandstone beige uniform of the Laymon PD, but rather the Prussian blue duds of the Sulfur Springs precinct. Another officer in an identical outfit, presumably this one's partner and nearly his doppelgänger, conferred with Nurse Marie at the desk. He twiddled her puffy gold sleeve with his fingers. She giggled.

"Yes," Gulliver answered. "That's me."

"I need you to accompany me to the station."

"Why?"

"Just to ask you a few questions, and take your statement about what happened to you and your girlfriend tonight."

"She wanted me to wait here for her—"

"She's in good hands, sir. Don't worry."

"But I promised her I'd stay," Gulliver persisted. "Can't I do my statement here?"

"No, sir."

"Why not?"

"This is not a request, Mister Huggens. You *have* to come with me."

"No." Gulliver shook his head. "I said I promised her. I'm not leaving."

"You either come along with me voluntarily, or I'll be forced to take you into custody."

Gulliver blinked as if he just had pollen blown into his eyes. He whiffled his lips in indignation. "Am I b-b-being arrested?"

"You are being detained for questioning. So please, don't make this any more difficult than it has to be." The officer overtly placed a hand on the silver cuffs he carried on his belt. His partner eyed them from the reception area.

Gulliver stood there stunned. "I really don't understand" was all he could mutter.

"It's okay, sir. Now if you please." The officer gestured toward the exit. "I won't ask you again."

The bewildered Gulliver nodded resignedly and allowed himself to be ushered into the S.S. patrol car parked outside, with its pistol-packing Pepé Le Pew emblem emblazoned on each of its front doors.

On the way out, all Gulliver could think about, all he really cared about, was if Kat would pardon his absence when she was discharged from the clinic. He couldn't help feeling he was abandoning her when she needed him most.

He hoped she would give him the chance to apologize, to vindicate himself. To set things right. To live happily ever after like they did in fairy tales.

Then, of course, this was no longer a fairy tale.

The fairies, as Kat called them, were all dead.

Morning broke. The Sulfur Springs officer—who had never formally introduced himself—chauffeured Gulliver, locked in the patrol car's backseat behind a partition of bulletproof glass, to Laymon police headquarters.

Upon reaching downtown, they cruised into what'd be considered, by Laymon's standards, pandemonium. Reporters mobbed the street, many holding microphones in front of ENG cameras, some of whom Gulliver recognized from TV. They flocked around the car, volleying questions at him: "Who are you?" "Are you under arrest?" "What's your involvement in the Crusher case?" The S.S. officer told him not to answer, just to ignore them, and keep his eyes faced forward. Gulliver did as he was advised, but felt he was being awfully impolite.

Officer No Name radioed in their arrival, and the tall entry gate adjacent to the station building opened. The car swung into the lot and parked near the rear entrance.

The officer let Gulliver out of the backseat and escorted him inside.

The interior of the station wasn't quite as hectic as it had been outside. Gulliver spotted one Laymon deputy, three more S.S. cops, and a pair of gray-suited men with mousse-molded hair. For some reason, there was also an Indian, all togged out like he was the keynote speaker at a Rainmakers Convention. Most everybody was on a phone.

Officer No Name brought Gulliver before the Laymon deputy, seated at a desk with a Spirograph pattern of coffee rings on it. They waited until the deputy hung up his phone.

"Gulliver Huggens," the S.S. officer announced.

The deputy, whose face was as pasty and bloodless as Dracula's, nodded and said, "I'll take him back."

Gulliver was led through the squad room and down a short corridor with only two doors. One was to the restroom. He was ushered through the other door into a small, cream-colored space, furnished with a plain wooden table and a few folding chairs. An interrogation room.

"Have a seat," the deputy directed.

Gulliver complied.

"Care for coffee? Water?"

"No, thank you."

"Wait here. The sheriff will be with you soon."

Gulliver nodded and the deputy withdrew from the room, shutting the door behind him.

An hour passed. Then another fifteen minutes. Perhaps more. There was nothing to read, nothing to even look at of any lengthy interest. A lone window with a view of an alley where miscellaneous construction materials were stowed served as the feature presentation. Gulliver grew antsy, chewed down his cuticles.

While he wasn't under arrest—not yet—he still felt like a prisoner. One who was innocent of any wrongdoing. Mostly. He wondered what they would pin on him.

Gulliver was directing his attentions to scraping the forest dirt off the soles of his sneakers when the sheriff finally entered

SAWNEY HATTON

the room, followed by one of the gray-suited men with the stiff hair.

The sheriff had puckered pink sacs beneath his half-open eyes. He appeared as if he had just woken up from hibernation.

"Mr. Huggens," he rasped. "I'm Sheriff Boone."

Boone extended his hand, and Gulliver shook it.

"Sorry to keep you waiting so long. It's been a trying day."

"For-me-too," Gulliver spurted. He hadn't been prepared for such a hospitable salutation.

"This here's Special Agent Rhodes of the FBI," said Boone, referring to the gray-suited man who now stood against the far wall. The two stuffed shirts had arrived only thirty minutes prior. While the sheriff had anticipated the Feds would meddle in the case, they seemed more intent on drinking coffee and texting on their cell phones than providing any perceptible investigative expertise.

"He's gonna be observing our interview, alright?"

Gulliver nodded.

Agent Rhodes was typing something on his Blackberry.

The sheriff settled into a chair opposite Gulliver, laid a red file folder on the tabletop, and flipped open his pad of notes.

"We have a lot to talk about."

Gulliver agreed. Everything that had happened with Kat, and Mr. Knox, and the Giants—it was this king-sized cabinet of unpleasant curiosities he needed to describe, even if he couldn't really explain it all. The truth, as they say, is frequently stranger than fiction. And it often bled as profusely.

"Can you tell me how Kat is doing?"

Boone screwed up his eyes in puzzlement. "Your cat?"

"No," Gulliver replied. "Katrina Klugerschmidt. The girl I took to the urgent care clinic... She was attacked tonight."

"Oh. Yes." The sheriff riffled through his folder. "Sorry. I don't know how she is. But I can have somebody check for you, after we're done here."

Gulliver nodded, but appeared no less ill at ease.

"We've got the facts just about figured," Boone continued. "And there are things you should know. Better it comes from me than some boorish newshawk hunting for a quote from you at two in the mornin', right?"

Gulliver again concurred, although now he had no idea what the sheriff was talking about.

Boone consulted the file folder.

"You had stated previously that some large individual—a 'giant'—had murdered your neighbor, Mrs. Jensen."

"Yes."

"Well, it weren't no giant that killed her, Mr. Huggens. Nor the others."

Gulliver batted his eyelids, incredulous. "Sure it was." Was the sheriff playing some sort of mental gambit with him?

"No, we can now reasonably say it wasn't... It was your brother. Dale."

"My bro—?" The sheriff might as well have slapped him with a slice of cold ham and told him it was the Mooseneck Lake Monster's flipper. "My brother's dead."

"No, he isn't. I realize that must come as quite the shock to you."

"It's not a shock. It's not true."

"We confirmed it with your aunt." Boone checked his notepad. "Augusta."

The sheriff cleared his throat before proceeding.

"Your brother didn't die in that car accident with your parents. But he was seriously injured. Disfigured. He spent several weeks in a children's burn unit, then months more in a convalescent home down in Tupelo. When he was set to be discharged, your aunt didn't want him. Claimed he'd become an 'abomination of God.' Which we assume meant she could not bear the sight of him. So your brother was consigned to a special living facility in Colorado. For what it's worth, your aunt did send him a Christmas card every year while he was there."

Gulliver scoffed at this. "Aunt Augusta would've told me."

"Well, she didn't. Thought it would be easier for you, a kid at the time, to handle your brother being dead and gone rather than what he'd become. Anyways, when your brother turned eighteen and was no longer a ward of the state, he left Colorado and returned to Laymon."

"You're wrong," Gulliver snapped back. This story—this fabrication—was absurd, an affront to his intelligence. "Dale would've come back to me."

"Your brother was so horrified by his own appearance, he became a recluse. Lived all this time in a cabin in the woods on the other side of the Devil's Horns. Primarily self-sufficin', scavenging for what he needed. Anything he couldn't grub himself, he ordered online and had it delivered to one of them unused mailboxes at Blessed Acres. He earned decent money telecommuting, writing tech manuals under the pseudonym... hmm, lemme see here... Leonardo Rot-wang. Or Ro-twang. However you pronounce it, he knew his machines upsides, downsides, and sideways. He just shunned people. Even you."

Gulliver said nothing.

"But he didn't forget ya. He kept very close tabs on you. Watched most everything you did." Boone pulled from the folder a stack of photographs he had retrieved from the cabin, slid them toward Gulliver. "He had hidden cameras and mikes all around your house. And he kept a photo diary of you. There are hundreds more of these, spanning years we reckon."

Gulliver fanned the snapshots on the table, scrutinizing them. Each had captured an arbitrary moment of his life in multiple places throughout Laymon. And, indeed, there were several taken inside his home. There was even one of him and Kat, sitting together on the sofa, moments before they had begun wading into each other's hot pools of carnal passion.

"And he knew about your, um, delusions."

"My delusions?"

The sheriff regarded him heedfully. "The little people."

Agent Rhodes glanced up at Gulliver, then reverted to diddling his phone.

"They're not delusions," Gulliver asserted, staring down the sheriff. "They're real."

"Your brother wanted you to have the normal life he was robbed of. Have a good job. A wife. Kids. But he figured these tiny fellas were keeping you from that. So he dreamt up a plan to rid you of them."

Gulliver entwined his fingers, knotting them up. He expelled a bitter chuckle, choked off by the sour bile rising up his throat. "This makes no sense."

"Your brother weren't much behavin' sensibly. Hope you understand, he's not well in the head. He believed if he could convince ya to kill off your little buddies, you'd be free of your delusions. Curing you, I suppose."

"But, the Giants—"

"Were made up by your brother. To scare you. And to manipulate you."

Gulliver shook his head. No, this couldn't be true.

"The messages, the murders. Abducting your girlfriend. All perpetrated by your brother. For your sake."

"No," Gulliver said vehemently, his eyes narrowing to slits. "My brother *is* dead."

"I assure you he's very much alive, Mr. Huggens. I spoke to him myself. That's how we know you weren't involved in these homicides. At least, not directly."

Gulliver's head twitched. "Dale is dead."

Sheriff Boone sighed, delved into the folder, and extracted one more picture—a freshly developed Polaroid, its chemical tang still detectable. He presented it to Gulliver.

"This is Dale. Taken at the hospital four hours ago."

Gulliver focused on the photograph. He'd braced himself to see a part man, part monstrosity. Instead, he saw something that wasn't a human face at all. It was a head in contour only, lacking lineaments, as if its creation were abandoned soon after the clay was set upon the sculpting stand. This was nobody he knew. This wasn't his brother.

"This is not Dale."

"He's not the brother you remember. But that there is Dale Huggens."

"Dale is dead," Gulliver reiterated.

He couldn't allow this blatant lie to metamorphose into an undisputed truth which not only resurrected his brother, but would label him a murderer in the annals of crime for all of history henceforth.

"Dale. Is. Dead." He repeated this mantra louder and louder to the sheriff, yet the lawman would not listen, could not be swayed.

"I'm sorry, Mr. Huggens" was all Boone would say. That, and "please calm down—"

"DALE IS DEAD!"

"DALE IS DEAD!"

"DALEISDEAD!"

A fusillade of white flashes inundated Gulliver's vision. These ubiquitous detonations were accompanied not by *bangs* or *booms*, but by the sound of gigantic bones breaking.

Or mighty timbers splitting.

Or universes winking.

Or timescapes ripping.

Or perhaps they were the twisty synaptic passageways of his own mind, fracturing then reforming. Fracturing and reforming. Over and over.

Within the blurry spaces between the flashes, Gulliver witnessed the room's ceiling buckling inward, raining debris down around him. It buried the sheriff and the FBI agent so quickly they hadn't time to react.

Gulliver sat there for a moment basking in the flood of sunlight, until a towering shape eclipsed it. A flickering hand the size of a harvest moon reached through the jagged hole above Gulliver, enveloping him, and his world went dark...

and deaf…

and numb…

Gulliver opened his eyes to somebody giving him the stink-eye.

"Dale?"

"Yep. It's still me. And it's still your turn."

His brother sat on a stump opposite him at a chiseled stone table. On it was set a Scrabble game in progress. Gulliver had five letters left on his wooden rack. He took an "E" and added it to the end of "FAT" already placed on the board. Double word score.

Dale was neither dead nor disfigured. Both Gulliver and the sheriff had been mistaken.

Dale studied his remaining letters and surveyed the board. He finally threw a hand up and harrumphed.

"You win again, li'l brother." *Dale shot him an additional stink-eye.* "How 'bout another game?"

"Sure," *Gulliver answered.*

While Dale collected the tiles and funneled them into the cloth pouch, Gulliver gazed around him.

Within this glade where they played was a circle of large rocks surrounding the smoldering embers of a campfire. Above, an awning of dense evergreen boughs blotted out the sky. From many tree limbs hung sticks formed into minimalist shapes.

There came an advancing rumbling noise Gulliver thought was thunder.

"Ah," *said Dale.* "They're back."

Out of the forest tramped a hunting party of a dozen Giant People, lugging a slain adult black bear lashed to a log. They all carried javelins and bows as long as semi trailers, wore mooseskin loincloths and waistcoats buttoned with deer antlers. Each must have been thirty feet in height, and their entire bodies, far as Gulliver could tell, were bald as newborn hamsters. On the shoulder of one perched an eagle, squawking like a parrot.

Dale smacked his lips. "Yum. Bear soup tonight."

Most of the Giants sat down on the ground, while a couple worked together to string up the carcass for butchering. One Giant scratched its rump against a tree.

"You pick first, Gull," his brother said, jiggling the tile pouch.

As he dug his hand into the sack, Gulliver commented on what was most mystifying him—not about how Dale weren't some deformed demon, or how he wound up living with the Giants, or even that he was alive.

"You haven't aged at all."

"Nope," replied the eleven-year-old Dale. "Don't have to here."

And then Gulliver understood, and he smiled.

Here he was safe.

ACKNOWLEDGMENTS

Brobdingnagian thanks to my übereditor Barney O'Neill.

Much love to all those who have given me invaluable and inspiriting feedback on my opus: Erin Zolkosky; Tsiphuneah Becker, Don Heistand, Ashley Hurd, Allen Taylor, and the rest of the scribes in the Central PA Writers Workshop; Jas Obrecht, Thom Daniels, Sue Whitmarsh, Jessica King, Jordan Myers, Chris Moriarty, and Chris Sutton; Taylor Atreides, Dianna Zimmerman, and Liz Scoggins Zolkosky.

Lastly, but not leastly, my heartfelt gratitude to everybody else who in some way supported my efforts to start/finish the damned thing and share it with the world: Russ Colchamiro, Ed Mazza, Chris Crane, Patrick Phillips, Dan Calvisi, Craig Kestel, Jonas Cohen, Renee Heath, Miriam McNamara, the Philbrick family, the Zolkosky family, the motley gang at Pac Ave, and all my Facebook friends who 'like' me.

ABOUT THE AUTHOR

Sawney Hatton writes for food, money, and superpowers. He will even write for fun—so long as it's accompanied by a fine meal, a good paycheck, or the psychic ability to locate hidden treasure anywhere across the globe. (X-Ray Vision an acceptable substitute.)

Other incarnations of Sawney have written screenplays, produced marketing videos, and played the sousaphone and banjo (not at the same time). He fancies himself as somebody you can relax and have a beer with, and encourages people to buy him beer in exchange for his company.

Visit the author's website at
www.SawneyHatton.com

Printed in Great Britain
by Amazon